TARGET MAYFLOWER

RICHARD HIRSCHHORN

TARGET MAY

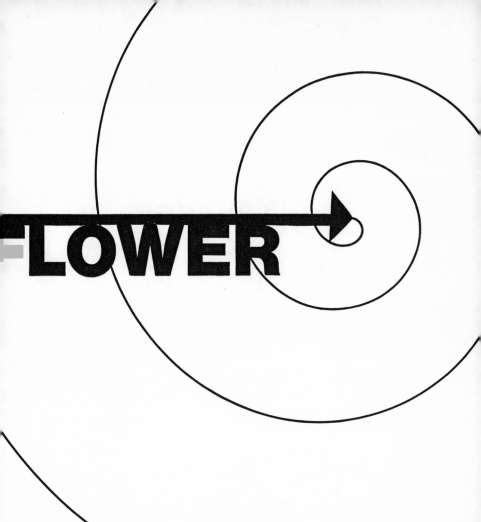

FLOWER

HARCOURT BRACE JOVANOVICH NEW YORK AND LONDON

.... to "Sunset Rock"
and all the lives it has enriched

Printed in the United States of America

Library of Congress Cataloging in Publication Data
Hirschhorn, Richard Clark.
    Target Mayflower.
    I. Title.
PZ4.H67234Tar   [PS3558.I675]   813'.5'4   77-7356

First Edition
B C D E

→ PROLOGUE

May 1944

By the fifth year of the war it was evident to the overlords of Nazi Germany that the tides of fortune were
shifting. No longer was the map of Europe drawn by
German will. England and Russia had persevered. Africa
was lost. Italy and Japan were reeling and doomed. The
invasion of France was imminent. Each day another ancient German city was bombed, its core obliterated, its
inhabitants incinerated.

The once-invincible Wehrmacht was not alone in this
military reversal. From the headquarters of the Kriegsmarine, next to the concrete submarine pens in Kiel, the
Admiralty staff could see the increasing number of slips
that stood empty and accusing whenever a decimated
wolf pack returned home. The walls of the briefing room
were now crowded with black-draped photographs. Earlier
in the war Goebbels had touted the daily sinking of Allied
ships. Now there was silence.

In the opening days of the Battle of the Atlantic in
1940, German U-boats had sailed on the surface, defying
the British and Americans, strutting across the sea lanes
like stormtroopers on the Wilhelmstrasse in Berlin. Nazi
scientists had poured out their inventions: the snorkel, to
recharge the submarine's batteries while it was moving
underwater; the E-torpedoes, electrically propelled so as
to leave no warning path of air bubbles. From 1943 on,
it all changed. American sonar and British asdic hunted
the Reich's U-boats without mercy. Contact "hedgehog"
depth charges destroyed without even a warning that the

enemy ship was on the surface. The new 9-centimeter radar, which the Germans insisted could never be built, drove the U-boats into the depths of the ocean where they scared only fish. And should the submarines open their mouths to send one radio signal even for a second, Allied high-frequency directional finders plucked them from the hidden valleys of the seas like a giant finger.

The wolf packs retreated north to Cape Hatteras, then further north to Iceland. Then east to the Azores, to the tip of Africa, to India. They were safe there, but what could they threaten in those warm, still waters?

The Nazi attack on the United States, code-named Operation Mayflower by the Kriegsmarine, was the brainchild of Grossadmiral Erich von Eyssen. A highly sophisticated idea, it exploited a dramatic potential in the accidental juxtaposition of certain chance elements. Originally conceived as an act of bravado, a fist shaken in the face of defeat, Operation Mayflower quickly expanded into a daring military adventure, one that would pose a credible threat to the Allied cause and sustain the last desperate hope of the faltering Third Reich.

Von Eyssen had heard rumors that the Luftwaffe had developed a revolutionary type of aerial bomb, self-propelled and self-guided. A few days spent at Peenemünde convinced him that the Vergeltungswaffe-2—"Reprisal Weapon No. 2"—was exquisitely suited to his purpose. The Grossadmiral knew that the role of the submarine in modern warfare had changed forever. The evidence of its failure was all around him. The U-boats had not cut the marine arteries which sustained Germany's enemies. Why not send these same ships to strike instead at the heart? he asked. No longer would the underwater vessel be a submerged cannon, shuttling bullets to within three hundred yards of the target and then spitting them out. Von Eyssen predicted the day when the submarine would be too valuable to waste on sinking oil buckets. Why not use the same submarines to ferry death and terror to the homeland of the enemy itself? Equip the ships with the means of transporting the air-

borne torpedoes under the protective screen of the sea,
and then unleash them behind the enemy's lines.

Look at America, von Eyssen said. The country is
playing at war! Their cities are lit up at night, their
coastal facilities inadequately defended. The Americans
will no more expect to see us rising out of the sea than
Rudolph Hess dropping down from the sky into a Scottish
hayrick. With the V-2, we can land and destroy and leave
again before they even awaken to our coming.

Suppose they try to stop us. Where will they start?
New Jersey? Florida? Maine? It would take armies,
hundreds of thousands of men to patrol the coast and
calm the terrified population living behind it. Look at
England when she expected the Führer to invade the island. The whole country was a military camp. At best
the tactic will paralyze the seaboard. At worst it will
cripple the transport of men and supplies to England and
delay the invasion of France.

The Grossadmiral assembled his colleagues for a final
presentation of his plan. Standing before a huge map of
the American east coast, the excitement in his voice
rising as he spoke, he stabbed at the United States.
Boston, he exclaimed, Boston is the target. One hundred
twenty thousand men are assembling there for the largest
convoy to be sent to England. Disrupt them and the
invasion of the Continent must be delayed, perhaps even
aborted.

He searched the faces of men who had seen thousands of their comrades sent to their death at sea. They
all knew Boston to be the pivot of the merciless antisub-
marine warfare campaign in the North Atlantic. Even
more, the city was the primary center for research on
sonar and radar. Cripple Boston, he boasted, and the
Reich will gain six months, maybe a year, until the new
"final" weapons are perfected for our eventual victory.

But there was one ingredient critical for the success
of the plan. There had to be a fail-safe maneuver to defend the submarines and their deadly cargoes during the
twenty-four hours required to set up the missiles. Von

Eyssen had wrestled with the almost insoluble problem for months, poring over maps, devising ingenious but ultimately futile schemes for the transport of troops to North America, until he realized that the army he sought was already in place, in the United States itself. Five thousand German prisoners of war, the cream of the elite Afrika Korps captured at El Alamein, were interned near the Maine coast. An army-in-being, the division of well-trained troops would first fall upon the American rear and provide the necessary time. Then, once the salient was secured, the Korps would execute a second maneuver: a short inland sortie to attack a railroad depot situated between the prison camp and the coast. There they would capture a solitary train traveling south from Canada.

Von Eyssen told no one why the contents of that train were worth the expenditure of precious men and time. Yet, he warned, this thrust was even more vital than the attack on Boston itself. Everything must be subordinated to this mysterious feint.

The train, the prisoners, seven submarines, and twenty-four hours, von Eyssen had concluded triumphantly—that is all the Reich needs to score a dazzling victory for the salvation of the Fatherland.

To head the mission, the Grossadmiral selected Wilhelm Rohmer, his prize wolf pack commander. At first, the thought of attacking a city of a million people with a handful of submarines had seemed to the U-boat captain like some sort of suicidal heroic gesture, a grand collective death wish on the part of the Kriegsmarine, with the seven crews playing the role of involuntary martyrs. Only when the U-boat captain studied the details did he acknowledge that the scheme stood an even chance of success—better odds, he grudgingly admitted, than the ones upon which he daily risked his life.

To the hard-pressed Reich Command, the von Eyssen plan was a low-cost, low-risk, high-option payoff concept. It had captured the imagination of Hitler himself. Whereas others on his staff disparagingly rejected it, the Führer was dazzled by the daring attempt to throw down

the gauntlet of Nazi power where the enemy would least
expect it . . . in his own vulnerable heartland. But it was
von Eyssen's creation, his alone, and only he knew of the
mortal dangers crafted within for each of the unsuspecting participants.

TARGET MAYFLOWER

→ ONE

Kiel, Germany

Wilhelm Rohmer always slept fitfully when he was not at sea. Twenty-seven years in the German Navy, the past eight spent sealed into two-hundred-foot submarines, had left him unaccustomed to the infinite spaciousness of his marital bed. He pitched and yawed all night, still responding to the corkscrew motion of the sea. In his underwater world, neither sun nor moon imposed their diurnal rhythms of work and sleep. On land, in deference to his wife, Rohmer followed the now-alien cycle, but it was a habit lost, never to be regained.

The dry crunch of car wheels below the bedroom window startled Rohmer awake. He moved carefully off the bed. His wife's flaccid body flowed into the warm vacuum and halted without a sigh. Of medium height, with thick neck and thinning gray hair, Rohmer stared at his own coarsened face in the mirror as he shaved. His eyes took in the photographs crowding the bureau top. His proud graduation from the Naval Academy at Flensburg. His wedding picture with Anna, awkward and embarrassed. The only offspring of that union, Wilhelm, named after his father and his grandfather . . . his first Communion . . . the final letter, ringed in black with the blood-red swastika on the letterhead. The end of the line. No more.

His dressing finished, Rohmer walked over to the bed. Love stopped him from waking his wife with a caress or a kiss. He cast a final glance around the room, wondering if he would ever see it again, and quietly left the house.

It was five-thirty in the morning, but an impenetrable fog darkened the dawn and kept back the day.

The large Mercedes field car was waiting, its motor rumbling with a dull synchronous throaty purr. The driver did not hear Rohmer coming. Only when the door opened to the touring back did the driver start up and apologetically greet his passenger.

"Good morning, Herr Kapitän."

"Good morning, Hans. Another foggy day." He looked up at the white screen swirling around him. "For us, today, it will be good." Noticing the worn leather suitcases and duffle bags lying in the front seat, he said, "I forgot about them, Hans. I am sorry."

"Do not be concerned, Herr Kapitän. Your wife called me yesterday. We packed them for you. It will be a long trip this time?"

"Yes. They are all long. They seem to get longer each time." He leaned back as the car crept quietly into the enveloping mist.

Rohmer liked the fog. It made him feel anonymous. Sunlight and open space frightened him, stripping him naked and vulnerable. But the fog, almost substantive, cloaked and protected him on land as hermetically as did the heavy fathoms of the sea. He inhaled the fog as if it were perfume and held it in his lungs for a long time.

Next to the fog, he loved his native city, Kiel. He could never imagine one without the other. Kyl . . . Kille . . . from the Saxon, "a safe place for ships," it lived up to its legendary origins. A deep, secure anchorage, the crown jewel of the Hanseatic League of the 1200s, property in turn of Norway, Sweden, Denmark, Prussia, Schleswig-Holstein, for a thousand years it had sent its sailors into the Baltic and North seas with the riches of the forests and factories of northern Europe. Now the prize of Hitler's Third Reich, it discharged swollen darts of destruction which killed without warning.

The descent from the bluffs overlooking the bay was treacherous. The car dropped lower and lower to the harbor below, pausing with each switchback almost in synchrony with the long, low bellows of the lighthouse horn. Halfway down the car stopped and Rohmer got out before his driver could open the door for him. He went over to the crumbling roadside shrine with its leaning crucifix bleached by the salt air, the Christ staring sadly back at him from under the leaking shingled half-roof.

Rohmer dropped to his knees among the cracked stone urns with their simple offerings of wilted flowers. He offered a silent prayer to the Savior, then crossed himself and rose. Suddenly, a loud greeting came out of the whiteness. "Wilhelm. Wilhelm Rohmer!"

The familiar voice was followed almost immediately by the thin figure of the postman on a bicycle which he stopped and leaned against the front fender of the car. Heinrich Lindemann had known Rohmer all his life, and Rohmer's father as well. He shook the commander's hand. The warm smile on Rohmer's face told of his affection for the old man.

"I will stop and look in on Anna, Herr Kapitän."

"Thank you, Heinrich," Rohmer said gratefully. "It means so much to her. Ever since young Wilhelm. . . . She has been very lonely."

They hugged in a clumsy fashion. Then each disappeared from the other's view as the fog neatly obscured their divergent paths. Their meeting was so innocent, so brief, that no one could have noticed the look with which the postman rapidly scrutinized the car and took inventory of its contents—the packed luggage, the attaché case with its escutcheon of secrecy and importance, the captain's rarely worn ceremonial naval uniform.

Soon after, when Herr Lindemann entered Lisa's, an establishment in the harbor's red-light district, it was not to give substance to his aging sexual fantasies, but to tell the proprietess of the luggage.

When Lisa left her whorehouse later that morning and went to the Church of Saint Nicholas, it was not, as the pious folk of Kiel thought, to buy salvation with her prurient gains, but to transmit to Father Kohler the knowledge of the packed bags.

When Father Kohler, the Catholic shepherd of his flock, climbed the bell tower, erected in 1572 to commemorate a particularly good year in the Flemish wool trade, no one would have thought it for any other purpose than spiritual meditation.

The cryptic message that spit from Father Kohler's wireless, certain obtuse phrases picked up twice by volunteer operators in Dover, was rushed posthaste to Room 39 in Whitehall, London. Its authenticity attested for, the message sped by undersea cable to the Atlantic Fleet, Anti-Submarine Division, in Boston, where the imminent departure of Rohmer's pack was immediately translated into the sudden lighting of seven small red lightbulbs on the vast map of the Atlantic painted on the wall.

Rohmer's car continued its descent to the harbor, winding through the old city with its narrow thirteenth-century streets and cobblestone pavements which not even a Mercedes could smooth out. It passed the University, then the Church of Saint Nicholas with its vigilant Father Kohler. It reached the broad thoroughfare of municipal and civic buildings and once-smart shops, now empty of goods and mostly vacant and boarded up. The fog was gradually losing to the hot sun in their perpetual matinal battle.

The automobile eased through the grimy waterfront district. Not even the Thousand-Year Reich could rid the harbor of its fringe of whorehouses. The car twisted and picked its way to the guarded submarine pens located adjacent to the seamy hotels, bars, social clubs, and flop-houses ... all leeches to drain the lonely sailor first of his money and then of his semen, both done with equally coldblooded efficiency.

Two sailors had dashed out from one such establishment, oblivious to the danger of the traffic, preoccupied only with adjusting the tight confines of their crotches. They forced the large Mercedes to swerve sharply to avoid them. Rohmer abruptly glanced up, taking in the gilt sign over the doorway.

Kiel had other whorehouses, those with gaudier decor and more expensive entertainment, but only Lisa's had that apparently inexhaustible supply of tight young flesh from the surrounding farm villages.

Passing through the barbed-wire gates and double sentry stations, Rohmer could feel a sudden tension which always accompanied the departure of his wolf pack from Kiel. It was a curious mixture of impatience and fear which he and his fellow captains could never overcome. Waiting in the assembly room for the final briefing, Rohmer looked through the window at the harbor. The bright sunlight blinded him for several minutes until his eyes accommodated themselves to what had become a rare transparent May day. The submarines bobbed gently at their moorings on the long jetty. The individual Korps flags were flying on their own flagpoles at the head of each slip, next to the red and black flag of the German Reich. The last-minute loading of supplies was taking place. The peaceful scene seemed incongruous for an active arsenal of death.

Von Eyssen entered at the front of the room. The Grossadmiral's uniformed body was short and stout, his head large and covered with sparse gray hairs plastered across the almost naked top, his round, deeply lined face framed with thin steel-rimmed glasses. Immediately he started in, his voice authoritative and curt.

"Gentlemen, we are giving you the three ingredients for success: numerical superiority, tactical advantage, and surprise. It should be of no concern that your force will be isolated and deserted three thousand miles away in enemy territory. Where we will place you both in time and in space, you will outman and outgun the enemy. By the time the Americans wake up and counterattack, it must take them two days to overwhelm you. Your task requires only twenty-four hours.

"I wish you well. Not luck. You will have no need of that 'mercurial commodity.' You cannot fail as long as you maintain the element of surprise. You will make the initial move, and if you keep the inertia of momentum, the Americans will always be one step behind you. They cannot catch up unless you either fail in the execution of any maneuver or you lose the protective cloak of surprise.

"Remember, Gentlemen, twenty-four hours. Keep

that element of surprise, and you cannot fail. The Fatherland salutes you. Heil Hitler!"

Rohmer's arm shot up in unison with the others, but his "Heil Hitler" was automatic and unthinking. His mind was still grappling with the intricacies of the plan—the split-second timing, the prisoners of war, the mysterious provocative gambit to the American railroad depot. His eyes focused through the window on the seven U-boats outside, but all he could see were the deadly new "missiles" now safely secured in the holds below. Forty-nine ominous black "torpedoes" that would never pass through the ejection tubes in his departing wolf pack.

→ T W O

Boston

Simultaneously with the departure of Rohmer's pack, thirty-five hundred miles to the east, the overnight train from Montreal was knifing its way deep into the old commercial section of Boston. The grime-covered train pulled slowly into South Station, bucking and jerking the

last hundred yards until it could go no further. Before
the train had quieted, the passengers streamed out from
every portal, bumping against one another in pursuit of
some critical mission which could brook no delay.

Lars Trondheim watched through the window of the
deserted dining car, as through a keyhole. The scene little
resembled a city at war. The soldiers walked by, their
limbs intact. The people were dressed well, unlike the
shabby crowds in the cities of Europe. They did not walk
with one eye and ear alerted to the sound of death from
above. It was "business as usual." Why not, he thought?
The skies bring only sunshine and rain and stars. Here
was the bustle of peace, not the tension of war.

He reminded himself that America always liked to
play at war, especially on someone else's land, in someone
else's cities, never upon her own soil. It would soon be
different. He thought of Rohmer and smiled. Trondheim
glanced at the *New York Times* near his plate. The war
continued badly for the Germans. Their once-swollen
perimeter of conquest was shrinking day by day. He knew
that the war in Europe was rapidly coming to an end. It
mattered little to him who actually won. He had no strong
feelings or sentiments about the righteousness or the
cause of either side. What mattered was that the Reich's
financial arrangements were inordinately generous to
successful agents like himself. His account in the Crédit-
Suisse in Zurich was impressive. Soon he could return to
Sweden, rich for life and not yet thirty-five.

Trondheim stood up and adjusted his clothes, brush-
ing them into decorous shape. He was tall, with a spare
frame, blonde hair, and a handsome Nordic face with
broad eyebrows, blue eyes, and thin lips. His immacu-
lately tailored suit shaped his long, angular contour.

He checked his wristwatch. It was time to leave. He
tapped his inner jacket pocket for the reassuring crackle
of the envelope secured there and left the train. His luggage, by prearrangement with the porter, would be sent
directly to the Parker House. He had no time to check in
now. Giving the cab driver the address written on the

outside of the sealed envelope, Trondheim settled back
for the short, jolting ride to the Boston waterfront.

Pietyr Aacher was engaged in a heated conversation
on the telephone when his secretary entered to alert him
that a salesman was waiting. Pietyr had forgotten the
appointment made several weeks before. He resented the
intrusion into his busy morning schedule. He motioned
for her to put the calling card down on the desk. Trondheim was still standing patiently by the reception desk
when she returned.

"Mr. Aacher is on the phone. He should be with you
in a few minutes." Somehow she felt guilty for keeping
this well-dressed stranger waiting in the cluttered ware-
house office. "You've come a long way. Is this your first
visit to Boston?"

Lars said nothing, but stared at her as if he were trying to decide something. She grew uneasy under his persistent scrutiny.

"Please take that chewing gum out of your mouth,"
Trondheim gently ordered. "It destroys the lines of your
face." Without knowing why, Rhoda removed the gum
and placed it in the wastebasket under the desk.

"Much better," he complimented. "Yes. See—that
didn't hurt."

He moved his hands to both sides of her face.

"Your hair. Raise it off the neck. This is much better.
Your neck is too lovely to be hidden. Ah, so," he mur-
mured as he lifted her hair, curling it on top of her head
in a soft swirl.

"There. That is better. See for yourself." He stood
back to admire.

Rhoda took out her pocketbook and passed the mirror
in front of her face. How did he know? Even so, what
gave this stranger the right to touch her in such a dominant manner? She had only met him moments ago, and
yet she could do nothing to stop him.

Trondheim did not move. His eyes continued their
inventory. A young girl, maybe nineteen, twenty at most.
Overweight and self-conscious. A pity ... for her. It

would make his job all the easier. Her face too round for his tastes. The breasts straining under her tight sweater, the lap fleshy and ample, bulging thighs pressed tightly against each other.

"Ah, excuse me," the Swede apologized in a disarming fashion. "I have no right. I forget that this is America. Here, you cannot admire a beautiful woman so openly. It is wrong. I apologize. Please, let me make it up to you. Have dinner with me," he begged. "I am a stranger in this city."

Before Rhoda could begin to think of an answer, the door opened with a jerk. Aacher held the stranger's calling card in his hand.

"Mr. Trondheim? Come in. Come in."

Rhoda stared after them as her boss closed the heavy door. Aacher was short, no more than five feet, five inches, and slight of build. Heavy horn-rimmed glasses, deep furrows creasing his forehead, and a perpetual frown made him look older than his twenty-four years. Trondheim represented the Göteborg Trading Company in Sweden. The appointment had been arranged by their Montreal office some time in the past without an explanation. Aacher waved the visitor into his office and closed the door behind him.

"Please sit down. What can I do for you?" he asked.

Trondheim did not accept the proffered chair. He took the envelope from his inner jacket pocket and handed it to Aacher. "I have merchandise to sell."

Aacher took the envelope and opened it, surprised at the sheaf of glossy photographs that spilled out onto the desktop. Suddenly he seized the pictures. His face contorted into a horrible grimace and turned white. His hands shook uncontrollably. He let out a cry of pain and revulsion. "You bastard. You fucking Nazi bastards!" He threw himself at Trondheim, "You murderers!"

Trondheim stepped aside at the right instant, turned quickly, pinioned Aacher's right arm, and wrenched it cruelly behind him. Aacher twisted in an unsuccessful attempt to break loose even as he continued to send a stream of curses at his composed guest.

Trondheim forced Aacher into a chair. "Sit down and don't ever touch me again," he warned, the words issuing through clenched teeth as he brushed off his clothes and straightened his tie.

Aacher cringed, trembling at the photographs of two old people, haggard, malnourished, with sunken eyes and sagging flesh, looking as if they would welcome death at any moment to deliver them from their present agony.

Trondheim looked at the seated figure with an impassive expression. "Pietyr Jacob Aacher. Born Amsterdam, the Netherlands, 11 April 1920." Trondheim intoned the words as if he were a judge in a court of law. "Son of Samuel Aacher, a wealthy importer, respected by the community—that is, until 12 February 1941, at exactly 6:00 A.M. From then on, a member of the Jewish Council. You do remember the Jewish Council?" Trondheim asked.

Pietyr remembered. On February 12, 1941, the Jewish Quarter in Amsterdam was sealed off by Seyss-Inquart's orders. From that time forth, no German set foot inside the ghetto until the very end of its existence. The Jews ran it themselves. The Germans told them how many people were to be delivered each day to the railroad depot for transport. The Jewish Council selected them.

Pietyr shrunk further into the chair, hiding from the facts which he had thought buried where they could no longer pain him. Aacher would never forget: Twenty leaders of the community. Lifelong friends of his father. Once pious, upstanding men who purchased sanctuary for themselves and their families with the blood of their coreligionists. No freight car to Westerbork for them. No deportation to Mauthausen or Belsen-Belsen for these men. No. The Jewish Council was exempted from the daily quota of bodies to be delivered up to the German occupiers for slaughter.

His father, each day, signing his name to new batches of mimeographed lists of Jews to be hunted down in the ghetto by *Jewish* police. Those who resisted beaten with truncheons. On 5 December 1941, when his father could no longer hide from his conscience, he resigned.

Two days later, Aacher and his family were put on the train for Westerbork. . . .

Trondheim stared at the Dutch refugee with a bemused expression. "What you don't remember, because you could not have known it at the time, is that your father had made preparations to escape to England. He liquidated everything he had left, at a fraction of its true worth. Twenty thousand guilders were somehow smuggled out of Holland to the Crédit-Suisse Banque in Zurich and were deposited there to the account of Colonel Hans Collmeyer, in return for his cooperation.

"At the train stop in Drente, midway from the Amsterdam Central Station to the transport camp at Westerbork, the guards on the last two freight cars carrying the prisoners somehow disappeared. It was night. By prearrangement, the Dutch Resistance broke into the cars and ferreted you and four others to Ijmuiden. You stayed there hidden for thirty-six hours, and then were placed aboard a ship for England. Six months later, you joined your father's brother in Boston."

Trondheim anticipated the question on Pietyr's face. "Yes, your parents were supposed to have been rescued along with you. But that was not the plan. *Our* plan. Collmeyer was Dutch—but also a Nazi. He took his orders directly from the head of German Security and Police for the Netherlands. Collmeyer had been ordered—by us— to approach your father and certain other families who had the qualifications we needed."

Pietyr followed the story with poorly controlled agitation and distress. Several times he wanted to jump up and scream out his anguish. It seemed he was hearing the story as if in a dream, a nightmare concerning people he only knew vaguely, by hearsay. Finally, he could contain himself no longer.

"My mother and father. What happened to them?"

"Oh, they were recaptured. Or, I should say, they were never allowed to escape. Think, Aacher. Do you imagine that with sixty thousand desperate Jews sacrificing their wealth, their religion, their families, clawing at the gates to get out, that you and your mother and father would be the ones to escape? Are you so naïve?"

He did not wait for a response.

"We let you go, but we kept your parents. We repeated this maneuver over and over again. There are many others like you. We think of you as seeds sown in the heart of every country fighting the Reich. When it suits our purpose, we harvest the crop so patiently planted."

Aacher was shaken both by this man, this unholy apparition, and by his loathsome story. He could only ask, "Why me?"

"You were perfect. In your twenties, intelligent, a rich uncle in the importing business in Boston. And guilty."

"Guilty?" Aacher could hardly control his floundering emotions.

"Yes, Aacher. Because you survived, not a day goes by that you don't think of yourself on that dock at Ijmuiden. Should you have stayed behind, you wonder, and waited for your parents to escape, or fled to safety and left them behind? Should you have died with them, or deserted them to live?"

He pushed his face to within an inch of his listener's. "It is true, Jew, isn't it? Say it! Say it!"

The weak nod told him everything. Then: "Aacher, your parents are still *alive*."

The words fell upon Pietyr like hot coals. He sprang to his feet.

"Alive? How can they be? They were still on the train. No one has ever come back from Westerbork."

"Don't be stupid. Your parents never went to Westerbork. What good would you be to us in America if your parents were dead? We went through a lot of trouble to get you here! Your parents have been kept in Theresienstadt, until last week, when they were transported to the Vichy French embassy in Madrid."

Aacher did not know whether to believe this incredible tale or to throw the stranger out. He could say nothing, but sat hypnotized like a mouse in front of a weaving cobra.

Trondheim's voice became almost soothing. "I do not expect you to believe me without proof. Last week we reserved time on the transatlantic cable for you. At three o'clock this afternoon, you will identify yourself to the overseas operator. Your call to the embassy is expected. Talk to your parents. Convince yourself that I am telling you the truth."

The whole story was preposterous, yet why else would this stranger dare him to test its validity? Aacher had accepted the fact that his parents had died in the concentration camp. Now he was suddenly engulfed by the oddest feeling, as if his parents were alive and actually in the room with him, as if he could reach out and make contact with their physical presence. He wanted desperately to seize and hold on to that illusion and, as he tried, the hope that perished on that desolate pier in Holland was suddenly born again.

Aacher said nothing for the longest time, allowing his emotions to recede. Reason slowly reasserted itself and argued to accept the Swede's story, to follow it to some conclusion, logical or otherwise. He felt, with a desperate compulsion, that in some way, through this bizarre encounter, he might achieve freedom for his parents.

"Perhaps your story is true. I will call Madrid. What then? You didn't come all the way to Boston to reunite a Jewish family."

Even as he asked the questions, Pietyr began to think of what it was he had or could do which was so important to the Swede, something that could justify the obvious barter that was about to take place. He was stymied.

"It must be something pretty damn important for you ... to 'harvest' me." He thrust the photographs at the Swede. "I can see your merchandise. Two hundred pounds, if even that much of Jewish meat. Well, what do you want for them? How much?"

"No, no, Mr. Aacher," pushing the photographs

away. "You misunderstand me. You think...? Oh, no. We are not selling your parents. They are *not* my merchandise."

Pietyr gave a feeble protest, "I don't understand."

"Look, Mr. Aacher, look at my card. I am selling forest products. The Göteborg Trading Company sells paper, timber. That is all I am selling. Newsprint, lumber. Please—please, understand my position."

"Paper!" Aacher jumped to his feet, his eyes thin slits of hatred, his heart pounding violently. "What kind of an idiot do you take me for? You come in here and tell me that my parents are alive after I have seen them taken to the concentration camp. You say that they are in a neutral country and I can talk to them in four hours. You tell me my whole life story and that you, not my father, arranged for my escape. Then when I ask you what you want in return, you tell me to buy your *trees?*"

His voice became high-pitched and strident with rising anger and disbelief. He hated this stranger who raked his flesh with the tines of his own conscience.

Trondheim ignored the outburst. He took a folded paper from his pocket and laid it on the desk.

"Yes, Mr. Aacher, only what I told you. You buy from us and your parents will go free. Here is the manifest for one of our freighters, the *Astra*. It is now loading in Göteborg. You are to send a cable to our head office there and confirm your purchase of the products on the ship."

Aacher stared at the tall mercenary. The wave of anger had passed and was replaced just as quickly by the leaden fear of the power his visitor had over him and his family. He picked up the paper and scanned the list, nodding affirmatively with each entry.

"The *Astra* will sail tomorrow. As a Swedish ship, and therefore of neutral registry, it will be in no danger from German U-boats."

He noticed Aacher's hesitation.

"It is not a trap," he reassured. "The *Astra* is bound for Santiago to pick up Chilean copper ore and nitrates for fertilizer. You will be able to dispose of our cargo anywhere in the world at a good profit. We would not ask a Jew to do business without his making a profit, even if it meant saving his mother and father."

Pietyr ignored the slur. He was still puzzled by the arrangements. On the face, it seemed open and above-board, a perfectly straightforward business transaction. But obviously it could not be. There had to be something more. The nagging thought persisted. What is so damn important about this ship? What else does the *Astra* carry? Why does this Nazi prick come all the way over here to do business with me?

Trondheim sensed the anxiety and bewilderment his proposition had provoked.

"Do not try to understand. You will not. That is only for us to do. All you must know is that the trans-action is clean. It will stand the scrutiny of your Ameri-can FBI. But . . . but there *is* one thing more."

Aacher's head snapped up, tense, but he was to be even more puzzled by this last condition.

"If you will reflect, the only detail missing is where you will take delivery of your cargo. Within the next few weeks you will receive a message with the name of a city. Send a second cable, to Göteborg also, advising them of the port of call—and then your parents will be freed."

Aacher got up and walked around the room. He paused several times to look at his visitor who followed him with his eyes, saying nothing, a tolerant smile on his lips. Once or twice Aacher started to speak but stopped, uncertain how to proceed. Finally, he said,

"Suppose that I did consider your offer. What guar-antee do I have that my parents will be released, that this isn't all some kind of sadistic trick?"

"That poses no problem," Trondheim replied blandly. "One week from the day that you send the second cable relaying our message, your parents will be released with their passports to the United States embassy in Madrid. Your American ambassador there will confirm their sanc-tuary. If they are not there on that day, you can cable us in Göteborg, cancel the sale, and refuse to accept ship-ment. You have nothing to lose."

Aacher countered, trying to trip up the spy. "Let us consider the reverse. My parents are released. What if I then turn around and cancel the order, leaving your ship stranded in the middle of the Atlantic Ocean?"

Trondheim did not hesitate, but rebuttled with good cheer, "That is no problem, Mr. Aacher. We have another plant, who upon receipt of prearranged instructions will cable our main office and purchase the cargo at sea. He will complete delivery to the port of our choosing at the time of our choosing. But *that* would be most unfortunate for you."

"Why?"

"We would kill you, Mr. Aacher. Kill you because you know too much."

Pietyr chewed his lip. What the Swede said seemed perfectly plausible. Weighing his words, he asked, in a deliberate manner, "If that is the case, what is to prevent you from killing me anyway after the *Astra* has docked, wherever that will be? That would cover your traces, eliminate a potential leak, and you would still have your precious cargo."

Trondheim smiled at Pietyr like a teacher delighted to see his backward student unexpectedly display a flash of intelligence. "You are thinking, Mr. Aacher. That is very good," he beamed again, his smile lacerating Aacher's fragile composure. "Yes, we considered the possibility. Conversely, you could have made a deal with the American authorities in return for protection. Of course, what would you have to tell them? That some tall, blonde gentleman offered to sell you some newsprint, and now you are afraid that he is going to kill you? Oh, no . . . ," shaking his head from side to side. "In the last analysis, Mr. Aacher, it all boils down to a covenant of trust in which each side gains something from the other and loses nothing in exchange. These are the best kinds of contracts, and the safest. We must trust each other. Am I not correct?"

Trondheim held his hand out to Pietyr, who did not take it. He looked at the outstretched arm with abhorrence and kept his own hands frozen to his sides. The rebuff did not temper the Swede's mood.

"Yes, think about it, but not too long. The telephone call is reserved for you for three this afternoon. If our home office in Göteborg has not received your first cable by tomorrow afternoon, your parents will be started on their journey to Mauthausen. There will be no second chance. Your usefulness and theirs will no longer exist. But place that cable on time—and as directed—and they will live. One week after the second cable, they will be set free."

Trondheim's smile was sweet and benevolent. "Perhaps you Jews do have a God in Heaven. I wonder if He realizes what wonderful and efficient ministering angels we Nazis make in carrying out His work on Earth?"

➤ THREE

The news from Father Kohler that Rohmer and his pack had left Kiel was now one week old, and Boston had yet to receive a single communiqué from the coastal observers who scanned the Baltic Sea exits for German naval traffic.

Michael O'Malley stalked up and down the length of his Boston office, stopping at each end to stare down at the activity below him. His office was a brightly lit glass-walled booth suspended halfway up the wall of the large map room. As if by levitation, the luminous chamber hung like a baleful eye over the dim beehive of movement below. A pair of ornate filigreed-iron staircases spiraled up the sides of the room to his office.

The chief of Anti-Submarine Warfare, Naval Intelligence, East Coast Command, was tall, his lanky height overshadowing his other proportions. His face was square with sharp vertical shadows creasing each cheek and cleaving his chin. A dense thicket of bronzed red hair covered his head. Bushy red eyebrows overhung his face where an incongruous scattering of freckles gave an adolescent cast to his thirty-one years.

His staff, working below, could sense his caged tension. Every time he stopped, his frame sliced the light streaming down from his office and made someone glance up at the dark shape silhouetted above. Michael searched the map in vain for evidence of Rohmer's movement. If the wolf pack had gone the long way through the Skagerrak, why hadn't he heard from Kristiansand or Skagen? If the seven U-boats had veered further north, Göteborg would have spotted them. Agents along the southwest coast of Sweden could operate even more freely and openly than in occupied Denmark or Norway. Suppose, on the other hand, he argued with himself, they took the shortcut through the Kiel Canal. All of the ships would have had to travel on the surface until they merged at Neumünster. There they certainly would have been detected before they burst forth to lose themselves in the vast North Sea.

Not a word. Not a goddam word!

Michael glared at the map, trying to provoke it into revealing Rohmer's position. His anxiety heightened. And to add to his worries, this! He clenched Bainbridge's message in his hand. Bainbridge . . . Michael had not seen his superior in over a year although they communicated often, the flow being mainly one way, from Bainbridge to O'Malley, like water seeking its natural lower level. The message contained information painstakingly culled from reliable agents in Stockholm which predicted attacks on Boston and London in exactly two weeks.

What the hell does it mean? O'Malley shook the crumpled paper at the unresponsive glass window as if expecting someone to shout back the answer. The room below simply ignored him.

The map room was designed for one specific function, to track submarines. The North Atlantic was painted blue on one long wall, with the coordinates of longitude and latitude carefully plotted to scale. The monotonous surface was relieved by shifting patterns of colored lights which signaled the positions of Allied convoys and the passage of enemy U-boats bringing death to those same ships gliding above them. Young girls and boys, nubile, smooth-cheeked robots shuttling back and forth in front of the map, moved the lights in response to invisible commands fed through long black wires which snaked across the floor, trailed around their legs, and terminated in black earphones clasped about their heads. Silently, they carried out their strange ritual dance as if before some unseen deity. Yellow lights for the ships, red for the submarines—it was absurd to imagine that these colored bulbs represented a life-and-death struggle in a cold and turbulent watery wasteland. The map seemed more an abstract montage than a symbol of fluctuating peril and terror.

Telephones were always ringing in the map room. The muted bells, the buzzers, the ringers, the mechanical, steady click-clack-clack-click of the decoding machines and the typewriters ... all blended into a diffuse background harmony, a dense acoustical perfume which somehow could never quite mask the staccato curses and other pungent signs of human activity under stress.

O'Malley's staff was hard-working, hand-picked to help him parry the underwater thrusts of Rohmer's killers. They adored him. He overworked them, underpraised them, and rarely criticized them. Other departments periodically tried to entice them away, but to no avail. To those who were unaware of his relationship to Bainbridge, Michael seemed to possess channels of power unexpected in one with his unkempt personal appearance.

Michael was that infrequent example of Nature perversely cloistering a fierce, driving intellect within a shy, retiring personality and leaving it fallow, unmolested, and unaroused for a third of a lifetime. Born and raised in a small town in northern Ohio, Michael had traveled east for four years of college on a full scholarship. Through some alchemy, he attended and graduated from Princeton without retaining any visible evidence of having ever been near that arena of sophistication. A master's degree in mathematics, coupled with his natural talents, easily purchased tenure in a small college back in the Midwest to which he gratefully receded. Unambitious by instinct, solitary by nature, a bachelor through inertia, he spent those dormant years as a currency of no value. Like a passenger on a cross-country bus, he passively viewed the world as a blur of motion sustained by another's activity.

That is, until the crescendo of war serendipitously intruded into his hermetic cocoon in the shape of Lawrence Bainbridge. That name, to those (and there were few) who had ever heard it, conjured up some legendary figure, quasi–State Department, quasi–Pentagon, quasi–OSS. A shadowy, formless *eminence grise* with Roosevelt's ear, he was the necessary catalyst, that ubiquitous ingredient in the formation of the myriad of agencies, departments, and task forces molded from a lethargic nation to cope with the strident victories of the Axis. The transformation of an apathetic peacetime Washington to a dynamic capital at war, no easy feat at best, bore the indelible imprint of Bainbridge and others like him in the National Defense Council.

It was Bainbridge who plucked Michael Francis O'Malley out of his vegetative existence and brought him to Washington.

Bainbridge had known of Michael years before they ever met. During the long years of the Depression, Bainbridge, a political scientist at Columbia, and Michael in Illinois were both amateur cryptographers. They belonged to the few cryptoanalytical societies which, like clubs of gloxinia propagators or colonial stencil collectors, were devoted to periodic mutual mental masturbation of a singularly esoteric and unproductive strain of human intellectual activity.

In those obtuse gatherings, Michael had achieved a sort of underground fame with his theories of modern cryptography. An effective code, he propounded, must conceal the message in such a manner that a finite number of technicians, working in a finite time period, cannot break the cipher before the message becomes outdated and worthless for military use, and even more, before another, equally effective code is substituted for it. The future of modern codes, he argued with conviction, lay with electronic machines which alone could spew forth the almost infinite number of variables required to hide, dissever, and encumber the vital message.

His theories were generally ignored by his peers, who preferred the traditional methods of code-making dating back to Machiavelli. Ignored by all except the Japanese and Bainbridge.

In 1938, when the possibility of war with Japan finally frightened the American Navy into action, Bainbridge was given a free hand to organize a select group to crack the electromechanical Imperial Naval Code. Michael, an intellectual gypsy, accepted Bainbridge's offer of a commission in Navy Intelligence. Within one year, the cipher was broken and the American Navy was decoding secret communiqués faster than the Japanese themselves could in their Washington embassy thirteen blocks away from where Michael worked. Michael would have drifted back to Illinois without a second thought, were it not for the Battle of Midway.

Midway: the battle plan Yamamoto had crafted after his spectacular victory at Pearl Harbor. A complex scheme to lure the shattered remnants of the American fleet into one last trap and destroy them. It would have taken the Americans five years to rebuild their naval forces, and by then, the Japanese felt, their empire would have been impregnable.

An elaborate plan was devised with four huge fleets pirouetting across the Pacific in a sinister dance of deception. Only if Nimitz was told where the main jugular thrust would come could he concentrate his inferior forces to bear in any viable attempt at parity. All the Americans knew was that the prime objective was code-targeted "Attu."

Over and over, Bainbridge analyzed the Japanese wireless messages, digested troop movements, cargo ship transports, and shore leave cancellations, and assimilated all the details which an attacking enemy must plan. The Aleutians, Hawaii, Australia were ruses, he argued, eloquently and with conviction. Concentrate everything at Midway. "Attu" is Midway!

Nimitz countered: Where is your proof? Bainbridge had none, for all his evidence was circumstantial and intuitive. Without that last crucial empirical link, Nimitz had no alternative but to divide and dilute his scanty forces into four inferior fleets, each certain to face overwhelming defeat.

The Rosetta stone was Michael's. He had said nothing during the meeting between Bainbridge and Nimitz, but his mind was not still. He remembered a fact buried somewhere in his cerebral cortex, a chance observation seemingly of no value at the time. Whereas Pearl Harbor had to communicate with all the other American Pacific outposts by radio, which the Japanese were constantly monitoring, Midway was still connected to the mainland by the old prewar underwater telephone cable, immune from Japanese detection. Michael had a message sent to Midway—by cable—instructing them to inform the mainland—by radio—that their water distillation plant had broken down. Within twenty-four hours after that distress call, the American wireless picked up the gleeful messages which crackled across the Pacific from Tokyo to Yamamoto's flagship that "Attu" had a serious drinking water problem. Midway was the apogee in the Japanese blueprint of expansion, and from that overwhelming defeat her "Greater Asia Co-Prosperity Sphere" steadily shrunk.

Bainbridge insisted that Michael get the credit, and he never went back to Illinois. Transferred to the Naval Anti-Submarine Warfare Command in Boston, he initially was attached there as their expert on ciphers. The scope of his activities expanded dramatically when Raeder intensified the Battle of the Atlantic, slashing the marine lifelines to the British Isles. In the early days—1942 and 1943—the Atlantic was practically a German lake. The Americans were stunned by the enormity of trying to comb the haystack of ten million square miles for an object only two hundred feet long and showing only four square inches of snorkel above the water.

Gradually, tempered by failure and experienced by success, the Command learned to use the newly perfected tools of sonar and radar. They began to integrate the vital information acquired from prisoner interrogations, chance sightings by passing boats and planes, and the "huff-duff" triangulation devices. Michael found himself in the heart of this complex process of correlating the constant barrage of data which poured daily into the office, demanding a practical synthesis. Almost without his being aware of any active impulse to do so, he developed a dedicated cadre of people around him who, before the days of those electronic monsters, functioned like a six-headed computer, absorbing and digesting the changing mountains of facts.

By early 1944, his group could, from three thousand miles away, pinpoint a submarine's position to within ten miles and call in the killer teams of ships and planes to sink it. This activity became routine and they dispatched it with quiet efficient skill. That Raeder was replaced by Doenitz was small tribute to O'Malley's skill in helping the Boston Command restore Allied hegemony to the North Atlantic. In an ironic twist, it was that very success that had compelled von Eyssen to plan an attack on the city, the deadly fear currently occupying O'Malley's attention.

There was a loud knock on the door before it burst open and Michael's five assistants filed in and took their seats. After one last forlorn review through the glass wall, O'Malley turned to his audience. His eyes picked out in the back of the room the bobbing blonde head of his companion of the night before. The attractive girl's hair was now trapped back into a forbidding bun. Her steel-rimmed glasses, several sizes too large, clung precariously to her tiny nose for survival. The lithesome young figure looked up to catch Michael's benevolent gaze and responded with a fast, knowing grin.

This newest recruit to his staff was becoming an increasing source of consternation to Michael. Over the years, many young girls had tried to catch him by flaunting their sexual invitations. Only this diminutive, blonde-haired girl had fathomed that his reticence toward the female sex came not from lack of interest but from an unexpected, reluctant and painful virginity, a stigma she had managed to remove with much tenderness and dexterity.

Michael had abandoned any pretense of considering himself immune from Elizabeth Chute's wiles. Instead, he had pragmatically expanded his cloistered world to encompass the novelty of her affection. In careful analysis, what probably bothered him the most was not her addicting feminine charms, but the gratuitous intelligence hidden within. It still astonished him that women could think. Although he drove them as mercilessly as he did the men on his staff, he had always considered their powers of reasoning as erudition misplaced. And, even more disturbing, she was damned clever! Although he often suspected that Liz considered the ploy as beyond his detection, she always made certain that *her* contributions in the office appeared as products of *his* perceptiveness.

Michael telescoped himself into the ancient wooden swivel chair moored in front of his desk. His back was defiantly turned away from the unfriendly map as if daring its hostility. He held the crumpled piece of paper in his fist, but before he could start to read it for the tenth time, his preoccupation with Rohmer broke through.

"Goddamn it!" he exclaimed. "We know von Eyssen's U-boats carry only enough fuel and supplies for a two weeks' transit here, two weeks to screw the Navy, and then two weeks to get back to Kiel. According to that timetable, they should be *here*."

He poked one finger at the small map under the desktop glass. "Right *here*," he kept stabbing at the desk. "They can't go through the English Channel. Today is their seventh day out. We should have spotted them at the Faeroe Islands, as we always do at this time. But we haven't got a fishing boat in those waters that's reported even a floating turd. Where are they?"

Disgusted, he turned with an air of wretched resignation to the bunched-up message clenched in his fist. He opened his hand and smoothed out the paper. He knew the words by heart, even though he did not know their meaning. He read them out loud, slowly and deliberately. Even as he was mouthing the warning of peril, his mind was grappling with the facts. The connection was, of course, absurd. But, then, attacks on London and Boston by a collapsing German military machine were absurd, too. Was it possible that Rohmer's yet-unexplained behavior could in any way be related to the warning from Bainbridge?

→FOUR

If morale was any index of the future success of von Eyssen's plan, it was fortunate that the Grossadmiral was not aboard the U-206 or the U-207. The two captains, Wachtel and Heinemann, were as moody as their crews. The jitters and tensions customary at the outset of a mission would normally have been dissipated by the routine monotony of two weeks at sea. Not this time. Four days out of port, they were moored off the fishing village of Allinge on the Danish island of Bornholm two hundred miles *east* of Kiel, deep into the southern reaches of the Baltic Sea, still waiting impatiently for two mysterious strangers to arrive from the German mainland eighty miles to the south. The crew, confined aboard ship for "security reasons," looked with envy at the picturesque but forbidden whitewashed village in the distance. The sea lapped at the subs, gently rocking them as the tide turned and moved to the shore. The men fumed and waited for their human cargo to arrive.

Generalmajor Walter Dornberger was unhappy, too, but for different reasons. He was in charge of the development of the FZG.76, or Flakzielgerät, antiaircraft artillery apparatus. Before the war he had been an aeronautical engineer with Fieseler Flugzeugbau of Kassel, where he helped design the Argus-powered Fieseler 196. Named the Storch ("Stork") by pilots enamored of its flight characteristics, it quickly became one of the Luftwaffe's prime weapons.

After the devastating fire-bombing raids of the RAF on Lübeck, his work changed. In anger, Hitler heated up research on weapons which he told the Reichstag could deliver "terror attacks of a retaliatory nature." Two

years of heartbreak and dogged work tempered by
violent deaths from premature explosions had finally culminated in success. It had been a proud day on June 13,
1942, when Dornberger and his key assistant, Wernher
Von Braun, demonstrated the first prototype, the V-1,
Vergeltungswaffe-1, before Albert Speer and General
From. And now, Dornberger thought bitterly, staring
across the dark, turbulent waters toward Bornholm
beyond the horizon, he was about to lose his two most
important engineers.

The Generalmajor took some slight measure of satisfaction that, after a horrendous battle he wished never
to repeat, he was able to wring one concession from von
Eyssen—to keep his submarines out of the Security Zone.
Secrecy was paramount at Peenemünde. Not that the
large, square, concrete buildings and vast earthen ramps
could speak, but no chances were being taken. Even the
French and Polish forced-labor conscripts who constructed the facilities a year before had been removed
from the area. Despite the RAF photoreconnaissance
missions which flew overhead regularly, Dornberger felt
confident that the Allies had not yet discovered the secret
of his "aerial bomb."

Only the two scientists bound for the waiting U-
boats seemed to have no opinion one way or the other. The
receding coast of Germany appeared immense to them,
even as it shrank from view, in comparison to the open
boat which was carrying them to Wachtel and Heinemann. The passengers looked straight ahead, except for
occasional nervous glances over the gunwales at the rushing gray foam. The two engineers, one Czech and the
other French, had worked for the Germans for the past
six years. Now they had another source of anxiety.
Despite their active collaboration, von Eyssen had transferred their families to Fallersleben, near Kiel, to be kept
there under "protective surveillance" until they returned in six weeks. It was, he explained to the two
gentlemen, "to insure your complete dedication to duty."

Arriving at the U-boats, on von Eyssen's orders the
engineers were assigned to separate vessels as a safety

precaution. In addition to a single small piece of personal luggage, each man carried, secured by a thin chain to his wrist, a worn brown leather briefcase, bulging with the paper tools of his trade. Taking a last fearful look at the sea, wondering if it was to become their unmarked grave, each disappeared through a U-boat's conning tower. The rasping grate of the hatchway clanked shut above each man's head, the metallic sound reverberating through the long hollow metal cylinders.

Even as each descended the tight spiral stairs into his new home with clumsy steps, a coded wireless message was speeding to Kiel, alerting von Eyssen that the transfer had been completed. He received the news with an expectant smile, but continued to stare at the empty berths on the Tirpitz Pier while tapping impatiently on the windowpane. He sustained this nervous habit for another two hours until the second message arrived, this one assuring him that U-204 and U-205, laden with another pair of clandestine passengers, had safely left Böknfjord, in southern Norway. The two Norwegians, who had made the long trek from the Norsk Hydroelectric Plant in Rjukan over the chilled, barren Telemark tundra in order to meet their submarines, were now safely aboard and, like their Baltic confreres, gingerly testing the claustrophobic confines of their new nautical world.

Unlike O'Malley, von Eyssen had the advantage of knowing where Rohmer's U-boats were. This knowledge, however, did not allay a feeling of apprehension as the aging admiral watched the late afternoon sunlight tickle the ancient wooden piers in Kiel Harbor. The jetty is old, like me, he thought sadly; if the war lasts much longer, they will have to replace it. The tide was low, exposing the worn pilings, with their well-demarcated tops disintegrating in the damp air. If he closed his eyes, he could see his forests near Königsberg where the sun and air raised trees straight to the sky. It is ironic, he mused, that here where the trees are dead, water will preserve the wood, while the tops of the trunks, bathed in sun and air, will rot and crumble. He remembered seeing in the King Gustavus Adolphus Museum in Stockholm a Viking ship dating from the tenth century, which had lain for a thousand years at the bottom of Göteborg Harbor preserved intact by the mud and slime.

The von Eyssen heritage was almost as old as that ship, but had not been dormant all those years. His ancestors came with the second wave of Teutonic Knights in the 1300s. Gradually subduing the heathen Prussians, they planted their own seed upon the vast conquered tracts of harsh Baltic heath and moor. His was a hardy, virile race of overlords. By adroitly shifting loyalties, by changing religion from Catholic to Lutheran to Calvinist, by deliberate intermarriage they lived and multiplied and prospered. Fighting in turn the Danes, the Swedes, the Austrians, the Poles, and the Russians, they emerged as the dominant Germanic state and served as the catalyst for Frederick the Great to weld the scattered small duchies into the First Reich.

Von Eyssen had no love or affection for the Nazi hierarchy. Like his father and grandfather before him, he complied with his ancient hereditary obligations to support the state which, in return, guaranteed his elite Junker class the sole right to acquire estates and to be exempt from taxes. For three hundred years, the fate of his class was inexorably intertwined with the fortunes of the Reich. This was never more true than now, a dire realization which made him fear and tremble.

Von Eyssen realized after the catastrophic disasters at Stalingrad and El Alamein that Germany could never defeat the combined will and power of America and Russia. He pondered the future of his nation. The defeat of the Third Reich would shatter the structures which had sustained his family for over three centuries. The Allies would be vindictive and hold the Prussian officer caste responsible for the holocaust which had visited Europe over the past five years, even though the true blame lay with Hitler and his coterie. It would be comforting to think that a peace treaty would confirm the continued existence of the Junkers, but he refused to allow such a sanguine hope to drug his concern for the future.

The sun was warm, and he pressed his forehead lightly against the cool windowpane. Looking at the empty slips, he wondered how many of the U-boats would come back. Rohmer would *not* return, although the Kapitän did not yet know this. War was cruel. Von Eyssen imagined he could hear the rumble of Russian tanks as they rolled across the low lying forests and sparse fields of Lithuania and Latvia, to turn at the water's edge and knife down toward his native Pomerania.

His estates below Königsberg would soon be gone, delivered into the hands of the new-day Tartars. Not in his lifetime nor in his children's would they again be free. After what we did to them in the Ukraine, he thought bitterly, it is unlikely that they will ever again let the land go. All eastern Europe will be converted into a sterile antitank ditch, a buffer between the Fatherland of the tsars and the fear of a renascent Reich. He pursed his lips. His eyes watered, blurring his vision, as he tried to hold back his sorrow.

He withdrew from his breast pocket the baroque cameo locket which had once belonged to his wife. Since her death, he carried it with him always. He looked at the photograph of Klara, and then of his son, Albert, missing in action in the Battle of Kharkov. He raised the locket closer. Expectation erased the gloom from his face. It won't be long now, he whispered to the silent visages, as he communed with them the secret promise.

Von Eyssen had reason this day for optimism. He had long thought his son buried in the frigid wilderness of Siberia. A year ago, thanks to his wife's family connections with the Wallenbergs in Sweden, he had learned that Albert was alive, though just barely. The knowledge of his son's existence stirred fires of ambition which had died when his only heir was taken prisoner two years before. The news rekindled his interest in the future. His family had retained its link with immortality. He must plan again. Think for the future. But how? Where was

the land into which to sink those tenacious roots? Prussia
was gone. It would never again appear on the maps of
Europe except as some inconsequential district of Russia
or Poland. No, he must look elsewhere. His forebears, in
coming to the Baltic, had hewn a country out of the
heathen wild land. He would do the same. Only today, he
would need to be more than a knight on horseback to win
a new start for the von Eyssens.

The Grossadmiral let out a quick, nervous laugh. The
future. So much depended upon those tiny ships travers-
ing the vast reaches of the North Atlantic. Seven fragile
vessels of hope. His future. The future of the German
Reich. How could the plan *not* appeal to Hitler? The
Führer always did like the heroic move, the dramatic
gesture. Well, von Eyssen concluded, as if his willing it
was the critical determinent, if it succeeds, and it must
succeed, it would once more prove Hitler's genius, which
like marching into the Rhineland and the Sudetenland
had astounded the world with its success. And so far, von
Eyssen thought with guarded optimism, it was succeeding. Everything was falling into place. Trondheim's two
plants in the United States were properly activated. Even
the American and Russian enemies were carrying out
their unsuspecting roles so perfectly that one might almost accuse them of deliberate collusion with the Reich
Kriegsmarine. Everything was on schedule, but timing
was crucial.

His face tightened into a worried scowl. Rohmer
must adhere exactly to the protocol and not vary by a
day, an hour, even a minute. The next message from the
wolf pack would originate from the American mainland.
The fingers of von Eyssen's left hand crept surreptitiously
over to his right wrist. They paused there and rested
lightly on the thready radial artery. The wait would be a
long and anxious one.

→ FIVE

The same nightmare again. His mother crying and push-ing him away. Unseen hands which trapped him. He broke loose trying desperately to reach his parents. His father's vicious slap stopped him in his steps. The hands reached out to encircle him again. The stench and roar of the boat engine as he kicked to get loose.

Finally freed, he sprang to the transom, only to see the dock ... empty. He screamed over and over until soft hands closed his mouth, suffocating him to wakefulness.

Pietyr Jacob Aacher cried and moaned as his wife turned and held him in a tight embrace. She said nothing. It was the same dream. For two years, he had slept freely. Now the terror of his early days was back, just as vio-lently as when he had first arrived from Europe.

Pietyr sat up the rest of the night in the dark, chain-smoking until dawn. He had talked with his parents. He trembled at the memory of that experience. His parents' static-clouded voices had seemed like disembodied frag-ments of the past suddenly brought to life deliberately to sear his soul. All he had been able to do was sob into the telephone, unashamed of his emotions.

He had sent the first cable as directed that afternoon. It was now one week later. Trondheim had not contacted him, nor had he received the message that was to be the signal for the second cable. Would there ever be one? And, if so, would it mock him with "contract void" or "sale cancelled"?

He shivered again as he saw the pleading faces of his mother and father writhe and die in the smoke twist-ing up to the ceiling.

Lars Trondheim had suffered no such recurrent nightmares these same seven nights. He usually slept soundly after pumping his acrid sperm into Rhoda's sow-like body. In Göteborg, he would have been embarrassed to be sleeping with someone like Aacher's secretary. His lean body craved the tall, thin women he had made love to in Sweden, their concave pelvic cradles bruising his abdomen, their long, sharp legs locking him in a painful scissors grip, narrow heels wedged deep into his back, digging in harder with each thrust. Rhoda's very fatness sapped his frustrated tumescence.

In her own simple way, Rhoda knew that Lars could easily obtain someone more sexually attractive than herself, and that knowledge kept the unanswered question— why did he choose her?—buried inside where it would not rankle. The feeling of being part of some exotic adventure with this handsome stranger was all the license she required to be a willing participant. Nevertheless, like Pietyr, Rhoda could not help wondering what mission had brought the mysterious foreigner to Aacher's office. As with her employer, she could never find a satisfactory answer and ended by accepting his presence for whatever hidden purpose lay behind it. Voluntarily and without caution, she entered into her own special relationship with Trondheim, one in which, ironically like Aacher's, each side gained something from the other and lost nothing in exchange.

As a reward for servicing his constant sexual demands, Trondheim confided to Rhoda that he had consummated a large business deal with her employer. He warned that competitors were following him. One week from the day he had first entered Aacher's office, Rhoda told him what he had been fearful of. Two men had called upon Aacher for questioning. Two men whom Trondheim knew were agents from Naval Intelligence.

Tronheim had been well informed about Michael Francis O'Malley in the extensive briefing sessions held in Kiel before he started the assignment. He had high respect for his antagonist's deductive powers. The Swede made a mental note. It was time to send Aacher that second cable. He had a premonition that he was next on the redheaded American's list.

———→ S I X

Michael looked up at the grey-white sky, slowly lightening in the early dawn. It was quiet, deathly still. The soft drizzling rain made him blink. Michael had a childish urge to take off his clothes and run naked among the drops, to let the cleansing water saturate his body, gather in rivulets, and tickle as it ran down his thighs and legs. He entered the South Gate of Harvard Yard, and then detoured past University Hall, whose dull Vermont granite walls were now stained by irregular blotches of rain. To his right loomed Widener Library, its overwhelming mass of stairs deterring the weak-hearted who might want access. As he passed, Michael wondered why men built libraries with such formidable physical and psychological barriers. Why could not libraries be built on the same level as the human being, or even lower, so as to entice people in? Michael made a mental note someday to explore that line of thought along with countless others that had flitted in and out of his mind over the years, enhancing his personal belief that life was just a kaleidoscope of coded messages waiting for someone to extract the hidden meanings.

Liz was waiting for Michael in front of Memorial Hall, that grotesque gothic monument to the post–Civil War era. She took his arm and gave him an affectionate kiss. As they proceeded north onto Oxford Street, Michael made a face back at the gargoyles perched precariously on the roof edges, wondering if they liked the rain as much as he did.

It was not yet seven o'clock in the morning when Michael and Liz entered the university building where the office was located. Only the white-gloved MPs flanking the doorway warned the passers-by that the property had been commandeered by the United States government for the duration. Few people knew the depths to which the Boston area's educational institutions were participating in the war effort. Marcus Ethier in the next building had developed a jellied gasoline, called napalm, with the ability to stick tenaciously to its victim until it had cooked him to death. Two blocks away, Spencer Kissielowsky had staked his claim as America's foremost explosives physicist until one day when he and his brilliant young assistant, Douglas Gatling, had suddenly disappeared. Few on the faculty knew of their clandestine relocation to a secret project rising to disturb the sluggish reptiles on the silent sands of Alamogordo.

Along the flat banks of the Charles River, two miles downstream, the wizards of MIT were spewing out fantastic instruments of detection, far surpassing the original crude and primitive radar devices designed by the British in the late thirties. One day, when the war was over, what incredible stories these taciturn ivy-covered walls would tell. But for the present, they were as silent as the two large bronze rhinoceri which guarded the entrance to the Biology Building across the street.

Michael was troubled. He had become more irritable and jumpy as the days passed since Rohmer's wolf pack had departed Kiel two weeks before. Each day brought a new load of random gleanings which could not be assimilated. Michael sorted and resorted all the facts, but his attempts to process them into an integrated theory were in vain. He was frustrated. He knew he had only to remove that last layer to expose the cipher like an ancient buried mosaic.

"Damn it," he said to his staff assembled in his office this Monday morning. "Something funny is going on with Rohmer."

Heads snapped up, conversations cut off in midair. With a noisy heave, Michael settled himself down in his cramped chair for what he knew would be a long and labored explanation.

"Look," he began, "look at the map." His audience strained to look over his shoulder down through the glass to the map on the wall below. Seven red lights marked the last known positions of Rohmer's U-boats off the European coast. His assistants turned again to their boss. They did not see anything unusual.

"Think for a minute. The pack left Kiel two weeks ago, all refueled and ready to strike. But what did they do? Rohmer's flagship went straight out just as he usually does. We sighted him at Skagen on his usual course. What about the rest of the pack?" He did not wait for an answer. "They all went off in separate directions." He paused for a minute, trying to discipline his thinking process to the slower pace of his audience.

"Take U-206 and U-207. After leaving Kiel, Heinemann and Wachtel went *up* the Baltic, to pick up two mysterious passengers from Bornholm. Then they retraced their steps and were sighted off Skagen, following Rohmer's course but well behind him. Why?

"What do we know about Bornholm? This past winter British Intelligence reported unusual German activity on the mainland near the island, at some place called Peenemünde. The Danish underground sighted unexplained explosions on the water near there, and even on Bornholm itself. The RAF flew over the area many times trying to discover what is going on there, but all they

came up with were large earthen ramps for some kind
of secret research. Are the Nazis developing some new
kind of weapon there? More important for us, how are
the two passengers from Bornholm connected with whatever is going on at Peenemünde?

"As for the U-204 and U-205, they were spotted by
observers at Bergen coming out of Böknfjord. The two
men they took aboard there were identified by the Norwegians as engineers from a hydroelectric plant five
hundred miles further north. Why the side excursion to
Norway? Is von Eyssen testing some new kind of submarine propulsion engine?"

Michael stopped for a moment to free some stuck
drawer in his memory. "If you recall, early in the war the
British ordered the Norwegian underground to blow up a
large scientific installation at that northern site, somewhere in the province of Telemark. No one here could
ever find out from the British what was so important
about that plant.

"Remember one thing," he shook his finger, "the
wolf pack didn't get its name for nothing. The days of
the solo U-boat are over. The submarines fight together,
not scattered all over the place. They cannot waste valuable time making detours to Norway and the Baltic like
a taxi service—yet that's just what they have been doing."

Michael gave a terse smile. "Suppose, as a hypothesis," he said, "von Eyssen is not going to use his pack
to sink ships. What if the seven U-boats are engaged in
some other activity whose purpose will become known
at a later time? Then all this so-called atypical maneuvering might make sense. The side trips. The separate
courses. The lack of concern over fuel. Then everything
that seems to us irrational and random becomes rational
—and deadly. Rational because it fits a tight pattern, a
Nazi plan. Deadly because we do not know what the plan
is. What we are seeing with Rohmer may be the opening
gambit of an entirely new game. But what the hell *is* it?"

The activity of the wolf pack was only one of the
mysteries that gnawed at O'Malley. It seemed that every

time he turned around, another enigma emerged. What disturbed him the most was his inability to know whether they were at all related.

The "ski slopes." During the winter, British Intelligence had transmitted photographs of strange slanted structures in northeastern France. Suspicious of anything that the Germans did, the RAF had bombed the hell out of them, just in case. The Germans tenaciously rebuilt them in other sites, relying on heavy camouflage to shield these yet-unidentified constructions. What were they for? Did they have any relationship to the activity in Peenemünde or Telemark or to the wolf pack?

Then there was the whole provocative question of the Russian ships. Michael had been following this fleet across the Pacific with more than cursory interest, ever since he learned that Nikolai Martov had authorized its departure. Although the Russians were America's ally, Michael had a high index of suspicion for anything, no matter how patently innocent, in which the furtive and powerful Kremlin Intelligence official was involved.

Leaving Vladivostok, the five ships stopped only once at Tokyo for a courtesy state call. It was ironic, Michael thought, that the Russians, who were fighting the Germans for survival, would curtsy before the Rising Sun, with whom they were ostensibly at peace, knowing that their host was locked into the tripartite Axis pact with Germany and Italy aimed at Russia's certain destruction. And here they were, blithely crossing the Pacific without worry of Japanese attack, whereas the Americans, their wartime partners, sailed the same waters at their peril. The task force of four destroyers and one battleship had passed through the Panama Canal. ConCinch in Washington and the British Admiralty had both confirmed that the fleet was heading for Boston and Montreal and then on to Murmansk.

It made no sense. Why would the beleaguered Russians send precious men and material on a round-the-world goodwill trip in the middle of a war?

"Let me know the minute there is any change in their

course," he instructed Moe Berkowitz, his senior assistant. "Let me see a copy of every message that they send or receive. I'd especially like to know if they are talking to any German subs in the area."

This last request startled the staff, and in fact Michael had no special reason for seizing on it. It was just another example of his casting about for chance combinations of isolated opposites to see if they would fit, like pieces of a jigsaw puzzle.

Finally, there was Lars Trondheim. They had kept a constant tail on the Swedish spy. They knew he was peddling his paper products during the day and screwing some Dutch refugee's secretary at night. When they questioned Aacher, they got a copy of the cable he had sent to Göteborg. It appeared, just as Trondheim had assured Aacher, to be a straightforward business deal. Yet the sale to Aacher was the only one Trondheim had made since his arrival in Boston.

The *Astra*'s sailing declaration, filed in Göteborg, showed that it was to stop in Reykjavik to unload shingles and framing studs. Michael insisted that the boat be inspected there. "Use any excuse, but get it searched from top to bottom. If you find anything at all, let me know!"

Lars Trondheim's role in all this perplexed Michael. Even his sex life. The agents who had the spy under surveillance reported that he was good-looking and had lots of money. He had no need for Aacher's fat secretary except as a lookout. But for what? Michael decided against taking Trondheim in for interrogation. His story would just corroborate Aacher's and frighten him away. They knew where he was at all times and could bring him in within minutes if necessary.

Michael was disgusted with himself. No matter what tangent he went off on, he always came back to the same place, like the hub of a wheel: Bainbridge's warning of simultaneous attacks on London and Boston.

Intelligence sources had said the action would be timed to coincide with the opening of the next session of the Reichstag, now only five days away. Hitler was planning a major broadcast Saturday night to tell the world about a new Nazi secret weapon. That was all that was known.

Michael could not help admiring the German daring. An attack on Boston at this time was brilliant. The Germans had enough fifth-column agents in the city to report every detail of the massive buildup taking place for the Normandy invasion. From Marblehead to Cohasset, tens of thousands of bivouacked troops were slowly boarding the troop carriers now crowding in the harbor. The warehouses on the long jetties with such names as Fisherman's Wharf, Tea Party Wharf, and India Wharf were packed to overflowing with guns, tanks, munitions, and the other supplies of war until the piers threatened to collapse into the dirty water under the unaccustomed weight. Within days, the logistics would mesh to form the largest convoy ever for the invasion of Europe.

The Navy had stripped the eastern seaboard of ships in order to protect the vital transit. Already in the harbor, these consort warships stretched to the horizon. Nothing could violate the juggernaut once it reached the safety of the high seas. In the meantime, the assemblage lay uncoiled and vulnerable.

Michael was prepared for sabotage on a massive scale. The Army Harbor Command, the Navy, the Civil Defense—all were alerted. Every ship was searched for time bombs. Frogmen scoured the harbor floor and the bottoms of hulls for magnetic mines. Every ship permitted access to the harbor was thoroughly inspected. Platoons of soldiers occupied all elevated sites around the port.

Bostonians, whose last encounter with soldiers taking up protective positions within their city was with the Redcoats, were treated to the spectacle of machine gun implacements around airports, railroad stations, power plants, water supply reservoirs and pumping stations, telephone exchanges, sewage disposal plants, and key subway junction centers. A curfew was imposed on the city for the second time in its history.

Although everyone in the city was cooperative,

Michael was still not satisfied. It did not add up. A dozen, even a hundred agents could be no more than a pinprick against the military behemoth occupying the city. Certainly the destruction and loss of lives would be staggering and would jeopardize the departure of the convoy to England, but a simple act of sabotage could not be the whole answer. And a handful of submarines could not do much more. There had to be something else. But what?

Could it be a one-shot overflight bombing raid from offshore carriers like Doolittle's raid on Tokyo, with a suicide landing in enemy territory? Or could the Germans have conceivably perfected a round-trip transatlantic bomber? The long-range fuel requirements would be incredible, but it never paid to underestimate German potential.

O'Malley turned to face his audience, searching for Morris Berkowitz seated in the back of the room. Berkowitz had been in contact with Whitehall, but as yet had been unable to get satisfactory answers to these perplexing questions.

At times, Michael was aware of a hard-to-explain intransigence on the part of British Intelligence. While they were quick to boast about certain daring exploits, at other times they held back information of quite routine nature. This annoying habit often made Michael wonder if his British counterparts realized that America was really fighting on their side. Some of the British reluctance, he felt, was due more to concern with protecting the secret sources of their information than to the content of the communiqués themselves. Perhaps the director of Naval Intelligence had reason to play his cards so tight to his chest, but this was one time in which Michael had to get the answers and damn the British.

Michael dismissed his staff except for Berkowitz, who waited patiently while Michael placed a long-distance call to Bainbridge at an unlisted number. His mentor readily agreed to Michael's short request without a comment.

"Moe," Michael said, his expression somber, "if you leave now for the airport, Bainbridge will have a plane waiting for you. When you arrive in London, go to White-hall and ask for this man." Michael handed Berkowitz a slip of paper upon which he had scribbled the name of Bainbridge's counterpart in British Naval Intelligence.

Michael looked up at the calendar on the wall facing him. Today was Monday. The Reichstag opening was scheduled for Saturday. Five days! Maybe they could make it. If . . . if . . . the British knew something that he didn't.

"The British must be as scared as we are, especially after living through the Blitz in 1940. Bainbridge will have cleared your way. Fill in DNI on everything we know. Tell them about Rohmer's odd behavior pattern, and Lars Trondheim and Aacher and the *Astra*. See if any of it makes any sense to them. Get some answers, damn it!" he ordered. "Ask them again about the power plant at Norsk, the explosions near Bornhold, what is going on at Peenemünde, and why von Eyssen would be sending a wolf pack here with passengers from those places. . . ." The words were now coming out in a rush: ". . . and don't forget about the 'ski slopes' and the Russian fleet. Above all, keep in mind the message from Bainbridge. It warned that London would be attacked at the same time as Boston. Have the English learned anything we don't know? What are they doing to stop the attack? And, Moe," his voice dropped to a low whisper, "tell them anything they want to know. Don't keep anything back. Right now, I couldn't give a damn in hell about security. Just get some answers!"

Berkowitz was young and darkly good-looking. Though highly perceptive, he was ill equipped conversationally to handle his boss's overriding intellectual superiority and dominance which, on important occasions such as this, left him painfully tongue-tied. Had he been able to speak, Michael gave him no opportunity for rebuttal. Berkowitz could see that Michael was aching to go himself, but could not.

"Three days. That is all the time you can have. Bainbridge will arrange a military transport to fly you back from Heathrow on Thursday."

Moe could not even get out a "good-bye." He just sat there, his tongue fluttering in the back of his mouth, trying to form words. Michael looked at his speechless aide, misinterpreting his silence. "Don't worry about packing. Everything you need will be waiting for you by the time you get to London. Bainbridge is very efficient. Just go. I'm counting on you."

Michael rose to shake Berkowitz's hand. He looked at the young man with a sudden worry. O'Malley had no illusions about the omnipotence of American or English security. He could not suppress a certain premonition of danger. "Moe," he added slowly, "please be careful."

—————→ S E V E N

Frenchman Bay, Maine

May was Barnard Hodgdon's favorite time of year. By then the spring rains had percolated through the soil, drying the boggy ground cover which cushioned the bedrock beneath. The vegetation was the light chrome oxide green of spring, and had not yet acquired the mature darkness of late summer. Through the air, still and hot, he could hear the dull metallic rhythm of the bell buoy bonging on Crabtree Ledge. The tide was coming in and the rapid waves increased the frequency of the penetrating sounds coming from the east shore of Adams Point.

Hodgdon was almost through his daily tour of the point. In another two weeks, this job would be over until after Labor Day. Winter inspection didn't pay much, only $2.50 per month for each cottage, and for that he had to check each property for water damage, vandalism, and blowdowns. Still, it was $2.50 times 60 and there weren't many jobs in Hancock County during the long winter season.

Adams Point was a broad, almost deserted peninsula which tapered to a blunt point jutting out into the middle of Frenchman Bay. There was always a friendly competition between the east shore and west shore inhabitants. The east side had the sunrise and the west got the sunsets. Those at the very tip got neither, but they had mastery of the panoramic view of the bay, with Schoodic Peninsula on the left and Mount Desert Island on the right, the two stretching out like attenuated arms to encircle the large body of water. Far in the distance, blocking the entrance to the vast saucer of blue, were the Porcupine Islands, named by Samuel Champlain for their bristling cover of tall spruce and fir trees.

Hodgdon commenced his tour on the east shore at the site of the Mount Desert Island Ferry, a solid mass of huge concrete pilings with a rusty ribbon of railroad tracks leading right out to the edge of the pier. Until 1940, a special train run by the Pennsylvania Railroad in the first week of July would collect the rich, perspiring residents of Philadelphia's Main Line and West Chester County. The long ride down east would terminate at the North Sullivan Junction depot just north of Ellsworth. There the train was shunted onto a special spur to Adams Point where the passengers transferred directly to the waiting ferry for the ride across the bay to Bar Harbor. In the fall, the process would reverse, and the summer folk of Mount Desert Island would once again return home to winter in their overheated mansions.

The massive iron and concrete pier was a discordant note on the primitive shore. There had been talk each year in Ellsworth, the county seat, of putting this terminal to a more commercial use. Nothing ever came of it for there just wasn't anything else in the county worth shunting a train to Adams Point from North Sullivan Junction fifteen miles away.

As Hodgdon rounded the tip of the point, he was hit by the strong, cool breeze which blew in from the northwest and puffed the balls of dust from his footsteps. Here the houses were farther apart, with large areas of untouched forest in between. Hodgdon's walk was disturbed by an occasional car with an out-of-state license plate. The occupants waved to him, but vanished in a trail of dust before he could see who they were. "Too many people!" he shouted after them as he sought refuge in the soft shoulder of the road. I guess I'll do some lobstering this summer, he thought, when he resumed his solitary walk. With the price up to 70¢ a pound, this year might turn out to be pretty special yet.

The day was lovely, the sky a deep cerulean blue. The waves sparkled like scattered sequins as the sun touched the tip of each crest, flinting it with diamond facets. He took in a deep breath and held it there. The air was good. The war was far away. If it ever touched the lives of the people here, or modified the traditional patterns of existence, such changes were minimal and certain to be transient. America might be galvanized to fight a battle for survival thousands of miles away. But here life continued as it had for generations, shaped by the tide and the weather and the exigencies of earning a living.

Barnard Hodgdon was indirectly responsible for most of Stephen Shoemaker's distress, especially these last four Friday nights when the ache in the young sailor's balls forced him to pull over to the side of the dark shore for relief. It took almost two loads before he was able to finish the lonely drive along the unmarked gravel road back to the naval installation at the end of Schoodic

Peninsula. Even then, his erection persisted and he was resigned to the taunts of his companions, who accurately deduced that once again Edith Hodgdon would not put out for him.

One more month and his rotation would be over at the radar station. He could not tell which he disliked most, the time spent watching the oscilloscope tube for the white glowing spots which detected surface intruders within one hundred miles of the station, the eight hours allocated for the domestic chores of the small concrete blockhouse he and his mates inhabited, or the eight hours in bed, trying to sleep with no incentive for the horizontal position other than perpetual priapism.

He realized how far away he was from civilization by the four-hourly fail-safe radio call from O'Malley's office confirming that the station was viable. The crackling voice from Boston seemed eons away instead of only hours.

It was Edith who tempered for him the silent loneliness of Frenchman Bay. Edith Hodgdon was a nurse in the Ellsworth Hospital, and Shoemaker had met her at a social held at the First Congregational Church in Winter Harbor, the town nearest to the post. By the second month, Shoemaker and Edith Hodgdon were together every day he was off duty. Stephen met Edith's father the first time he called for her. The old man had said nothing as both of them waited in the small parlor. Barnard Hodgdon looked his daughter's caller over very carefully. The boy seemed like a clean-cut chap, especially compared to some of the riff-raff that had been stationed out at the post before. There had been a few bad times with the enlisted men there, and only quick transfers and much diplomatic maneuvering on the part of the Navy and the town fathers had averted a virtual blockade against the radar station.

"You seem a decent enough fellow," Hodgdon had finally allowed, spending his words as if depleting his verbal inventory would render him bankrupt. "But take care. I don't know what you have on your mind. I never tell my girls what to do or what not to do. They know what's right, living in this house and watching Mrs. Hodgdon and me. But do her no wrong. If you hurt her, I'll cut your pecker off and use it for lobster chum!"

Stephen had not known what to answer. He grew red and stammered some inane reply. Even in retrospect, he could never discover a rational answer to that warning. Hodgdon was all pleasantness when Edith came down, and the old man never alluded to that subject again.

Hodgdon did not have to warn Stephen. On their third date, when he reached over and started to pet Edith's breasts, she did not object. Her parents were asleep upstairs and it was late. When, mistaking consent for further invitation, he groped under her skirt, she firmly removed his hand and placed it back on her breast.

"Stephen," she said in a matter-of-fact tone, "I have nothing against sex. I have five brothers and sisters and we all know what my mother and father do in their bedroom. There is nothing wrong with it. But I don't plan to have sex with you or anyone else until I'm married."

Shoemaker had heard that story before, but with Edith it stuck. She would never let him explore below her waist. When Stephen, several dates later, settled her hand on his bulging fly, she said gently, "Stephen, do you really want me to? All this will do is make you feel worse, like you always tell me." That usually stopped matters right there, and was the reason why the Schoodic Peninsula road received its weekly fertilization of Shoemaker seminal fluid.

It was strange. Stephen could not explain it. As the months passed by, he resented less and less the mental and physical isolation imposed by the climate and topography. Through Edith's eyes he saw the evergreens march down to the water's edge with only a rugged demarcation of rocks and tumbled boulders to mark the separation. The rising and ebbing of the tide twice a day as the moon, with a galactic shove, hoisted the ocean over the barricade of boulders, but, like Sisyphus, without ever achieving more than an emphemeral beachhead. The days on end of nothing but dense fog, that offspring of the Gulf Stream which had traveled thousands of miles north to mate its Caribbean warmth with the Arctic chill of the Labrador Current. She showed him how the water mirrored the colors of the sky until one could see them merge into a oneness at the distant horizon.

Stephen had decided to return to the area after the war. A gasoline station would be a natural for this location, he told Edith. If only he could get some of the Kraut prisoners at Gouldsboro to teach him automobile mechanics, he would be all set. It was his dream, and Edith did not discourage him.

Master Sergeant Mario Steffanelli also had a vista of Maine, but *his* view was confined by a fourteen-foot-high barbed-wire fence and did not arouse a pastoral surge in his heart. He manned one of the four corner outpost towers ringing the Gouldsboro Prisoner-of-War Camp. Looking out onto his sector of the vast compound, he could see the geometrically monotonous rows of austere two-story barracks spread out beneath him like hotels in a Monopoly game. Ten rows of barracks, gray, peeling, poorly insulated, each with a smoking stovepipe chimney, even in this May weather. On the other side of the square stockade, the assembly field was bordered by the mess hall and the recreation hall, both used in shifts, for by 1944 the prison population was increasing faster than the ability of the Army to house it.

Just outside the northwest corner, beyond the wire fence, were four large Quonset huts, with grease-stained windows and spreading blotches of crumbling orange rust on their pitched sides. Mario could hear emanating from them, without a pause, the constant din of machines and tools being worked against resisting metal as the prisoners sweated to mend the shattered vehicles from the African campaign of the American Third Army. Scattered over the dozens of acres surrounding the repair and maintenance shops were thousands of tanks, jeeps, armored personnel carriers, trucks, and mobile artillery pieces which had either just arrived from Boston for rehabilitation or were about to be driven, fully restored, back to the railroad depot at North Sullivan.

God, how those fuckers work! Mario listened to the steady noise of labor. He shook his head in disgust and shifted his Garand to his other arm. The Germans came out of the Quonsets each evening, with dust and grime glued to their skin by hot sticky sweat and grease. But no matter how tired they were, they all stripped and showered completely before putting on the rough clothes they used after work. There was a mechanical precision in the way they worked, showered, ate, and even played. Mario could almost imagine them all lined up in a row, their pricks out at right angle, on their hands and knees, fucking in unison as their colonel, Werner, called out the timing. I'll bet they'd all come off at the same time, too, he thought to himself.

Mario was ashamed to admit that the Germans ran everything themselves, unlike the Italians who had occupied the camp up until six months ago. It was rarely necessary for the guard platoons to issue orders or to make arrangements for the logistical details of food distribution, clothing requirements, or hygiene for the five thousand men. The Germans maintained their own rigid military hierarchy and functioned as if they, and not the Americans, were in command of this desolate outpost.

The Army had chosen the camp site with unusual thoroughness. Placed far up the Maine coast, about fifty miles from the Canadian border, it was as isolated as any place could be on the American mainland. Schoodic Peninsula was a rocky fist thrust twenty miles out into the Atlantic Ocean. On three sides, freedom lay three thousand miles away across the hostile north sea. As for the mainland side, it *was* possible for the prisoners to escape, but to where? Ten thousand square miles of impenetrable forest without food or roads lay north and west. And going south would only lead to large population centers. No, the site was excellent. The Germans were prisoners, isolated physically and trapped psychologically. With bureaucratic overconfidence, the Army had deliberately undermanned the camp defenses.

Looking at Mario's short, fat body and dull-witted expression, one would have been hard put to say that he was doing anything at all, but beneath his thick, double-folded eyelids he was methodically sweeping his assigned sector for any unusual activity. He squinted because of the glaring sunlight and, as he did, the scene lost its three-dimensional appearance. Everything became flat and artificial, resembling a stage-prop setting with paper cutouts pasted on a painted backdrop. The optical distortion could play funny tricks, he realized with a sudden feeling of alarm. For a moment, from his elevated stance, Mario imagined that the Germans below were the freed men, and he, up there enclosed in his small wooden box, was the prisoner in a suspended cage. He blinked hard and, to demonstrate who was the master, spat widely over the railing.

Those bastards, he conceded grudgingly, are certainly resourceful. It was true. The prisoners lived almost as well as the guards, thanks to a ploy they were exploiting to the hilt. The war had called up most of the able-bodied garage mechanics in Hancock County. Hesitatingly at first, and then with increasing confidence and ease, the local farmers and factory workers brought their ailing cars, trucks, and tractors to the prisoners, who quickly put them back in running condition, often with filched Army parts. The Germans could not accept payment for their work, so there quickly developed a thriving barter service by which the inmates obtained all the sundries not provided by the United States government. Extra food, chocolate, cigarettes, blankets, and even a radio appeared. The camp command did nothing to discourage the practice. It kept the prisoners busy, saved the taxpayers money, and, most of all, served to dispel the initial anxiety and lingering fear in the surrounding population that the presence of five thousand foreign soldiers had originally engendered.

The last few weeks, the Germans had been working harder than ever. Colonel Werner had obtained permission for his men to return to the shops after evening meals to work on a large collection of tractors and harvesters which the farmers had brought in after their spring plowing. As the prisoners worked late shifts, the lights and noisy racket marred the pitch blackness and silence of the star-spangled night.

Now those bastards are really crazy, Mario and his companions commented to each other over a beer one evening. When questioned about the sudden interest in sprucing up their uniforms, Werner explained that it was for a dress parade to celebrate the founding of the Weimar Republic.

"No Nazi crap, Werner. You bastards can march all you want, nice and spiffy-like, but keep your damn Hitler stuff out of my camp." The warning also applied to the cardboard swastikas Barracks 5-A had cut out of thick pieces of foot-square cardboard stock, which had cost the Germans two valve jobs.

The sun was bright today, and Mario leaned back against the searchlight stand to seek the cool shadow of the tower roof. He spat over the side again and waited. That was all he had been doing for sixteen years. He was a twenty-year man. Four more years and, if the war was over, out on half-pay. It was a good job. A good life. He never cared where the Army sent him. He just did what he was told, drew his pay, saluted his superiors, and pulled rank on everyone with fewer stripes. He never went into Winter Harbor on his time off. It was not that he was deterred by his physical unattractiveness—he always expected to pay for female companionship—but by sheer sexual inertia. He got his three squares a day, clean sheets, and was as happy as a well-fed basset hound. He patted his expanding paunch, content with his existence.

"Hey, get away from that fence!" he suddenly barked. "Get your fucking ass away! You know the rules." He leaned far out over the railing.

The figure below looked up at the menacing silhouette and smiled. He saluted Mario good-naturedly and made a token bow from the waist as he clicked his heels. Oberst Otto Werner was tall and thin, with a lean, pinched-in look that gave his otherwise boyish face an acerbic cast. He wore steel-rimmed glasses. His sandy blonde hair was clipped in a short crewcut.

It was okay, Werner assured himself. They *do* watch us, even when we do not think they do. Especially Steffanelli, that fat Sicillian. This is good. They watch us all the time to make sure we do not break out. He continued his pacing of the perimeter to test the same ploy with the other three towers. Just as long, he nodded with a devious smirk, as they do not watch to see if we are breaking *in!*

Mario watched the retreating figure with contempt. "Got to be on top of those bastards all the time," he muttered aloud. He continued his surveillance. The rising waves of heat from the ground below mixed with the dust and shimmied the spatial planes of sight. His eyes skipped over the dividing fence and took in the whole panorama as a single composite picture. The blatant disparity in manpower between the multitude of prisoners milling below and the too few guards. The Germans doing calisthenics over in the opposite corner, the running and crouching, oddly enough looking more like commando tactics than pushups. The static parade of vehicles all finely tuned, fully gassed up, washed and waxed, waiting only for pressure on the accelerator to spring to life by the hundreds.

Without his being aware of the subconscious process, his mind began to weave these visual fragments together. He gasped with mental pain as a sickening thought took shape. Aw, c'mon now, Steffanelli, you'll be having nightmares next! Sharpen up. But he could not repress the fear which rose to mock him. He scanned the now-ominous landscape again. Never! They will never! he muttered to himself, actively alarmed. Why should they escape? What for? Where would they *go?* And with that comforting conclusion to slay the chimera, he leaned back into the cool shadow and spit once more over the side.

Otto Werner, too, stopped to take in the same scene as Mario. The sight did not frighten *him*. He had been in captivity too long. A soldier should be shot, not caged. He sighed, for just an instant, and then turned toward the east as if the cool breeze touching his face was a messenger from his native land across the immense distance.

"When?" he had asked impatiently over and over, up until one month ago.

"Soon," came the reassuring answer, not on the wings of the wind, but hidden in a side of pork delivered each day to the camp kitchen by the purveying firm of Schneider and Son from Presque Isle where Lars Trondheim had stopped to make another "sale" on his busy trip down from Canada, not too long ago.

About the same time that Mario leaned over the side and cleared his throat and spat five times in as many minutes, Agreen Crabtree and his thirteen-year-old son Homer looked up and down the deserted double track of the Maine Central Railroad.

Half a dozen long trains passed through North Sullivan Junction each day, but rarely did any of them stop there. Passengers now had to go to Bangor and get the train or bus from there. Even the Bar Harbor Special had been discontinued for the duration. To build a whole spur just for a bunch of summer people? Crabtree shook his head in a gesture of disgust. The ways of the rich and mighty never set well with him.

During these war years, the shoreline route of the Maine Central was busy with freight, hauling the paper and timber products of the rich forestlands, as well as the endless cars of dried fish caught off the Grand Banks and destined for the civilian centers of Britain. In the fall hundreds of boxcars of potatoes from Aroostook County would pass through on the way to eastern markets. Only in late August would Agreen Crabtree throw the semaphore switch to signal the 6:05 A.M. southbound to stop at the nondescript depot and couple on the long line of boxcars laden with the blueberry crop of Hancock County.

Crabtree had more than the usual reason to stare at the empty tracks this late Friday afternoon. The day before, George Hazelwood, the county superintendent, had paid one of his infrequent visits to the North Sullivan depot. It was to tell Crabtree a rather incomplete story. "I'm telling this to you, Agreen, so's you won't be calling me up in the middle of the night and waking everybody

up. The train isn't going to be scheduled. It'll just come
along at any time with one car."

He looked pompously at Crabtree, shaking his finger
into his face. "So's don't be bothering nobody and scaring
nobody when it comes through. Do you understand?"

Crabtree maintained the same impassive expression,
looking squarely at his superior. Hazelwood felt a little
foolish and hastened to add, "I can't tell you any more.
I don't know ... oh, it's some secret Army business. They
won't tell me. They won't tell anybody. Only I've got my
orders like everybody else. I'm going down the line telling everybody just the same's I'm telling you."

The finger kept poking, almost defensively. "It's
coming from Canada, I heard." He moved closer to whisper the furtive words in Crabtree's ear. "It's coming
straight down from some lake with a funny name up in
Saskatchewan, and it's going up through Boston to some
place in Tennessee. The Canadian Pacific is taking it to
the border and we're coupling it from there."

He paused for a minute, for effect.

"They're going the long way around to get to Tennessee, if you ask me, but that's none of my business. I
don't know what the bejeezus is on that train, but someone is going to a heck of a lot of trouble and spending a
heck of a lot of money to haul it special-like all the way
up to Boston."

He stopped, aware that he was running on. "So's
remember," he warned in a solemn tone, "keep quiet and
don't bother nobody when it comes on through."

When George Hazelwood had left and was recount-
ing to himself the outcome of that very satisfactory conversation with Crabtree, he realized with a start that not
once during the whole time had Agreen said a single
word.

→ EIGHT

Rohmer was impatient. It was over three weeks since he had left the Tirpitz Pier in Kiel. He lay waiting at the designated grid sector for the other six U-boats to join him. His position was off the coast of Maine, one hundred forty-one miles northeast of Mount Desert Island, just beyond radar range of the Schoodic Station, whose maximum area of accuracy was between eighty and one hundred miles. He paced back and forth on the bridge, chain-smoking to assuage his anxiety and making his Oberleutnant, Kern, very miserable.

Finally, Rohmer stopped his nervous activity and, in the failing light of dusk, stood next to his executive and first-watch officers, elbows cocked on the cold rusty metal rim of the bridge, scanning the horizon for the last time with long, slow sweeps of his binoculars. Suddenly, a black speck broke the glassy stillness of the water. Then, like a conjuring of Merlin, out of the deep void, living parcels of human beings, friends, companions, memories of the past, and hopes for the future—all appeared, without a warning, from nowhere, on time and in position. Another and another and another. It was a startling sight, impressive to the uninitiated, and still thrilling to a jaded old sailor like Rohmer watching the maneuver for the thousandth time.

The vessels moved in closer as loud cheers of greeting were shouted across the still water. The rendezvous had not been scheduled to boost morale. Von Eyssen had often sent his men out for as long as eight months during which time their whole world consisted of a hermetic cylinder pierced only by an occasional static-clouded message. There was a purpose for this meeting, and Rohmer saw that it was dispatched. Almost immediately, the two scientists from Peenemünde emerged and were ferried from boat to boat in inflated rubber dinghies. They looked at the scene around them. Quiet black dots bobbing on a plane of gray which mirrored the clouds above until one could not see where the water and sky drew their boundary lines. It was an eerie sameness, as close to a sense of being suspended in infinity as they were ever to experience.

It was amazing, too, how their perspective had changed, conditioned by the tangible parameters of their new world. They thought back to that first day and the wet, precarious ride from Peenemünde to the waiting submarines at Bornholm. How solid and immense the mainland had appeared, how tiny and vulnerable the U-boats. Never, they had concluded simultaneously to themselves, could forty human beings live and work and breathe within that thin skin of iron, constructed like a patchwork quilt with panels of riveted metal stuck onto a spindly oval framework. A loose rivet, a stress crack in the metallic fabric, a fissure in the smooth gray film which somehow kept out the tons of water, and their lives would be extinguished in an instant.

They thought back to those long days when they traveled submerged with only the snorkel wake to mark their existence. How much their lives depended upon this frail umbilical pipe which sucked in the necessary mixture of nitrogen and oxygen which God had insisted every human consume every minute of his life, even when he was in a place where he had no business to be.

And the scientists' hesitant exploration of the submarine itself. Von Eyssen had seen that they had free run of the ship. They inspected cautiously, venturing outward a little more each day, fore and aft, widening their beachhead of familiar conquered terrain. How the vessel got larger and longer each time they traversed safe and friendly landmarks!

They almost missed the hidden sleeping quarters of the crew, two-by-six-foot shelves hung as an afterthought between the hot- and cold-water pipes, whistling metal arteries of oil, compressed air, and effluent, and miles of electrical cables.

They peered into the "wireless room," no more than a closet where one hydrophone operator sat impassively, earphones on his head. For the duration of this mission, he would not dare send a single electrical spark. His job was to monitor the constant barrage of disjointed messages from the communications center in Lorient which meant something to some recipient somewhere in the Atlantic. Patiently, he waited, marking his endless vigil with the special hourly coded communiqués which assured the seven U-boats that the Kriegsmarine still considered their mission viable. If one hour passed without picking up that signal intended only for them, the attack would be aborted and the pack would turn for home.

The scientists spent much time in the forward engine room, marveling at the two powerful four-stroke diesel engines, each capable of forging twenty-two hundred horsepower at full speed. They saw the eighteen cylinders with their synchronous sliding pistons of oiled and burnished steel marching back and forth like a row of goose-stepping soldiers. The two diesel engines which coupled vile-smelling petroleum with pure, sweet oxygen to produce electricity. Electricity to propel the motors when submerged, purify the air, remove human waste products, and even raise and lower the whole vessel to and from the ocean surface. They admired the intricate intermeshed complexity of the whole process, standing back to take it all in like a Léger painting of the early 1930s.

It was in the forward torpedo room that they really felt at home. That is what they had come for. They slowly ran their hands over the sleek cylinders, one end tapered like a conventional torpedo, the other end flared into a fimbriated terminal with sharp fin guides like a bomb. Their hands explored and checked that swollen protrusion near the head which puzzled the sailors, but which the scientists knew contained the brains of the lethal instrument, the inertial and magnetic gyroscopes. At the launching site, they would totally degauss the large metal cylinder, thus demagnetizing it prior to imprinting into

the electronic memory the exact coordinates of its destination. The ingenious mechanism would then lift the pro-
jectile up into a smooth, unerring trajectory two hundred
miles long and bring it down on target within an accuracy of one mile, to destroy an area ten city blocks in
diameter.

Like an artist's signature, the imperial swastika of
the Third Reich was stenciled on each side of the nose
cone. The scientists' fingers lingered on the blood-red
symbol as if it were warm and comforting. They thought
again of their role in producing this inhuman weapon
and their expressions turned proud.

They are a strange lot, thought Rohmer when they
came to inspect the missiles in his submarine. They barely
glanced up at him when he greeted them, ignoring his
station as beneath them. "I hope that von Eyssen has a
damn good lock on them to make sure they do what they
are supposed to," he worried aloud to Kern. "Especially
that Frenchie. I don't trust them any further than I
have to."

Rohmer met the Norwegian passengers when he paid
a call to U-204 and U-205. Although they were more
congenial then the Baltic bunch, he found that he had
very little to say to them either. They were Nazi collabo-
rators from Quisling's crowd and lost no opportunity to
praise Hitler at any chance. Repelled by their unctuous
sincerity, he complained to Kern that there was no more
fanatic a believer than a convert.

Rohmer only knew in vague terms what the Norwegians' job was. He was to capture the train from Canada and deliver the contents of the freight car to them.
They were to verify the shipment and repack the precious
material into large, empty, bright yellow canisters which
were carried in the stern bulkheads of each submarine.
Rohmer did not know why the Third Reich was so ob-
sessed with this mineral. He was no physicist and uranium meant nothing to him, but he could still hear von
Esseyn exclaiming its importance as he punctuated his
sentences with short jabs into the air.

"Rohmer, the train! That is your primary goal. I

cannot emphasize enough the urgency and strategic importance of the contents of the train. The safety of our men, yes, that is important. Do not neglect them. But they are not as important as that train. *If necessary, sacrifice them! All of them!* Save only enough to get you and your U-boats back here any way that you can.

"The missiles, the attack on Boston. That, too, is important, not only for us, the Korps, but for Germany. You know that. A chance to rub the American's faces in the shit they have been dropping on us. But do not let emotions get in the way. Do not let your zeal and personal feelings sway you from the real goal of this mission. Get that material!"

He clasped the captain on the shoulder.

"There will be other times, other cities, other missiles, but only this one opportunity to seize the ore. I don't understand its importance fully, but this I can confide. If you fail, you will be sealing the fate of your Fatherland and the home of your father and fathers before you . . ."

He tried to communicate to Rohmer an inspiring image of the triumph that could be his.

"Succeed, and the Führer himself will congratulate you. Rohmer, our salvation is riding on that train. You must succeed. You must!"

Rohmer watched as the rubber rafts returned the scientists to their home submarines after the last inspection. As soon as they were taken aboard, the U-boats would submerge and remain in place, hidden, until told to continue on to the mainland. Everything had gone as planned . . . so far.

As the two Norwegians climbed out of the rubber dinghies, they could not help commenting to themselves on the irony of how they, who could hurl fistfuls of death through the heavens to destroy whole cities, had entrusted their lives over the past hour to a flat balloon of air held in place by a sandwich of rubberized canvas. With a sigh of relief, they scampered up the slick sides of the U-boats onto the rotting wooden deck slats, which now seemed as solid and secure as the mainland of not too long ago.

Rohmer monitored their safe delivery and issued the order for general descent. The next time they would all see each other again, God permitting, would be on the shores of the United States. Turning away so his first officer could not see him, Rohmer crossed himself and sent a small but heartfelt prayer to an unseen guardian far up above the heavy layer of clouds.

→NINE

The recipient of that German prayer was Morris Berkowitz flying at two hundred seventy-two miles an hour in a passenger-converted B-24 Liberator. He was passing over the northern reaches of the Maine coastal waters and in another hour-and-a-half would be landing in Boston. Leaving England one day ahead of schedule, he had sat for hours hunched forward on the seat, tense and anxious. Michael had been right! The British had answers, but with them came new unexpected questions which only compounded the danger that loomed ahead. With a mingling of dread of the known and panic of the yet-unknown, Moe urged the lumbering plane on faster, as if every mile served to stave off the eventual Nazi nemesis.

Moe had not been prepared for the historic grandeur of the British Admiralty. He entered the complex guarded by the statue of Captain Cook surveying the green stretches of the Mall. The Director of Naval Intelligence occupied a three-story Georgian red-brick building to one side of the grassed-in park area. To the left lay the small enclosed garden of No. 10 Downing Street where Winston Churchill labored. Facing it across the Mall, he could see the Foreign Office and the Guards' War Memorial. And on his right stood the soot-drenched buildings of the Horse Guards and the old Admiralty building dating back to the days of Elizabeth I and Sir Francis Drake. The Mall itself, now ringed with sandbags and barrage balloon stanchions, still showed the vestiges of its former dignity as the parade ground used by the Guards for the Trooping of the Color, a tradition shelved for the duration.

The inside of the building quickly brought Moe back to the harsh realities of the business of war. Room 39. The heart of British Naval Intelligence. About thirty feet square, with creamy beige walls setting off the Norwegian rose marble fireplace, it was filled with a dozen desks occupied by persons busy talking, writing, or transfering "dockets," thin combinations of cardboard, string, and paper, from one station to another. The room was noisy, with an occasional oasis of relative quiet around either end of the Adam mantel where several persons were carrying on low-keyed private conversations.

Whether it was Bainbridge's magic or the extreme urgency of Moe's mission, Berkowitz realized that his British hosts placed high priority on his visit. It was obvious from the credentials of the two men assigned to him: Geoffrey Fleming and Merrit Hedley-White were both personal assistants to the first lord of the Admiralty and had been engaged in the life-and-death struggle with Canaris and German Intelligence since the middle thirties. Both were young, articulate, concerned, and, by pedigree, civilians.

The two men listened politely to the information Moe had brought with him. However, they were unable to avoid viewing with bemused indulgence and forebearance the colonial's attempt to practice counterespionage. As Hedley-White informed Moe with friendly condescension, his department had been in existence when Lord Burghley was using double agents with ciphers in beer barrel bungs to trap Mary Queen of Scots for Elizabeth I, while Indians were still fishing in Boston Harbor. Britain had been at war for as long as time itself. Not only with Hitler, but with European threats going back a thousand years. Despite her insular position in respect to the Continent, it had always been vital for His Majesty's Government to divine the plans of her European neighbors who, the English were convinced, were only waiting for a singular drought to dry up the English Channel, then to sweep across that precious moat and vanquish them as did the Celts and the Normans. Living in a constant state of preparedness, the British had developed an exquisitely perceptive Intelligence arm which, though always kept finely honed, was brought up to peak capability by war.

The Germans are planning long-range rocket attacks on London, O'Malley's assistant was told. At first, Moe could not comprehend such a weapon and found it hard to grasp the import of such a sinister development. Separated from the schemes of the Nazis not only by three thousand miles of ocean, but by a history of relative peace, he was not sensitive to the peril it posed to the island country whose borders were no more than thirty miles away from enemy territory.

The British knew a great deal about the German rocket research program. Hedley-White handed Moe a recent photograph from a reconnaissance overflight of Swinnemünde. It showed a rocket in place on an earthen embankment that pointed out over the Baltic in the direction of Bornholm. The rocket itself was easily identifiable. It was no more than twelve to fifteen feet in length, and small enough to be easily transported by almost anything, boat, truck, or even a hay wagon, and assembled within hours.

The British hypothesized that the "ski slopes" in France were related to the vast slanted earthen embankments seen at Swinnemünde and Peenemünde. Whereas the experimental rockets were being tested over the Baltic Sea, in France the "ski slopes" were all pointing toward England. The square buildings attached to the ramps were thought to be storage depots, although no actual rockets had been seen in place. Because of the danger that the rockets were self-propelled, the British felt that they would not get sufficient warning prior to a launching to destroy the missiles on the ramps. With no other alternative, the RAF waged a prophylactic war of attrition, pounding every site they could find.

Moe realized the inescapable logic of the situation. Why else would the U-boats make a detour to Bornholm and assume a completely erratic pattern of activity unless they were up to something more than hunting convoys? Fleming pointed out that it would not be difficult for von Eyssen to convert the submarines to carry the rockets. All he would have to do is modify the forward bulkheads and knock out the torpedo compression tube chambers, which he wouldn't be using anyway. In that way, he could deliver twelve to sixteen warheads per U-boat.

At this point, the deductive process broke down and left the British just as baffled as their guest over how the rockets were to be launched once brought to the United States. In the case of England, the Germans were in control of the Channel countries and the "ski slopes" were already built. In the case of the United States, the problem assumed a more complex nature.

First, the launch platforms, though simple structures, were still large and cumbersome, and difficult to transport or to conceal. Second, British scientists theorized that setting the rockets' gyroscopic systems would take at least twenty-four hours, during which time the Germans had to possess territorial mastery. DNI reluctantly left both these perplexing problems unresolved.

What caused Moe to despair was the realization that the British were not sanguine about stopping the rain of missiles. He could see all too well how the logistics of the simple, easily concealed warhead could defy advance detection or stopping. London prepared for the worst. Every day, thousands of children were sent out of the city to the surrounding countryside. Women and the old and infirm crowded Victoria Station for relocation elsewhere. Factories were dismantled and then reassembled in outlying counties. London was becoming a deserted city. What the Luftwaffe could not do in 1940 during the nine months of the ferocious Battle of Britain was occurring now from fear of the unknown, fear of what a devil incarnate like Adolph Hitler could conjure up when in command of the intellectual and scientific resources of a plundered Continent.

On Moe's second day, Hedley-White took him to see first-hand the "Divers Belt," a long strip of England which faced the expected stream of guided missiles. The protective shield reached back to a depth of fifteen miles from the English Channel and stretched in length from St. Margaret's Bay to Cuckmere Haven, a distance of seventy miles. Twenty-three thousand men and women manned thousands of antiaircraft guns and searchlight batteries. The skyscape was dotted with man-made clouds of balloons like floating Portuguese men-of-war trailing their long fingers of contact detonators. All this to stop the avalanche of rockets which the English knew would be hurled down upon them.

When Moe saw the vast preparations to counter the Nazi threat, he had a sickening feeling at how defenseless Boston was. Never, he realized, had Americans ever been afraid to look up into the sky. And not since the Civil War had Americans died on American soil in defense of their own cities. Was Boston or any other city in the future to become another London, paralyzed and decimated by fear? Would Americans accept the massive translocation of a metropolis to avoid a disaster they could not comprehend or envisage? Moe could barely restrain the impulse to bury deeply in his subconscious all the brutal facts he had just learned.

His hosts primed Moe with everything else they

knew. Lars Trondheim? Moe thought that in some per-
verted way, they admired the cocky bastard. They had
followed his previous "sales trips," the last one being in
Spain where he hovered near the British fortress of Gi-
braltar, trying to secure local agents for infiltration.
Nothing ever came of it, but Fleming was forced to admit that the modus operandi with "plants" and "hos-
tages" was "bloody clever." Hedley-White admitted that
on more than one occasion they had been able to feed the
spy with false information for the Abwehr, and had kept
him viable for this purpose.

The Göteborg Trading Company? It was a blatant
Nazi front, useful in converting the Jewish wealth of
occupied Europe into cold cash to finance espionage in
Allied countries. But it was Swedish and thus could not
be touched.

The *Astra?* The British could add only one rather
curious fact. The passenger list claimed six Latvian engineers traveling under Swedish passports to install a
fourdrinier for a Chilean kraft paper mill. The odd thing
about this—and it made absolutely no sense to British
Intelligence—was that six months before all of the men
in question were officers serving aboard the Soviet destroyer *Arakcheev.* However, as far as the cargo of the
freighter was concerned, it was clean.

Hedley-White and Moe realized that Trondheim's
activating Aacher tied the *Astra* to the Swedish spy. But
for what purpose? The Germans did not waste agents or
plants. Were Trondheim and Aacher and the *Astra* connected to Rohmer's U-boats, or were they part of yet
another plot? Sitting in the ministry that afternoon, no
one could tell.

The Russian fleet floored them completely. The British had been following the cruise with more than cursory
interest. Moe got the feeling that they still considered the
ocean as their private preserve and took umbrage when
anybody else used it. "Let the Bolsheviks hang out around
Vladivostock or Port Arthur where the Japanese blew
them out of the water with one hand tied behind their
backs," they complained to Moe. "It was your Roosevelt

—Teddy—that bailed them out that time." The British soon found out that their American visitor knew less of his country's history than they did.

"What the bloody hell are the Russians going over to the Grand Banks for? They didn't come all this way to go fishing. Nikolai Vasilyevich Martov is up to something," Fleming assured Moe, which only heightened his anxiety.

The side trips to pick up the scientists from Telemark made the English prick up their ears. Since the 1930s, Leo Szilard and British physicists had been alarmed by reports coming out of Germany from Otto Hahn and others of the possibility of constructing an explosive device, theoretically of great military value, using an entirely new kind of scientific principle. The British guessed that there was also clandestine research on this secret weapon in the United States which most people did not know about. Their reasoning was based on the fact that many of Hahn's coworkers who had fled to England when Hitler came to power in the thirties were now in the United States—physicists with names like Fermi, Teller, Fuchs, names that meant nothing to Berkowitz, who made a mental note to have O'Malley use his subrosa channels to pursue the matter.

During his forty-eight hours in London, Moe was constantly aware of Bainbridge's men hovering about, ready to protect him and supply his needs. But not even the agents could erase a furtive tail that shadowed Moe whenever he left his hotel. Shortly after making his hasty decision to leave England twenty-four hours ahead of schedule, Berkowitz was violently sideswiped by a car that must have been waiting two blocks from the British ministry. If it had not been for the fortuitous appearance of a food truck backing out of a nearby loading platform and forcing the speeding Jaguar to swerve, he would have been crushed under the wheels. As it was, the car barely missed him. Maybe it was all his imagination and nerves, but why had the two faces in the car stared long and hard after him as their car disappeared down the street? And where were Bainbridge's men?

The incident only reinforced his compulsion to get back to Boston and persuade the authorities into invoking protective measures against the potential horror of a missile attack. Laden down with an acute sense of fear for the future, Berkowitz departed on a modified transport which his British hosts had placed at his disposal.

Had he been able to look down through the carpet of gray clouds which shielded Rohmer from detection, Moe would have seen the wolf pack starting to dive, like a school of thin, sleek whales, pairing off for a delicate underwater ballet. The young American knew *now* what terror those marine inhabitants carried within their bellies.

➤ T E N

Hugh Denis O'Connell was in an irritable mood as he surveyed his office for the five thousandth morning. He had been mayor of Boston for sixteen years and he was tired. I must be getting old, he sighed to his secretary as she set before him the packed schedule of interviews, General Court sessions, visiting dignitaries, and routine paper work which filled his ten- to twelve-hour day. Not that he would have given up even one minute of it. In the late 1800s the Irish had foreclosed their mortgage on the political life of the city, and here, in his office, lay the keys of power.

O'Connell was in his late sixties, his pure white wavy hair set off by the baby-pink complexion of his fleshy face. He wore a pair of gold-rimmed bifocals and a constant half-smile on his face. A custom-tailored suit of brown cheviot attempted without success to disguise his heavy figure. Brown wing-tip shoes and a gold keychain across his vest completed the dignified image.

The office was a large, dark, oak-paneled room with high ceiling and wide casement windows overlooking the Boston Common. An old radiator hissed and clanked behind its fancy pierced-iron grille. It worked at the same pace both summer and winter, oblivious to the weather. Two flags stood behind the massive mahogany desk, one with the seal of the Commonwealth of Massachusetts, the other with the Stars and Stripes. A worn Kashan stretched from the desk, across the pitted floor, to the double doors leading to the antechamber.

O'Connell was a conscientious mayor, but he never fooled himself into thinking he was anything else but a willing political hostage of the faithful Irish Catholic vote. The O'Connells had an emotional hold on a large segment of the population who obtained from his family's steady ascension to power a sense of identification with their own hopes and saw in the biennial besting of his Republican opponent a belated retaliation for the Battle of the Boyne.

O'Connell got up and cast a worried glance through the window. He had been briefed by Naval Intelligence on the anticipated sabotage attack on the harbor. He interpreted the German threat as a personal affront, and had tended to the security precautions with a zeal usually reserved for the March Saint Patrick's Day Parade. In the distance, the green oasis of the Boston Common absorbed his attention. Even now, in the third year of the war for America, Hugh maintained the patrician tradition of the swan boats on the pond. "As long as I am

mayor, those goddamn boats will float, if I have to pay for
them myself." And as a contrary symbol of his plebian
administration, this gracious relic of the city's past had
persisted.

He turned back to his desk, his eyes taking in the scattered photographs. He would never be "Catholic Father
of the Year" with only five children, but that was all the
good Lord would grant his wife, Jean. He looked with
affection at the sepia-toned mezzotint of his grandfather,
standing in his saloon, which had also served as the
Democratic headquarters of the Irish-dominated Eighth
Ward. Next to it stood the austere picture of his father
in his flowing judicial robes. He could hear his father's
admonition ringing in his ears, as if the stately old gentleman were still alive in the room with him. "There are
a lot of micks in the States who have money. Only we
have a city. Keep this city and you will control the state.
Hold onto the state and some day, one can never tell, you
may control the country. *Never forsake our city!* The
Hebrews have a saying over two thousand years old, 'Let
my right arm lose its strength, O Jerusalem, if I should
forsake thee.' They are right. This is our birthright, our
burden."

As O'Connell remembered his father's words, a shiver
ran up and down his body. He never scoffed at his father
the way many of his friends did. The judge could be
right. America was changing. The Irish had broken out
of their provincial mold. They had had wealth for a short
time, and political power on a local level for a long time.
Someday, they would have national power.

The mayor remembered that fateful creed, "his
birthright and his burden." He had sons and grandsons.
Let the O'Connells hold the city, treasure the affection of
the people, and return it with sincere gratitude, and
maybe someday his seed would ride down Pennsylvania
Avenue.

He bent forward and leaned across the desk to pick
up the photograph of his eldest son John with his other
three boys and girl. He suddenly straightened up, and
rubbed his hand under his right shoulder blade to ease the

burning stab of pain. The past few months, he had noticed an almost persistent ache which started under his rib cage on the right side and pierced straight through to the back. It must be arthritis, he thought. It wasn't his heart. Even he knew that angina occurred on the left side. But for that occasional cramp and a general fatigue, he felt in good health.

It's this damn sabotage business, he would say to his secretary. Jennie would nod in agreement. It did not pay to argue with O'Connell, but privately she reserved her opinion that he had shown less energy for the past four or five months. He looked drawn and older. She was afraid to mention it, but even his face looked thinner. For the first time, she could see the bony outline of his usually well-padded cheekbones. Had she mentioned this fact, the mayor would have been delighted. Without making any attempt, he found that he could leave the table without finishing his food, let alone asking for seconds. His appetite had lessened, miraculously. His clothes hung better and his belt was looser. He was delighted, almost afraid to talk about it, as if that would dispel whatever magic was finally taking the fat off his bones.

It was not magic, though, that was reducing the human bulk of this third generation of O'Connells in America. A cancer of the head of the pancreas was growing, gradually, insidiously, weaving its tentacles around the nerves issuing from his spine, infiltrating the retroperitoneal space alongside his vertebrae, pinching off the biliary ducts draining his liver, strangulating his intestines and occluding the tube from his right kidney, until one day his complexion, usually florid and healthy, would begin to partake of the sickly yellow-green hue of cirrhosis, coloring his sclerae and staining his urine, and by then Hugh Denis O'Connell would dream no more.

He did not know this now. He replaced the gold frame on the desk, still rubbing his back.

"It's this damn German business," he complained to himself. "When I get that settled, I'd better go down to the State House gym for a workout or at least a massage."

With that comforting thought to ease his pain and

conscience, he pressed the intercom and ordered Jennie to bring in the first of his appointments. As he stood waiting for his guest among the ancient tokens and relics of his office, a handsome young stranger who had traveled three thousand miles across America was circling above the city, a man who before a fortnight was to pass would demand from Hugh O'Connell the brutal sacrifice of the city he loved.

→ **ELEVEN**

The last thing he heard before his head dropped back against the soft back of the seat was the mellifluous tones of the loudspeaker announcing that the plane would land in Boston within forty-five minutes. The stewardess moved down the aisle to see if any passengers in first class wanted more of her coffee or Danish pastry. She stopped at the sleeping figure. One could not help but be taken with the natural handsomeness of the man. About thirty-five, six feet tall, deeply tanned. The curly blonde hair which pressed against the white antimacassar must have continued over his chest so that it could peek out from under his sleeve ends. His unlined face, with finely chiseled features, was closely shaven. His seersucker suit, wrinkled from the ten-hour flight, clung to his muscular frame, pulling up in creases around the swelling between his legs. High cowboy boots, the only discordant element, gleamed as if from a GI's spit polish.

The stewardess disengaged his hand from the paper cup of tepid coffee which was threatening to spill. Feeling her soft skin touching him, the passenger smiled in his sleep and shifted his weight. He reached for her arm with his other hand. His motive was evident as he casually moved her fingers to the bulge below his lap.

"Oh, no," she whispered in his ear, "that's an old trick. I've been around too long to fall for that."

She completed her extraction of the cup and moved down the aisle.

Through half-closed eyes, Douglas Evans Gatling IV watched her retreating buttocks swing from side to side as she tried to keep her balance. Oh, well, sometimes it worked and sometimes it didn't. He smiled, not really caring. Soon she would be back again. He settled himself snugly in the corner of the empty row of seats and resumed his happy half-dream.

The sudden change from his physics laboratory at Harvard to the arid, dusty sterility of the American Southwest was the greatest shock Douglas had ever experienced. The absence of rolling moist greenness made him despondent for months. The landscape at Los Alamos was bleak and barren. Mesquite bushes tried to prove that the soil was not all that hostile, but only centipedes and scorpions were convinced, as they alone took advantage of the sparse ground cover.

It was either too hot or too cold, up to 110 degrees during the day, while the air turned frigid and brittle when the sun sank below the Sangre de Christo Mountains, blue and purple in the West. And always it was dry. The dust got into Douglas's nose, his ears, his pores, his soul. It would never leave, even during the infrequent trips from the Atomic Testing Grounds to Albuquerque when he would check into one of the heavily booked-up hotels and soak in tub after tub of steaming water.

The work. That was the reward. He had leaped at the chance when Conant and Bush secretly recruited him and his department chief, Spencer Kissielowsky, for the Manhattan Project. Edward Teller, with his impossible Hungarian accent. Enrico Fermi, the ebullient and gregarious Italian. Klaus Fuchs, the accommodating, brilliant German who could always be counted upon to baby-sit for the mothers or to fill in for bridge. The others, from every country, speaking every dialect, mixing like a modern Tower of Babel.

The temporary barracks, the inadequate and oppressive routine and diet. The rush, rush, rush of time, racing them for success. The complaints of the mothers over the schooling of their children, of the fathers for improved living conditions for their families, and of the wives over the laundry water in which the alkali scum would reharden before the clothes were even dry.

Above all, the lack of privacy. The crowding together into a makeshift Army camp of unique intellects who had previously flourished like hothouse orchids in the rarefied air of staid, ivy-covered halls of erudition.

There was constant antagonism between scientist and bureaucrat, between the thinkers—represented by Oppenheimer, the genius of slight build whose towering imagination and brilliance had attracted and held these superscientists in the desert—and Leslie Groves, the quartermaster clerk cum tsar, whose incredible zeal and ability to connive and commandeer scarce equipment and personnel in the middle of a war had created a billion-dollar empire out of nothing in two short years.

That they functioned together and that it all succeeded was due to fear and faith. Fear for the future should this awesome force be discovered first by the Nazis, faith in the magic powers of science to cure all the ills of mankind with an incredible new panacea. They all knew, no matter what their background, what they were trying to accomplish. To drive together some infinitesimal pieces of matter they could never see, with a speed they could never clock.

They were testing two types of nuclear material:

uranium-235, which was laboriously refined from the more common but heavier U-238 ore in Oak Ridge, Tennessee; and plutonium, a new, artificial element whose extraction in Hanford, Washington, required an industrial complex spread over 430,000 acres and absorbed the electricity of a Detroit. Dissimilar in many ways, these two elements had one unique property. Compress them into a critical mass, and they would set off a chain reaction, exploding outward with the heat of the sun and the raw energy of the solar system.

To perfect the untested mechanics of this jamming-together, Kissielowsky and Gatling worked twelve to fourteen hours a day, risking limb and life. The building they worked in was constructed in anticipation of their violent death. Three walls were cinderblock, the fourth thin wood, so that in the event of an explosion the force would be dissipated through this opening and away from the other laboratories.

The two men were casting explosive material into the shape of a "lens" so when it was detonated, the force would be confined to one sharply defined vector instead of spreading out in all directions. Oppenheimer was to put the uranium in the center of a large hollow globe, covered with dozens of the molded lenses. The force of the simultaneous implosions would be directed inward to bear upon the critical center, driving the U-234 atoms together in a millionth of a second. In that space of time, the nuclear material would kiss and the fission triggered off release energy undreamt of by all the philosophies in the universe. The detonators were finally perfected, the lenses cast. The men rested, all limbs intact, waiting with barely uncontrolled emotion for the first test at nearby Alamogordo.

There was on hand, in addition to the test device, enough nuclear material to make only two bombs. If the enemy did not surrender after they were dropped, the Americans would be placed in an embarrassing position. It would be reasonable to expect the Germans or the Japanese to look upon the bomb only as a freak, some unperfected experimental device, which should not be taken seriously. Without a backup arsenal, the terror of this weapon would be mitigated and the war prolonged.

Oppenheimer and Groves finally convinced Stimson and Roosevelt that the Americans must be prepared to drop bomb after bomb until unconditional surrender was achieved. This decision meant the delivery of vast amounts of uranium ore to Oak Ridge to isolate the fraction of deadly powder and send it to the desert for assembly into a stockpile of weapons. Twelve hundred pounds of the yellow ore cake, the whole production of uranium from Lake Athabasca in Sasketchewan for the past nine months, was on a special train making its way through the endless dark forests of northern Canada, skirting the deep glacier-blue lakes, detouring around towns, traveling on innocuous routes before meeting the Maine Central which would escort it through the blueberry junction of Ellsworth to Boston.

Douglas Gatling could still see Groves, sweat beading on his forehead, corpulent belly pushing against the desk. Oppenheimer slowly pacing the room, deep in thought, his head inclined forward, hands clasped behind him. Kissielowsky sitting almost hidden in the corner, a quiet unassuming man of fifty, bald except for a fringe of gray hair, his mind dancing with thoughts behind his flashing steel-rimmed glasses. The naked lightbulb casting bizarre shadows against the raw clapboard walls, making the four men look like caricatures of archconspirators or criminals.

"Douglas," Kissielowsky was speaking, his voice soft and intimate, "we cannot go ourselves, the test is too near. You must meet the train in Boston and take over from the Canadian authorities. Carlisle at MIT knows all about the shipment and will help you verify the contents. You will then accompany the ore to Oak Ridge."

He saw the disappointment register in Gatling's face and was ashamed to meet his glance.

"I know this means you will miss the test at Alamogordo . . ." he apologized. He turned away, saddened, unable to add anything to soften the blow. The other two men shook hands and left. One hour later, Douglas was airborne.

Douglas Evans Gatling IV remained pleasantly half-asleep, suspended above Marblehead in a circular holding pattern, dreaming of the optimal coefficient of friction between satisfied stratified squamous vaginal epithelium and turgid penile skin. His hand, consciously or not, slipped over the armrest and dangled loosely in the aisle. The stewardess was on her way back to the forward cabin. At first, she started to move aside to avoid his arm. She stopped and reflected. Boston could be a lonely city. Yes, she accepted.

She picked up his hand and gently stroked the palm with her index finger. Then, while whispering into his ear, she replaced the hand firmly over his crotch. She held it there until his fingers tightened over hers in a protective squeeze. His eyes opened and the small overhead reading light picked out the iridescent blue of his irises. An innocent smile reassured her.

→ **T W E L V E**

The two days during which Moe was gone dragged with indeterminable slowness for Michael. The large clock over the map in the lower room seemed to mock him by comparing its own unrelenting progress with his slothful inertia. The Reichstag meeting was only three days away. There was little that Michael had accomplished since Berkowitz's departure for London. The large pile of unmatched clues remained inviolate. He had spent time talking with the bureaucrats responsible for the safety of the city. The whole attempt at civil defense was so futile, so amateurish, that it made O'Malley turn away in sorrow.

The Russian ships had come and gone. That was another fiasco. By refusing them access to the inner harbor until they had been inspected, the Navy nearly provoked an international incident. The Harbor Command insisted that American pilots guide the ships to their designated berths. The Soviets would agree to none of this. In a fit of pique, they aborted their intended stay and steamed out of the area, despite frantic appeasement efforts of high-ranking officials flown in from Washington.

Michael was at Nahant on a routine visit to the Coast Guard facility, and from East Point he could see the ships passing about ten miles off the coast. He was just as happy to see them go. He didn't like the Russians any more than he liked the Germans. They probably feel the same way about us, he thought. All of which led him to ponder on the strange bedfellows that war makes. If the Russians were so suspicious in time of war when they were our allies, God help us in time of peace when they would not need us.

The report that had come in from Reykjavik on the *Astra* was of little help. While frogmen working in ten-minute shifts in the cold Arctic water combed the hull bottom for concealed hatches or mines, the inside of the ship was searched thoroughly. Everything was in order. Rolls of newsprint, each approximately ten feet long and four feet in diameter and weighing over a ton, were lying neatly on their sides in the hold. An occasional roll was detached from the pile and examined. The same procedure was repeated with the heavy rolls of kraft paper destined for a corrugated container factory in Santiago.

The lumber products consisted of various lengths of rough-cut milled spruce and fir. Some boards were stacked in horizontal piles with spacers every two feet for air circulation. Other struts were bolted together to form bleacher sections for a sports arena in Manueles, outside Valparaiso. Finally, there were two hundred barrels of pitch and resin consigned to an aromatic distilling refinery in Lima, Peru. This latter shipment was to be unloaded in Chile along with the paper and lumber and then transshipped by the consignee there.

Nothing! Nothing! But there had to be something! Michael pounded the desk in frustration, an act which surprised his staff sitting opposite him. Liz had just finished reciting the number of tons of shipping lost in the preceding week to submarine sinkings which were at an all-time low. It was obvious O'Malley had not been listening.

He swiveled around in his chair and stared at the map on the wall below. There were the Russian ships, heading north on a bearing of fifty-eight degrees, a course which would bring them along the coast of the Maritime Provinces and then to Cape Breton Island. Beyond this point, in order to enter the Gulf of St. Lawrence for the long three-hundred-fifty-mile trip to Montreal, they would have to turn one hundred ten degrees due west. Michael observed that if the Russian ships were to maintain their present course and *not* veer west toward Quebec Province, they would soon be in direct contact with the *Astra*, which had suddenly changed to a bearing of two hundred fifty-eight degrees south-southwest, in response to a cable by Aacher.

That disturbed him. Why should Trondheim instruct the Dutch refugee to divert the *Astra* away from its present course through the Panama Canal to Chile and instead order it to Boston?

"First of all," he told his staff, "we must assume that everything that Trondheim is doing is purposeful. It is possible the *Astra*'s course change is a feint, the *Astra* itself a decoy to divert our attention. If it leads up a blind alley, we will have lost only sweat. If it is tied in some way with the attack on Boston, and we do not pursue it, we risk disaster."

O'Malley went over the facts for the hundredth time, slowly and in chronological order, trying to evoke a hypothesis. "The original port of destination," he repeated, "was Santiago. Aacher purchased the cargo from the Göteborg Trading Company in a bona fide sale from Trondheim, the overt intent being to sell the cargo to mercantile interests in South America."

"That would be no problem," Liz interrupted. "The merchandise is grade A, and even without the black market, Aacher's firm will make a great deal of money."

"All right, Liz, then what is the purpose of Trondheim's shifting the cargo to Boston at this late date? More profit to Aacher? If that were the case, Aacher wouldn't need Trondheim to tell him where to direct the ship. Aacher owns the merchandise and can land it anywhere he wants. No, if transferring the ship's contents to Boston was simply to benefit Aacher's pocketbook, then I don't buy it. A Nazi doesn't come all the way over here and go out of his way to give a Jew money. No, it just doesn't make any sense. The diversion of the *Astra* to the new course to Boston *must* benefit Trondheim. But how?"

"What if the team in Reykjavik missed something?" a voice from the back of the room countered. It was Wibby, always sitting at the rear so he could tilt his chair against the wall and lean backward. Michael made a mental note to detach Wibby from the group. He was too relaxed.

"It's possible, Wib, but for the moment let us accept the Reykjavik search as valid. No bombs. No cordite masquerading as toilet paper. No detonating caps shaped like coffee cups. But even if you're right, the change in sailing course is *too late*. Liz?"

Liz's glasses bobbed perilously on the end of her nose as she covered a corner of a page with calculations. After a minute or two, she looked up and pointed her pencil at O'Malley.

"You're right, Michael," Liz reported with a puzzled expression. "The *Astra* can't possibly make Boston Harbor in seventy-two hours. In three days, they will be just about..." She went over to peer at the small map under the glass on Michael's desk. ". . . here—right about here. Isle au Haut Bay, at Rockland. The ship wouldn't even get far enough south to reach the Navy base at Portsmouth until the night of the fourth day. No, with a maximum speed of eighteen knots, she will still be twenty hours shy of Boston when Hitler enters the Reichstag."

"So you see, Wib," Michael added, "it can't be. If the *Astra* is tied in with the attack on Boston, I don't know how. And if it isn't, I can't figure out why Trondheim would activate Aacher to maneuver it there."

Liz was listening to Michael's narrative without commenting, her wrinkled brow signaling pursuit of an elusive thought. Suddenly, she asked, "What if it isn't going to Boston?"

"Sure," Michael replied with a hint of sarcasm, "the *Astra* may not be going to Boston any more than von Eyssen is not sending Rohmer over here to sink convoys. If it isn't going to Boston, then where the hell is it going?" Michael leaned over the desk to examine the jagged coastline starting from Nova Scotia. "I don't see it. There is nothing along that whole coast of any value, except Portsmouth, and it would be suicide to approach the Navy base there. It is too well guarded, day and night. No, Boston is the only major target on the coast that is both valuable and vulnerable enough to attack, and yet the *Astra* won't make it in time to join the party."

As he was talking, his hands were describing patterns like ouija board markers, the left index finger starting up from Boston and the right one moving down from Cape Breton. The two fingers moved at the same speed until they met. Michael looked down at the junction. He bent closer, to examine the junction in detail.

"Mount Desert Island," he exclaimed with surprise. "In three days, our mystery ship from Sweden will meet our perverse friends from the steppes at Bar Harbor." Reflecting on the foibles of the rich summer colony, he added, "I don't think they will be invited to dinner."

The room filled with laughter, breaking the tension. Maybe everything wasn't so bad after all. Michael laughed along with his staff, but his eyes were drawn back to the chart, mesmerized by the question which still hung there, unresolved.

"Bar Harbor? Mount Desert Island?" He shook his head, just as perplexed as before.

He was still shaking his head when the buzzer on his desk notified him that he had a call. It was Moe, a day early. He was at his apartment and he sounded scared.

It took Michael at least forty-five minutes to get across town by car. When he arrived, he found the door unlocked. He knew something was wrong. The lights were off, but with the help of the fading afternoon light, Michael could see Berkowitz on the floor, trying to crawl to the telephone on the table in the hall. He had been shot twice and was rapidly losing blood. One shot had entered the right side of his body, just missing the heart. It had torn open the chest cavity below the eleventh rib, lacerating the entire right lung. Missing the major blood vessels, the bullet, in passing, had ripped open a flap of bone, muscle, and rib cartilage, creating a one-way flutter valve. Each time Moe strained to breathe, the valve opened, trapping air into the thoracic cavity. The increasing accumulation, contained under mounting pressure, began to compress the critical mass of lung tissue needed for oxygen exchange. Ironically, in a vicious cycle, the more Moe struggled to breathe, the more he was sealing his own death warrant.

He fought desperately to tell Michael something of great importance. His eyes motioned Michael closer. Berkowitz tried to speak, but the other bullet had entered the right side of the neck, grazed the carotid artery, and turned slightly upward to pierce the throat through the soft palette. The root of the tongue was half torn off and hung loose, oscillating back and forth in a pool of air, bloody froth, and saliva.

Michael bent closer, straining to catch every audible sound. He looked at Moe, pleading with him. Both men must have realized that death was inevitable, and too few minutes remained for possible communication between them. Michael was seized by the fear that Moe would die

without talking. Sensing this, Moe motioned for Michael
to come yet nearer.

Michael knelt down. He cradled Moe's head on his lap
like a disembodied object. Berkowitz tried to say something, but the sounds came out as gurgling blood-tinged
foam. All that O'Malley could hear distinctly was the
intermittent hissing of the compressed lung which was
throttling the weakening life on his lap.

"Moe," he cried, panicked more by the prospect of
losing the information than its bearer, "Listen. What is
von Eyssen up to? What is Rohmer going to do? Does it
have anything to do with Boston? Think, Moe, think. Give
me a word. Not a whole sentence. Just a single word,
one sound. I will take it from there. I promise you. Please,
please Moe. One clue. One sound. A single syllable. Anything at all!"

Moe's head began to wobble as the anoxia ascended.
His eyes rolled back and clouded over. The breathing became shallower and less labored. More and more circuits
in his brain shorted out. He was giving up the fight to
survive, but he still had not lost full consciousness. He
was no longer thinking of himself. Pain was being han-
dled at a lower reflex level. He struggled to traverse the
infinitely large gap of inches between himself and Michael.

He looked up with a triumphant look on his face. His
lower jaw moved, almost imperceptibly. He saved up one
last breath and then let it out slowly, using the precious
air to form the sounds with his half-paralyzed vocal cords,
his shattered neck, and his mangled tongue. The words
came out, sandwiched between jets of blood which ran
down his neck onto O'Malley's long thighs.

"R ... Rock ... Rockets ... twenty-four hou ..."

He looked up with horror at the disbelief on O'Malley's face. Had his boss not understood? He could not
repeat the effort again. Only an inaudible gasp came out.

"Rockets? Rockets? Missiles?" Michael rapidly shot
back for confirmation. "Twenty-four hours? Twenty-four
hours for what? Till the attack?" He shook the dying

head. It was too late for Moe to repeat. His eyelids only blinked, terminating the fragile communion.

"Roc . . . ," and the jaw hung loose. The blood ceased to exude from the neck. The hissing stopped, the chest was silent, and the head fell, a dead weight, off O'Malley's lap to rest on the floor at his knees.

Michael rose awkwardly, trying to wipe off the blood which was already congealing on his lap. It adhered to his fingers like red paste. How could blood, he wondered, so thin and watery in the living body to carry vital oxygen through the finest microscopic capillaries, turn into an obstructing gelatinous mass when exposed to the same oxygen outside the body? He went into the bathroom to wash his hands. A plan of action was forming even as he looked through the bathroom door at the still form on the floor.

"Rockets." That explained Rohmer's erratic behavior. So far, so good. But the "twenty-four hours?" Did Moe mean that the attack would start in twenty-four hours? If so, it was already too late to stop it. But if that were the message, Moe would have said "tomorrow." Twenty-four hours must signify something else, some critical data he should know. What clue could be described by "twenty-four hours?"

His heart skipped a beat. Time. Time and rockets. They must be connected. But how? Twenty-four hours to launch a rocket attack? Michael panicked, a cold film of sweat washing his skin. He had three days left before the opening of the Reichstag. There was no time to send someone else to England to confirm his deduction, assuming the man would even return alive.

Michael managed to calm his fear. He began to explore the deadly parameters of the new knowledge. An attack on Boston would have to come from some site accessible to the wolf pack. That meant a seacoast. Jesus Christ! he cursed. If he didn't have any better clue, the Air Force and Navy could spend weeks searching four thousand miles of shoreline between Maine and New Jersey. He looked at his watch with dread. Seventy-two hours to go. Bainbridge could provide the military hardware, but only if given the exact coordinates of Rohmer's destination. Michael thought hard for a moment. The answer was not long in coming. He had no other choice. There was *one* lead.

First, he called Bainbridge.

"Morris Berkowitz has been shot. He is dead ... in his apartment. Please take care of him for me." Bainbridge assented without comment. There was a long pause while he waited for O'Malley to continue. Without knowing exactly why, Michael did not reveal what Moe had told him. He replied only, "I will be back to you in the morning. I have a lead to follow."

As he hung up, O'Malley observed that the callousness of men seemed to increase in direct proportion to their power over life and death of others. He recalled his own momentary guilt and sadness at Moe's death. Yet here was Bainbridge who never said a word of regret or query as to the manner or motive of the death.

Michael realized that he was being silly. It was no dark secret why Berkowitz had been killed. The Germans must have known he was on to something important after spending two days with Hedley-White and Fleming and then cutting his trip short to race back to Boston. What better way to prevent him from spilling his guts than to kill him?

Just before leaving the apartment, Michael made a second call to his office. Standing there in the hallway, waiting for the operator to locate Liz, Michael looked down at the dead figure, his anger mounting. He pursed his lips. No, he vowed, making a double pact with the devil and with the silent figure on the floor: *Trondheim would not get away with this!*

"Liz," the words slammed into the mouthpiece, "take Lars Trondheim in. I don't care on what pretext, but get him!"

He paused to think for a minute. "Call Alex Templik, and tell him ... his services are required."

As Michael returned to the body, he was overcome with a wave of remorse and doubt. Should he have called for an ambulance or sought medical help instead of extracting Moe's last breath for his own purposes? It had been a difficult decision.

He had made the right choice. The few minutes wasted might have been all the time Moe was allotted, and if lost, never recovered. Suppose Moe had lived, but had not regained consciousness for days. The information would then be useless.

No, he made the proper move. He was certain. Yet, if that were true, why long after Moe had ceased to breathe did Liz find Michael kneeling on the floor with the young man's head once again cradled in his arms, crying softly for his guilt?

⟶ THIRTEEN

Michael walked rapidly as he passed the Brattle Street Historical Society where he had once delivered a talk before the good spinsters and widows. He could still recollect thin, peeled slices of cucumber, tucked between circumcised Wonder Bread cut into triangles and trapezoids, the geometry somehow confirming his suspicion that the finished product was symbolic rather than substantive.

He turned south on Boylston Street and crossed the busy intersection opposite the Wursthaus, where he had often indulged in sauerbraten and a stein of Tuborg until it became unobtainable. One block further, he entered the indoor parking garage. The attendant, a slovenly, club-footed youth, recognized him and got up to get his car. Michael waited, anticipating the hollow, echoed roar of his patched-up prewar Plymouth coupe reverberating through the concrete ramps. He was almost hit by the screeching car as the would-be-warrior halted it an inch from his toe with a silent "olé."

Michael drove as quickly as he could, dodging the pedestrians as he wove up Massachusetts Avenue. In Arlington, he turned onto Route 2A, still going north. The rutted road jostled the car. There were no lights, no center white line. Michael swerved from side to side to avoid the pits and depressions, hoping that no one was coming in the opposite direction. Each time he swung back and forth, the headlights would skip over a pothole and he would be shaken as one wheel and then its successor struggled out of the harsh trap. He slowed down at each group of rural mailboxes until he located what he had been searching for, a small, neatly varnished signboard with large black letters painted on it, "The Masyzck Farm." He hoped Trondheim was already there. He did not feel like waiting. He looked at his wristwatch. Time was running out.

Trondheim's training had conditioned him for the day when he would be apprehended, even tortured, and possibly killed. Rhoda was the one who was flustered and scared. The insistent pounding on the apartment door did not give her enough time to put on a nightgown. She shouted to the loud knocking on the door to "wait a minute" as she wrapped herself in a cheap bathrobe.

The three FBI agents barely looked at her. "Trondheim—where is he?" they asked, their tone brusque. They released the safeties on their Smith and Wesson .45s and moved cautiously toward the still-closed bedroom door.

"Pete," the leader of the group ordered the youngest

member, "get outside and watch the fire escape. We'll take him from here."

The agent did not have time to leave the room before the door opened and the spy came out. He was naked, a cigarette in his mouth, its arrogant tilt paralleling the rake of his erect and glistening penis.

"Gentlemen," he said in a flippant, insolent manner, "I will be right with you. Please give me a moment to dress."

He pointed to the agent whom he decided looked most ill at ease, "You may come in to watch me and make certain that I do not disappear into my hat like a rabbit."

Rhoda sat in the corner, her knees and arms pressed tightly together, looking at one man and then at the other, trying to make some sense out of the confusing tableau. Nobody said a word to her. She might not have been there for all they cared. Rhoda started to cry. The hot, salty tears passed down her cheeks, streaking the remains of her makeup.

Trondheim entered the bathroom, leaving the door wide open so that his captors could monitor his toilette. He lathered up Rhoda's face towel with soap and water, and sponge-bathed his genitalia. He then cupped on scented talcum powder, creating dense clouds of dust which coated the agent watching from the doorway.

"C'mon, Trondheim," the leader called out, angry at the delay. "We're not going to any fucking party! Get your pants on."

"Be civilized, my good man," the Swede replied, refusing to alter the pace of his fastidious dressing.

Finished, he emerged from the bedroom and took one last glance around the dingy apartment. He looked at Rhoda, trying to imagine how she would look in about fifteen years, disgusting in the dark, let alone in the light. He went over to her and stared down into her eyes with a look of affection that she had never seen before. He brushed the tears off her eyelids with light strokes of his fingertips. Taking her face gently between his hands, as he had done that first day at Aacher's office, he spoke to her in a low voice so that no one else could hear.

"Rhoda, you are a very beautiful woman. You make love as wonderfully as any woman I have ever known. I will never see you again." He hunched his shoulder in the direction of the three agents. "Never forget me or what I tell you now. You are a good person and deserve someone even better than you think I am." He kissed her full on the mouth, while looking into her eyes without blinking.

Then, with a curt gesture to the men, he strode out of the apartment leaving the three agents to snap to attention and race awkwardly after him.

→ FOURTEEN

Trondheim had been blindfolded during the hour-long ride, his arms pinioned behind him in handcuffs. Not until he recognized the acrid odor of rotting manure did he realize that he had been taken to a farm. Once he entered the large, harshly lit, high-ceilinged room, his blindfold was removed. His eyes gradually accommodated to the glare of the fluorescent bulbs which hung from the dangling fixtures running the whole length of the chamber.

He could see along one long wall a row of white, ceramic-tiled stalls, each four feet wide and eight feet long with a waist-high partition separating it from its neighbor. Each cubicle contained a large rusted drain in the center, and in the corners four rings embedded in the concrete floor. Along the top of the partitions were a similar series of iron rings. At first glance, the whole appearance was that of a series of shower stalls except for the absence of shower heads and the presence of menacing iron bolts. Along the facing wall was a low slate table with scattered groupings of laboratory instruments. In the center of the room, a long table supported a large black box with various dials and current gauges. From the box, a pair of black wires ran to each cubicle. Hung on the back wall of the room were dozens of molded metal cups about four inches in diameter and curved iron rods varying in length from eight to ten inches like random-sized steel bananas.

Trondheim did not know what to make of the room or, for that matter, the "farm." He seemed almost relieved when O'Malley walked in. His American antagonist was a frame of reference in this alien setting. But he could not identify the three other men who flanked the tall naval officer. Two of the men were obviously Slavic, apparently twins, in their early forties, with stocky, flat faces, high cheekbones, and slitlike eyes and only a suggestion of eyebrows. They wore clean but threadbare plaid shirts, faded blue denim trousers, and high leather boots with metal toeguards. From the manner in which they were conversing, Trondheim determined the Slavs must own the farm.

The last man was about the same age, five-feet-ten, with short, muscular arms and legs. His heavy head sat on top of his shoulders apparently without benefit of a neck. The coarse white face, rutted with acne scars and shaving cuts, glared with contempt at the spy through eyes almost buried in pockmarked rolls of fat.

Alex Templik had carried out enough interrogations for the cold-blooded routine to be long since divested of any emotional effect for him, and he was impatient to get started. As Trondheim looked at the man, their glances crossed. A wave of cold sweat started from the spy's groin and traveled up to his throat. His bladder compressed and his anus tightened as a knot of duodenal spasm caught him in the abdomen. He felt cold and scared. Defenseless.

The FBI agents removed Trondheim's handcuffs. The spy rubbed his wrists to restore the circulation. Templik moved to his side and ran his eyes up and down the tall body as if appraising a carcass for butchering.

"Take your clothes off, Trondheim," he ordered.

Trondheim looked about, not quite knowing what to do.

"You heard me. Strip—or we will do it for you." He pointed to the agents, who were slowly fingering their pistols. The two brothers stood by without making a gesture or a sound. Michael watched, ill at ease, his fingers rubbing against each other as if they were still sticky with Moe's blood. He had an instinctive dislike for what had to be done. He hoped that Trondheim would cooperate . . . for both their sakes.

The Swede undressed quickly this time, dropping his clothes uncharacteristically in a heap at his feet. He felt that it would be unwise to provoke his interrogator.

"Your shoes and socks, too. Put them over there." He pointed to the table in the center of the room. The spy took a quick glance at the instruments on the table-top, as Templik had hoped he would, but could not divine the significance of the menacing apparatus.

The agents took Trondheim over to a middle stall and chained each ankle to an iron ring, spread-eagling his legs and forcing him to tense his leg muscles to maintain his balance. They then fastened each wrist with steel chain to a ring on the partitions, pulling his arms out widely, making it difficult for him to move without falling forward and cracking his head on the floor.

Templik walked over to the far wall with the two brothers and carefully appraised the strange metal appliances hanging there.

"Take the largest," he ordered. "He's got big balls."

The spy stared at the apparatus with a petrified expression. The two brothers moved swiftly in concert. One gave Trondheim's head a savage downward thrust, forcing the upper half of his body to the horizontal position where its further descent was limited by the painfully twisted muscles of his arms and shoulders.

The other brother moved behind the spy, spread the buttocks apart, and thrust one of the curved rods deep into the rectum. The act was over before Trondheim could even cry out. The brothers released the spy, who contracted his rectal muscles in a vain effort to eject the foreign body. It would not budge.

The brothers placed a cupped plate under the testicles and lashed the metal terminal tightly to the scrotum with thick leather straps. Finally, they picked up the pair of wires hanging loosely by the side of the stall, attaching one to the scrotal plate and the other to the protruding end of the rectal probe. The whole operation had taken less than two minutes. Templik looked at the Masyzcks with admiration. He respected professionals.

Trondheim looked around him, his eyes pleading for release. Michael had turned away, debating with himself whether to permit the horrible scene to continue. He knew that when he had asked for Alex Templik something like this might occur. Michael had heard rumors of Templik's brilliantly effective interrogations. Somehow, where other agents had failed, he was always able to extract the desired information. No one could ever find bodily evidence of sufficient torture to explain such automatic compliance from even the most hardened Nazi agents. Nothing . . . except for some odd superficial lesions on the skin of his victims, which everyone was hard put to make anything of.

Looking at the agent, repelled by Templik's indifference to the human being immobilized in front of him, Michael was filled with a sense of dread that he himself was the trapped spy instead of the naked form in front of him. But each time Michael's anger softened and his purpose became less resolute, he would think again of the bloody foam choking Moe to death in his lap and evision the many mangled bodies soon to die in Boston Harbor. O'Malley ended by keeping his eyes fixed to the floor, as if to shield his soul from the torment he knew it would hear, and he remained silent.

"Let me introduce you," Templik said politely to Trondheim, indicating the twins. "I have known these two brothers, Jacob and Stefan Masyzck, since 1940 when they emigrated here from Czechoslovakia. They were originally professors of animal husbandry and pioneers of many new techniques used throughout the world in the genetic upgrading of dairy stock. The United States government was very happy to give them sanctuary after they fled Europe. Right now, they run an experimental agricultural station for the University of Massachusetts and"—Templik gave the spy a chilling grin—"they often assist me in interrogations of Nazi agents.

The Swede stared at the two Czechs, who continued to watch him with expressionless faces. Trondheim wondered what their connection was with this unholy activity. Templik divined the question.

"I think the reason will become patently clear, Trondheim. These two brothers were born in a little town about forty miles from Prague. Each summer, they would send their children back to their native town to visit the grandparents. One fall, the children did not return home. Jacob had one boy and one girl, and, if I am not mistaken, Stefan had three sons.

"These men never saw the bodies of their children, nor of their parents who were murdered at the same time, nor even their graves. You must have read about it. Goebbels and Himmler took great pains to publicize the episode all over Europe as a warning to the occupied peoples."

Trondheim listened to this story with a puzzled expression. Once or twice he gave a nervous shudder, as if he was afraid of being sucked down into a pit of terror, the full depth of which he was to plumb with pain, and possibly his life.

"You must remember," Templik teased with a bitter smile, "just a little town near Kladno, outside of Prague. It was called Lidice. I said 'was' because it is no more."

At the mention of that name, Trondheim turned white. His body trembled as he looked at the two silent, unmoving men.

"You must also now remember the name of Reinhard Heydrich, the Gestapo chief for Bohemia and Moravia. The date, May 29, 1942, a lovely spring morning. Heydrich was assassinated as he was driving out in the country. Within twenty-four hours, the Germans had executed over thirteen hundred Czechs whom they suspected of aiding the terrorists. On June 9, 1942, Lidice was surrounded by ten truckloads of German soldiers. Every adult male was shot. The women were shipped to the Ravensbrück concentration camp and gassed. Four pregnant farm women in labor were allowed to deliver. The babies were used for bayonet practice. The children of the village, now orphans, the Masyzck's included, were gassed at Gneisenau. The empty buildings were dynamited and leveled with tanks. Only the last rite, the plowing of salt into the bloody earth, as the Romans did at Carthage, was forgotten in the passion of the moment. Not even a roadside marker tells where the town existed."

Trondheim cried out, terrified. He strained at his bonds. "No. No. Please. I had nothing to do with it. I have never even been in Czechoslovakia. Please, tell them!"

Templik placed both hands on Trondheim's shoulders to reassure him.

"They know that, Trondheim. This is just a small ritual payment for the loss of five Czech children, and" —he added harshly, turning to Michael—"one American Jew. Just a token. You must certainly understand that."

The first bolt of current hit Trondheim without warning. Then the second. The varying intensity and timing of shocks from the inducer was random, preventing the spy from anticipating or preparing for the charge.

The hot current seared through his scrotum as the electricity tried to escape, seeking in vain for the other electrode in his rectum to complete the circuit. The current twisted through his pelvis, frying his intestines, convulsing his muscles, causing arteries and veins to shudder spasmodically, occluding the blood supply to his vital organs.

Each of the billions of nerves occupying the raw living tissues between the metal electrodes triggered off its own message of excruciating pain which ascended higher and higher in the spinal column, until they crowded the brainstem and invaded the thalamus. An involuntary, blood-curdling shriek tore from his lips. His jaw flung open trying to heave out the unbearable agony which tore again and again through his body. His stomach contracted and vomit gushed from his mouth, spilling down the sides of his jaws. His bladder emptied as did his colon, sending jets of yellow urine to mix in a slurry on the floor around his legs with the deposits of brown feces which escaped despite the obstructing probe.

Over and over his body convulsed. He screamed unhuman cries, his head thrashing wildly, his body lunging first this way and then the other, attempting to escape the next inevitable lash of pain to come whipping out of the machine.

Michael was forced to go outside to relieve the waves of nausea which poured out of him. He stood in the damp barnyard, his skin sticky with chilled sweat, trembling, the sour taste of stomach contents poisoning the back of his throat, his hands firmly pressed over his ears, still hearing the shrieks penetrate his head. He had wanted to cry out to stop, to let it be, but he could not. In his own way, he suffered along with the Swede.

Suddenly, during one pause in the rhythm, Templik raced over to the spy and pried his mouth open. Evading Trondheim's vicious bite, Templik shouted to the Masyzcks.

"Quick, a bit!"

A moment later, the metal bar was wedged deep in the back of Trondheim's throat, preventing him from closing his mouth. The interrogator pried out the cleverly hollow crown. He held it on his palm and wiped off the bloody saliva. Of course Canaris would have equipped his agents with a suicide means. With a triumphant grin, Templik showed the concealed pill to Trondheim.

"Not this time, my friend. No. Not yet."

With the execution of this maneuver, whatever resistance was left in the spy vanished. Alex Templik knew the time had come.

"The *Astra*. Why is it so valuable? Where is Rohmer going? What about the rocket attack?" Trondheim looked up, startled. "Yes, I know about the rockets. Are they being carried on the U-boats?"

Trondheim tried to hold back the answer, but a deadly howl came out of his mouth as a high bolt of current squeezed his body in a vise of pain.

"Yeh, yes..." The metal bar gagged him. Templik removed the bit.

"Are the rockets being delivered by the U-boats?"

"Yes, yes."

"The date of the attack?"

The questions came too fast. Trondheim was still toying with the idea of buying time for his seared brain to devise some way of making a deal.

"No, Trondheim," Templik whispered, "just answer my question, or..."

A small wave flicked out from the machine, touching Trondheim's testicles in a gentle squeeze, to remind him that pain was waiting, eager to pounce.

Trondheim capitulated, "The date of the attack... in three days. To coincide with Hitler's speech in the Reichstag."

"And the *Astra*. What is in it?"

"I don't know," Trondheim beseeched his interrogator. "My orders were only to activate Aacher. I gave him the cables that I was ordered to. Only von Eyssen knows why the *Astra* was to be diverted. I don't know. I don't know!"

Templik elected to defer this point for the moment and turned to the crucial question, "Where does the attack take place from? Where is Rohmer heading?"

" 'Winter,' 'Winter,' that's all I know. I accidentally

heard von Eyssen discuss the attack and mention the word 'Winter.' I don't know any more than that. Believe me. I don't know. Von Eyssen would not give the full plan to everybody. Just because something like this might happen." He indicated the room with a weak nod of his head. "Believe me. 'Winter' ... that's all that I know—and I wasn't even supposed to hear that."

"Winter"? Templik was baffled. He turned to Michael who had returned and was now cringing back in the far corner of the room. Michael shook his head. The word had no meaning for him. Trondheim had been his trump card to locate the rocket launch site. Now, after having gone through all this, O'Malley had little to show for it, and time was rapidly fleeing.

Templik let out a curse as he looked at the torn body hanging in front of him. He was not accustomed to failure. He drove bitterly for another try. The machine moved into high and Trondheim shrieked his guts out, but nothing further could be obtained. The spy finally gave up fighting and lost consciousness.

Templik reviewed the extracted information with O'Malley. They had confirmed the date of the attack and the purpose of Rohmer's mission. But the *Astra* was still a mystery. And the site of the rocket launching was only the name of a season. Even Trondheim's response to Moe's death was puzzling. Despite racking the Swede's body to the limit, Templik could produce only an incredulous denial of guilt. What Templik did not know was that the Swede, his body broken but his mind intact, had kept back, through his pain, mention of the Gouldsboro Prisoner-of-War Camp and his plant in Presque Isle, knowledge of either of these two being sufficient to pinpoint Rohmer's destination.

Trondheim's body hung forward. A trickle of saliva and blood ran down from his mouth like a red stalactite. Michael could see the scorched area under the scrotum where the sweat had been turned to steam by the electrode.

"He will heal," Templik assured Michael. "You should come out here some day and observe how these instruments are used for artificial insemination. That poor bull has quite an ejaculation! This technique is really quite modern, although the concept is not original. When the captors of Edward II of England wished to kill him, they faced an age-old dilemma. Because of the tradition against violating the person of the sovereign, his murderers had to be very circumspect so that when the body was examined no evidence of foul play would be seen. They were really very clever. They inserted long, thin, red-hot wires deep into the monarch's body through his rectum. His screams were reported heard throughout London that night. Peritonitis from perforated intestines completed the job."

As Templik talked, the two brothers cleaned Trondheim and gave him some water to drink. The first two mouthfuls gagged him. The third he swirled around and let dribble out. The fourth he swallowed. The men were very gentle.

Seeing Trondheim recover, Michael felt as if he had shed a heavy weight. He went over to the spy and started to touch him in a gesture of apology. His eyes crossed the spy's and shamefully turned away. Without saying a word, Michael left the room for the long trip back to Boston.

Templik was happy to see Michael leave. It was not often that he had failed to obtain the information he had been charged to get. A compulsion for revenge tore at him. He pointed to the raw inflamed tissue hanging between the spy's legs.

"I don't think the Swedish Crown will find the goods very damaged. At least from what we have done to them."

Trondheim was puzzled. He looked at the two brothers. Were they planning a further agony?

"Tell me, Trondheim," Templik asked in a curious tone, "did your northern Swedish education ever expose you to sixteenth-century Italian literature?"

He did not wait for an answer.

"I could imagine not. Let me tell you a little story written by a Benedictine monk of Vallombrosa who lived in the early fifteen hundreds. It tells of a very vigorous young priest who catered to the needs of the good citizens of Vittorenza. Apparently he was more than just the spiritual shepherd of his flock. When the men were out working in the fields, he would make love to the women, married and single alike. One afternoon, several men surprised the priest in bed. They chased the woman from the room, chastening her with a few blows. The priest cowered in the corner of the room, naked, his long, thin penis and ropy testicles swinging in front of him.

"There was an old massive oak chest in the room. The men dragged the priest over and opened the lid. They took his balls and put them in the chest, then closed the lid down and locked the clasp securely with a large iron lock. The chest was old and there was a small amount of clearance under the lid so, at first, the priest did not suffer anything more than embarrassment and fear. The men picked up a long, sharp razor and went over to the father. To his surprise, they merely left the razor on top of the chest and departed."

While Templik was droning the tale, the two brothers had walked over to Trondheim with a long length of chain. Jacob seized the spy's scrotum and wrenched it down while Stefan wrapped the chain around the attachment of the testicles to the body until the blood supply was pinched off. Assured that the tissue could not be withdrawn, Jacob bolted the two ends of the chain to the iron rings on opposite sides of the stall. The Masyzcks released Trondheim's ankles and wrists. The spy started to move but found that he was completely immobilized by the chains to his genitalia.

Up to this time, Trondheim had paid only scant attention to Templik's tale, his body still numb from the previous ordeal. He slowly became aware of a dull cramp in his groin. He tried to remove the chains but the manipulation only increased the agony.

"Yes, Trondheim, you can imagine what happened next. Within an hour, the blood supply was completely cut off. The poor man screamed with the unrelenting pain. Twice he looked at the razor and shuddered. The third time he picked it up. The pain of excision was nothing in comparison to the agony he had been suffering. With one strong blow, he freed himself from his prison, as well as from earthly temptation forever. It is reported that the good father led an exemplary life the rest of his days."

Templik walked over to the spy and handed him a long, shiny knife.

"If you decide to follow the parable literally, you are free to leave. Your clothes are over there. A car is waiting outside with your passport. If, on the other hand, you cannot bear to be parted from your possessions, in one hour the pain will be more excruciating than anything you have experienced so far today. The pain of rotting flesh is so unbearable that in days when amputations were done without the benefit of anesthesia, soldiers with gangrenous extremities begged for the mercy of the knife. The Masyczks will leave you to your thoughts for three hours. If at the end of that time you are still here, they will kill you."

Dumbfounded, Trondheim looked up at Templik and then at the brothers. He pleaded for help from each in turn. He looked at the knife. The pain was intensifying.

"Oh, yes, before I leave—let me return all your property." Templik placed the cyanide capsule hidden in the molar crown in the spy's hand. "I suppose that this, too, is an alternative . . . of sorts."

The three men walked out without a backward glance.

"Cyanide," said the two brothers in unison as if casting dice.

"No, the knife," said Alex Templik.

Alex Templik was right. Lars Trondheim knew also he could never go back to Boston. The Germans would naturally assume that the spy had been released because he had told Naval Intelligence what they wanted to know. If that wasn't the case, then he should have been dead by cyanide. With that irrefutable Teutonic logic facing him, the Swede realized that he had better vanish rather

than risk from his fellow Nazi agents the same fate that
the two brothers had in store for him. Trondheim quickly
sorted out the possible alternatives. Canada. There to lose
himself until he was safe. He had money enough, God
knew that.

What neither Lars Trondheim nor his Diety knew
was that Templik had earlier passed the knife through
a steaming patty of fresh cow manure. The American
was acquainted with the life cycles of the clostridia and
tetanus bacilli which teem by the trillions in barnyard
excreta. By the time Trondheim had reached Concord,
New Hampshire the microbes had started their rapid
multiplication. Before the spy had turned off Route 3 at
Montpelier, Vermont, the deadly toxins were coursing
through his bloodstream, producing the characteristic
twitches, the facial rigidity, the headaches, the vomiting
and pharyngeal spasms, the salivary foaming. Two days
later, when the car finally skidded off the road and rolled
over into the soft shoulder outside of Burlington, Lars
Trondheim was dead of lockjaw.

Looking at the elegant clothes, the manicured nails,
the bloodstained silk underwear hiding the empty scrotum, the manacle burns on the wrists and ankles, the
County Coroner succinctly commented, "No balls," and
then added parenthetically for the benefit of his assistant,
"That's what happens when you play round with those
faggots up Boston way."

During the bumpy ride back to Boston, Michael ran
the interrogation over in his mind. The hours spent with
Trondheim seemed wasted. "Winter." Trondheim could
not have meant the season. That did not make any sense.
Michael let his mind go blank. Sometimes this trick allowed a fragile thought to float through to his consciousness. Thirty seconds passed.

Suddenly, he slowed the car down and pulled over to
the side of the road. He opened the glove compartment
and fumbled through its contents. He bent forward to
capture the weak light from the dashboard. He rapidly
ran his finger down the Maine coast on a dog-eared road-

map. He saw what he was looking for. There straddling the road from the naval radar station at the tip of Schoodic Peninsula was the town of Winter Harbor.

It all clicked into place. The landing, the radar station, the long-range missiles. As far as he knew, the Germans had not yet landed. Today was *Wednesday*. Bainbridge could move the Navy, or what was left of it, from the Portsmouth Naval Base to anywhere on the Maine Coast in twenty-four hours. Hitler would enter the Reichstag on *Saturday*. There was time to stop Rohmer. O'Malley urged the car on faster through the dark searching frantically for an open gasoline station to call Washington.

Bainbridge, unperturbed as usual, said he would leave immediately and told O'Malley to meet him at the Ritz-Carlton in about four hours. Michael's drive back to Boston seemed never-ending as he replayed in his mind the chance sequence of events which had culminated in his sudden success. Oddly, a feeling of triumph was absent. Without his knowing why, a queasy sense of doubt eroded O'Malley's enthusiasm and rendered him unsure and anxious, feelings which were to increase dramatically by the time his superior had finished with him.

→ **FIFTEEN**

Michael entered the Arlington Street entrance of the hotel. The aide who opened the door ushered O'Malley into the opulent eighteenth-century French and English Suite. In the foyer, sparkling lights from an amethyst and crystal Bacarrat chandelier glinted off the highly polished white and black marble squares covering the floor in an intricate diamond pattern.

In the living room, two Sheraton settees covered in light green watered silk faced each other in front of the fireplace. Mahogany Chippendale lamp tables with pierced stretchers stood at either end of the settees. The portrait of an American colonial mercantile prince done in the style of Whistler hung over the mantle.

At the far end of the richly furnished room stood a Louis XVI bureau plat, with bronze ormulu sabots. A man was seated in a large mauve velvet covered Regency fauteuille behind the desk. The shade on the girondole was tilted and the strong light hit Michael full in the eyes. It threw Bainbridge's lean figure into the penumbra where he blended with the soft shadows of the velvet until one was hard put to say where the fabric texture and the human texture parted company.

"I agree, O'Malley, the carpet, the carpet. Yes. Yes," Bainbridge said. Michael looked at the small carpet under the desk, not knowing what he was expected to say to this opening remark.

"It doesn't belong. An Ardebil Kerman, an old Isphaghan, or even a Savonnerie, but definitely not a Holbein. Never. Never. Too geometric for these lines." The wraithelike form indicated the room with a weak sweep of his arm. "If you had kept me waiting any longer, either it or I would have been forced to change rooms." The words echoed hollowly in the large room a fraction of a second after they were uttered.

The speaker rose from the pale inlaid desk with difficulty. He gripped both gnarled hands on the carved sides for support. He hesitated, straining to overcome gravity. With an awkward jump, he sprang from the chair. Pushing off from the side of the desk, he ran forward so as not to lose any of the precious momentum his pained effort had gained him. As he crossed the highly varnished parquet floor, his heels clattered on the Fountainbleu walnut and oak pickets, adding a chorus to his words. The smoked mirrors flanking the walls repeated his wizened form over and over again.

He was short and thin, his head far too large for his stooped body. The long, fine hair was pure white and gracefully swept to one side. His forehead was high, lips thin and moist, cheeks sunken, the skin tightly drawn over his face like a mummy, yet oddly pink with an overall tracery of fine, crinkly lines. The eyes large and clear, but full of water. His nose a formidable beak which rose out of the center of his small features, to terminate in miniscule nostrils.

He scurried, his aged body leaning forward. He looked as if he was continually about to fall, his lower half rushing up from behind to prevent the upper half from toppling over. Michael resisted the impulse to put his hands out and catch the man as he moved toward him in a mechanical shuffle. He knew that at the very last minute the elderly gentleman would miraculously stop and rock back and forth on his heels to let the momentum dissipate.

Then, the hand shake. The arm elevated in jerks like a toy soldier trying to salute. The fingers grasped Michael's waiting hand only to have the act initiate an uncontrolled paroxysm of shaking. The other hand reached over to dampen the tremor, but was itself affected by the same disabling spasm. O'Malley gently disengaged his fingers and allowed his host's tremor to fade. The little man rested opposite his guest, his back

hunched over, eyes fixed to the floor, a Maître Hauche-
come of Breaute, perpetually looking for that elusive piece
of string.

The performance did not upset the victim. He had accepted everything. Even the name of the disease, paralysis
agitans. The doctors at Queen's Square in London were
kinder and had called it Parkinson's disease, as if an
eponym would divest it of its malignant prognosis.

Bainbridge had wanted to retire and spend his last
years with his family on his salt-water farm near New-
buryport where, on a clear day, he could stand on the
shore and look across the vast expanse of ocean toward
the land of the Saxons from which his ancestors had
sailed. But with the war in its third year, he was trapped
in a succession of formal offices as advisor to the presi-
dent just as his mind, still intact, was incarcerated in the
failing garment of muscle and bone and nerve.

Bainbridge touched Michael's arm in a light gesture
and guided his way back to the desk, repeating his incredible shuffling gait. He motioned for O'Malley to take
the chair across from him. Tilting his own chair way
back to include the tall guest in his narrow field of vision,
the frail figure waited patiently for his visitor to begin.

"Well, Michael," he urged in a gentle tone, "tell me
all about your great adventure."

O'Malley reviewed the case. The wolf pack's atypical
behavior. The strange detours. Michael's suspicions which
led to the London trip. Berkowitz's information which,
tragically purchased, told not of sabotage, but of long-
range missiles. Trondheim's confession which confirmed
the use of the rockets. Finally, the launch site itself,
deduced to be Winter Harbor, Maine.

When Michael was finished, he leaned back in the
fragile wheelback chair and waited. For long minutes,
Bainbridge said nothing. His fingers rhythmically tapped
on the table in front of him making a soft patter like
dropping rain. His eyes traveled slowly around the room,
savoring the paneled walls, the crystal sconces, the lofty
ceiling with its embellishment of carved plaster cherubs,
flowers, and urns. This whole room, he thought to himself,

was a relic of an era when gentlemen sat drinking tea and decided the affairs of continents. When wars were tidy sessions of hired mercenaries fighting neat ballets like tin soldiers on a tabletop. It was all getting so complicated, he sighed with a resigned shrug. The business of America should be business, not politics or European wars.

Bainbridge looked again at the seated figure in front of him, and asked, almost wearily, "What about the launch pads? You mentioned 'ski slopes' in the Ardennes pointing at Britain. That solves the problem very nicely for our European allies, but how are *our* rockets to be launched?"

Michael had no answer other than to suggest the possibility that the *Astra* might be tied into the landing.

"But you said that the *Astra* was clean."

"Maybe we overlooked something. We did not know about the rockets at the time."

"Or perhaps"—Bainbridge's voice was stern and severe—"perhaps there is as much likelihood of the *Astra* helping to launch the rockets as there is having the Russians send them aloft. I understand from ConCinch that the Soviet fleet will be in Maine waters at the same time as Rohmer." He gave a wry laugh.

Michael could say nothing. The weak points in his case were as glaring and disturbing to him as to Bainbridge. He was totally unprepared for the old man's next cryptic comment.

"What if the Germans have found a way to launch their missiles from a submarine? If that is possible, and I do not say that it is, there is nothing we can do except patrol the entire coastline out to a distance of however far we would expect the range of their rockets to be."

Bainbridge stared at Michael in a worried manner, almost as if he was blaming him personally for the troublesome situation. If Michael did not know better, he would have sworn he detected a sudden flash of alarm which flitted across his host's face. Finally, Bainbridge motioned to an aide who had stayed well back against the wall. Michael was surprised to see him step forward. He

had not realized that a third person had been in the room
the entire time. Men like Bainbridge, he thought to himself, have to have subalterns lurking in the shadows behind them, to wait for fingersnaps.

Bainbridge whispered something to the man who
quickly left the room. Michael could not hear the words,
nor could he make out the low-pitched telephone conversation in the foyer. The aide returned and signified that
the matter had been tended to. Bainbridge appeared
relieved and took up where he had left off.

"All right, Michael," the words came out slowly,
almost with reproach, "let us review the facts and follow
them to some logical conclusion. For the sake of a working hypothesis which we both must have and which we
hope our Nazi brethren have likewise, let us accept your
story, *holy* as it may be," punning the word.

"Suppose I go to the Secretary of War with your tale.
I tell him about the aberrant wolf pack tactics, the rocket
experts from Peenemünde, the long-range missiles to fall
on Boston Harbor, the attack site in Maine."

It all came out sounding so childish and far-fetched
that Michael wondered whether it was a deliberate ploy
on Bainbridge's part.

"Suppose they pick up the weak spots, the unanswered questions. The absence of the missile launchers,
the spatial proximity of the Russians, the possibility that
the whole thing is a decoy, just a plant. What would you
expect Washington to do? Strip the Boston convoy of its
protective cover? Send the whole Navy up to Maine . . .
to trap lobsters?"

Although Michael had come to the meeting to urge
a strong military move north, his mentor's scorn made
such a maneuver seem inappropriate and of doubtful
value. Instead, O'Malley found himself agreeing with
Bainbridge's next suggestion that the Portsmouth Navy
Base be notified and a small task force sent up the coast
to try to head off any landing. Bainbridge tossed off the
proposal as if trying to humor the whim of a likeable
subordinate.

"And, of course, notify the radar station to be on the alert for submarines," Michael volunteered.

"Of course. Will that satisfy you?"

With that, the interview was over. Bainbridge faded back again into the fauteuille. The aide led Michael back into the foyer.

"Oh, Michael," the reincarnated voice came wafting out of the room he had just left. "I intend to remain in Boston for the next several days. I am looking forward to your visiting me again. I seem to have misplaced your explanation of the detour to the Norwegian fjord."

Michael ignored that last sarcastic riposte. He could accept Bainbridge's rudeness and condescension as the price of associating with the man. It was true, however, about the scientists from Telemark: Michael had no explanation for their presence. If only Berkowitz had lived longer . . . he might have learned more. He felt that Bainbridge did have the answer, but would make him work hard for it.

As O'Malley crossed the foyer to leave, his shoes skidded on the slick marble surface. He did not stop to admire the delicate Sheraton chair nor the Federal sideboard, nor even the restored Zuber of Washington crossing the Brandywine. He saw none of these precious antiques. His mind was busy churning with the realization that Bainbridge seemed to be teasing the situation, not dealing with it boldly or decisively. If the Germans were to land with missiles, then massive countermeasures should be taken. If, on the other hand, the hypothesis was invalid, then why send even an inadequate force?

Michael's disquiet increased. The oddest sensation came over him. That someone was pulling hidden strings and he was responding like a disjointed puppet. Just as he dropped off to sleep, the telephone awakened him. It was four-thirty in the morning. Bainbridge was calling to tell him that the Portsmouth Fleet had weighed anchor for Winter Harbor and was already at sea heading north.

But for the departing sailors, as well as O'Malley, it was too late. They had no way of knowing. At the same time as Michael turned his back on Bainbridge, Kiel, in response to a sudden message from the American mainland, was sending out new instructions to the waiting wolf pack to advance the landing by twenty-four hours.

──────➤ SIXTEEN

The dense, yellow-pigmented ore started its trip at the newly resurrected mining town of Eldorado on the eastern tip of Lake Athabasca. It had taken eighty years for the glacial waters to purge the tailings, left by earlier miners, of the yellow ore that gave the settlement its name in the 1800s. Now the lake was muddied again by thousands of tons of new leavings dumped by those seeking another yellow ore, this one unknown to history. The ore was placed in a single freight car, its openings sealed with riveted panels of thick steel. Slowly the train snaked its way across the barren tundra surrounding the southern reaches of Hudson's Bay.

The course had been carefully picked to use low-density freight routes and rarely used spur lines. The train traveled the open country by day. It was rushed through switching depots at night and always without explanation for the clandestine passage. As the train moved south, avoiding the major cities of the middle provinces, the terrain grew greener. Trees now grew thick and tall below the timberline, and the air became moist and warm. The train never stopped except for fuel and water and crew replacements.

The international border with the United States posed the greatest risk to security. The main conduits from Canada passed through the highly industrialized eastern provinces where German agents honeycombed the railway yards to report concentrations of munitions and troop shipments. In a little-inhabited area of northern Maine, at the foot of Louise Mountain, the two countries were divided by a rocky crevasse. Woburn Gorge had been spanned years ago by a steel trestle, eight hundred sixteen feet long and two hundred fifty-four feet high. Now rusted and abandoned, the spidery filigree of girders had once shivered under the weight of the surrounding forests on their way to Bangor for transport to the massive paper machines along the Penobscot River.

Over the past weeks, oddly suited hunters were seen reconnoitering the gorge and testing the span with wires and black boxes of electrical instruments. Passenger trains, whose cars were empty behind their closed window blinds, passed back and forth each day. Those who were curious about the unusual activity were even more puzzled when the strangers took down their tents and departed almost immediately after a powerful locomotive pulling a single car slowly traversed the gorge at two o'clock one rain-drenched morning.

The train paused briefly on the United States side of the pass to allow the engineer and firemen to be replaced by Americans, and then it started up again in a shriek of steel rasping against steel. As the thick, black smoke of the steam engine disappeared in the distance, Woburn Gorge fell silent once again.

Rohmer was still submerged and silent ten miles off the coast of Maine, waiting fretfully each hour for the coded message to initiate the final lap. Crossing the Atlantic, they had traveled by night on the surface and by day at periscope depth, relying on the snorkel to supply fresh oxygen and to exhaust the engine fumes. Rohmer remembered when the snorkel—or "big nose," as Doenitz named it—was first installed. The Dutch invention was highly touted as the means by which the U-boat Division would regain mastery of the North Sea from the Allies.

When the new invention was being tested, its built-in peril did not become obvious until a score of sailors had died. The snorkel contained two tubes. The first brought in outside air for the diesel engines and crew. The second tube, shorter and thinner, exhausted dangerous internal combustion gases as well as man-made carbon dioxide. The whole air mast was raised and lowered by an ingenious hydraulic oil-pressure valve.

The snorkel had originally been equipped with an automatic flutter valve which closed when a high wave hit it, to prevent flooding. When this happened, the diesels, deprived of surface oxygen, sucked in air from the hull and threatened the crew with death from carbon monoxide poisoning. After much bitter wrangling, the Hamburg manufacturers finally developed a means to provide the diesels with an extra reservoir of air so that the snorkel could be used when traveling in stormy seas.

For the last one hundred twenty miles to Schoodic Peninsula, the pack had traveled underwater both day and night to avoid radar detection. Guided only by dead reckoning coordinates, they were as deaf and blind as they hoped were the senses of the Eastern Coastal Watch to knowledge of their silent passing.

"Hasn't the telegraph room heard anything?" Rohmer barked impatiently to Kern.

"Nein, Herr Kapitän, not even a fish on the hydrophone," came back the respectful reply.

Eight bells—2000 hours. Perhaps now they would hear from Kiel. Rohmer stared soberly through the periscope eyepieces. He could see in the fading sunlight the fog layering out on top of the cold water. How many more sunsets would he live to count?

Rohmer knew by heart the frightening statistics for the U-boat service. In any other branch, the problem of recruits would have been horrendous. Somehow the Korps managed to retain its romantic aura and there was never a shortage of volunteers, even during the last days of the war when most patrols never returned and one's first assignment was apt to be the last.

"Thirty-two thousand men. Dead!" von Eyssen had confided. "Seven thousand survivors left out of thirty-nine thousand. And the U-boat losses? Only forty left out of eight hundred twenty. The rest sunk with their full crews aboard." He pursed his lips bitterly, "And you wonder why the Kriegsmarine considers your mission our last chance?"

Rohmer had known that casualties were high, but eighty to ninety percent! What were his own chances? This was his seventeenth patrol. Would he be forced some day to the surface and end up in a Stalag in Bormanville on the shores of Lake Ontario, or would he go down with his ship like Prien and Hauptmann? Would he have a choice?

There was a scraping noise on the ladder. The whiskered face of Obersteuermann Reche suddenly appeared. It had taken no more than four minutes for the message to reach them from headquarters in Kiel, relayed via the Kerneval wireless Navy transmitter located in the medieval stone fortress town of St. Louis at the mouth of the Bay of Biscay.

The decoded message from Lorient was thrust into Kern's hand. A quick glance and it made its way to Rohmer like a baton being passed in a relay race. The U-boat captain took one look at it and gave a big smile.

"This is it," he shouted like a schoolboy. "Twenty-four hours ahead of schedule." He pulled Kern to him in a boisterous bearhug, clapping him on the back. Giving out a loud roar, Rohmer swung down the round hatch passage, descending arm over arm, on the metal rungs. Kern followed immediately behind him, pausing only to turn the wheel over his head to secure the hatch cover. The control levers were pulled. The klaxon alarm shrieked through the steel shell. With a powerful surge, the diesels roared to life. The vents were opened to let in the cold ocean. The submarine sank fast as air fled from the main ballast tanks with a loud hiss. The bow went down first, tipping at an angle of forty degrees. Rohmer held onto the overhead pipes for support. It only took a scant moment as he passed through the control room, but with a practiced eye he checked the rudder and hydroplane valve controls. He stopped for an instant and waited. The smooth leveling off of the sub at sixty meters told him that trim had been properly compensated and descent stopped. He nodded to himself, satisfied.

He proceeded swiftly on his course, weaving by the radio room, the hydrophone listening room, the petty warrant officers' wardroom, ricocheting between outstretched hands alternately balancing on strategically placed ballast cells and petroleum and water tanks. He reached his private locker and drew the curtain for privacy. For the hundredth time, he reread the instructions from von Eyssen.

For the first time since he had left the long jetty in Kiel, Rohmer did not worry whether the landing would be detected or repulsed. Those were circumstances over which he had no control, any more than over the fates which had allowed him to live when his colleagues had long since perished in the ocean he now sailed. His mind grappled with the intricate timing of maneuvers which must be integrated to the minutest detail ... the neutralization of the radar station, the breakout at the prisoner-of-war camp, the unloading of the missiles, the preparation of the waiting launching ramps, the capture of the train with its precious cargo. All to be accomplished within twenty-four hours. A solitary day, during which Germany must seize and maintain sovereignty of her beachhead.

"After then," he quoted von Eyssen, "for the Americans, it will be too late." Even as he spoke those words, the wolf pack was already gliding silently toward the American mainland, impatient to release its caged birds of prey.

------→ S E V E N T E E N

Stephen Shoemaker received a warning from ConCinch Command in Boston telling him to keep a special watch for U-boats in the vicinity, but when he checked in with the Command at midnight, he had nothing to add to his report of four hours before. The sweeping radar arms monitored only the slow progression of the *Astra* eleven miles offshore. The radar tube glowed with an eerie luminescence in the semidark room. The radius of light swept clockwise, one revolution spreading every fifteen seconds to arouse the phosphors trapped in the fluorescent surface.

The previous watch had spotted the Swedish freighter's sudden appearance on the oscilloscope almost simultaneously with a distress call radioed from the ship for the nearest medical facility. The *Astra* reported a sailor burned severely when a high-pressure steam line cracked in the boiler room. The Coast Guard advised the captain of the ferry terminal at Adams Point with sufficient draught to accommodate the freighter. An ambulance would be waiting to take the victim to the hospital in Ellsworth. With a profusion of "taks," the captain altered course for Frenchman Bay.

A shout by his partner outside brought Stephen to the door. The fresh air felt good after sitting in the cramped viewing carrel. Stephen sucked in deep lungfuls and did several knee-bends to loosen his muscles. On the horizon, he could see the brightly illuminated hull of the white ship, passing them to starboard on its way into Frenchman Bay. Allied ships sailed at night with all lights extinguished. Neutral ships, in accordance with the Geneva Convention, were festooned with dazzling drapes of lights. The glittering sight was lovely against the inky blackness of the water. The surf could be heard cresting rhythmically on the shore, where rising inroads of white foam were already covering low tidal pools.

Offshore, submerged, the U-201 telegraph operator was carefully monitoring coastal radio stations. He pulled in signals from Ellsworth and Blue Hill nearby, and from Bangor forty miles away. By means of the radio bearings, the operator obtained a triangular fix. Rohmer glanced at the coordinates. With protractor and compass, he located his position on a copy of U.S. Coast Chart No. 306—one of dozens purchased by the Kriegsmarine before the war.

Rohmer looked down at the chart and grunted satisfaction. His submarine lay well in the lee of Turtle Island, whose rocky promontory would block the rays of the radar station's klystron tube, thus shielding him as if by a dense lead curtain. He gave the order to surface. The diesel-powered pumps blew water out of the ballast tanks. The U-boat began to rise ever so slowly, with perfect trim, until it was eight feet below the surface.

"Periscope up," he ordered, his voice tense and worried. He straddled the saddle at the base of the periscope shaft and rotated the narrow field of vision. "Perfect!" He smiled. The U-boat was exactly where he had planned. One mile away, he could make out the indistinct shape of Gouldsboro Peninsula, with the waves crashing on the very tip.

The U-boat was now too close for radar to be effective. Rohmer had turned off the diesel engines for fear that the radar station might have the underwater sonar detectors which Kiel had warned about. The submarine was now running on electric motors.

Three hundred yards from shore the U-boat surfaced. The hatches opened and as Rohmer and Kern watched nervously from the bridge, five rubber rafts were made ready. Leaving only enough crew to protect the U-boat from surface attack, Rohmer filled each raft with six men, fully equipped with wireless sets and submachine guns. Paddling silently with muffled oars, dressed in black with faces darkened so as not to reflect a glint of whiteness, the armada moved into shore. The lead man in each bow jumped out and pulled the craft high up on the beach as the other occupants moved onto land. The tide was coming in and they had no desire to be stranded in several hours. The men split into two columns and quickly surrounded the blockhouse.

Shoemaker was drinking a cup of coffee, his chair tilted against the wall with his feet propped up on the wooden table in front of him. The other two men on his watch were intent on monitoring their screens. The door burst open. The sudden apparition of strange men with soot-darkened faces resembled a Halloween masquerade, but the submachine guns readied under each arm dispelled any hope that this might be a charade perpetrated by their off-duty comrades as a prank.

Shoemaker still did not believe that he was face to face with the enemy until the sailor on his right sprinted for the door. A short stab of bullets caught him in mid-run. He fell, dead before his body reached the floor. The loud noise ricocheted through the tiny cinderblock room.

Another sharp burst of bullets killed the second sailor even though, like Shoemaker, he had not moved a muscle or said a word. Shoemaker shuddered. His mouth was open, tongue unable to move. His bladder contracted in an involuntary spasm, squeezing a few drops of urine into his clothes. He felt chilled and clammy and sick to his stomach. The gun turned in his direction. He instinctively put up his hands to ward off a death he knew was certain to come.

"Over there!" Instead of bullets, the words came out in English clipped with a German accent.

"Get over to your post," Rohmer ordered harshly. "Do not leave that chair. You are to tell me of anything that you see on that screen. If I see or hear any ship or plane before you have warned me that it is coming"— he pointed ominously to the two dead bodies on the floor where the blood was gathering into sticky puddles—"this will happen to you, too."

Stephen was paralyzed with fear and could not move.

The gun poked into his back, shoving him off his chair.

"Get over there. Immediately!" Stephen, trembling, did as he was told.

Leaving two sailors in charge of Shoemaker, Rohmer checked to see if the rest of the blockhouse had been secured. It had gone as planned. At this stage, Rohmer did not have enough manpower to waste on guarding enemy captives. Every American had been killed. He viewed the bodies in the bunks. Some were in the act of throwing back the covers to see what had happened and their bodies were exposed. Others were shot as they slept, huddled under the coarse ration blankets. One soldier was found outside. Stupidly he had come out of concealment and was shot. The freshly lit cigarette was still burning between his dead lips.

Rohmer counted the bodies. Eight. Plus the live American made nine. According to his information, there should be twelve. Shoemaker confirmed that the other three men were off duty. One was in Winter Harbor. The other two were drinking at some roadside café in North Sullivan, near the railroad depot. Von Eyssen's figure tallied. Rohmer turned and left, satisfied with this first phase of the plan. The remaining maneuvers would be more difficult. Von Eyssen's admonition came echoing back to him as strongly as when he had first heard it in Kiel: "You cannot fail as long as you maintain the element of surprise. You will make the initial move and, if you keep the inertia of momentum, the Americans will always be one move behind you. They cannot catch up unless you either fail in the execution of any maneuver or you lose the protective cloak of surprise."

That "protective cloak of surprise"!

Rohmer smiled again, pleased. Despite the coolness of the night, he felt pleasantly warm and flushed. He stepped carefully over the dead bodies of the Americans. For the first time since he had left Kiel, the U-boat captain felt confident.

Rohmer was aware that as an isolated event, the slaughter on Schoodic Peninsula was of limited value. It was a tangential move aimed at providing the German beachhead with advance warning of any American move in their direction from the sea. A move that, to be effective, must come within the next twenty-four hours. After that period, the missiles would be armed and any American parry toward Frenchman Bay would place Boston in instant jeopardy.

Kiel could provide the initiative, the command hierarchy, the missiles themselves, even the ammunition and communication linkages to sustain a military holding action for the required twenty-four hours. But only Gouldsboro could supply the missing factor which von Eyssen could not ferry over from Germany. It was not manpower. If the prisoners had not been available, the Type-XXI U-boat, with its displacement of fifteen hundred tons, could have transported ten times the crew complement of Rohmer's U-201.

No. At the very moment that Stephen Shoemaker in fright urinated in his pants, Mario Steffanelli saw that essential ingredient brilliantly illuminated through the dark of the night, in the longest split second of his life.

⟶ EIGHTEEN

It was Steffanelli's luck to pull the 11:00 P.M. to 7:00 A.M. shift. He cursed at the powerful searchlight beam attracting every flying insect, it seemed, within miles. He swore and swatted, trying to shrink far back from the fierce whiteness. To make things worse, he could hear the noise of tractors being driven back and forth as the Germans tried hard to make good on their promise to the local farmers. The unmuffled roar of motors accompanied the headlights crisscrossing the yard in their eerie do-si-do.

Had Steffanelli listened more carefully, he would have heard, under the blatant noise of the machine shops and tractor transmissions, another, more martial rhythm which, constant in tempo, grew slowly louder and more persistent. It filled the entire camp, coming from every direction. He looked over the side of the fence but could see nothing. He did not bother to swing the searchlight off the prisoner barracks to penetrate the outer perimeter.

The sentry wrapped his hands around his neck, trying to squash any biting creatures that might have settled there from a moment ago. The clanking noise was definitely louder, groaning and shaking the ground at the foot of the tower. Concerned, Steffanelli swung the beacon around. *Something* had to be going on down there. "Those sons-of-bitches, playing around at midnight with their fucking tractors. Goddam grease jockeys!" he swore, spitting over the railing.

The light stabbed through the night, illuminating the base of the tower. Nothing! The mechanical rumbling grew strident, now from all sides, overpowering everything else. Deafening. Blocking out all other sounds. Wildly, he flung the light in increasingly wider circles. Until . . . until . . .

He gasped and tried to scream. He never did get the shout out as Sherman M-4 and Patton M-46 tanks, by the dozens, hatches sealed, were upon him, each crushing with the weight of fifty tons.

A stampede of prehistoric monsters, they simultaneously cracked into all four control towers, crumpling them to the ground. They rolled back and forth over the fallen structures like giant feet wiping out insects. Convinced that no life remained, they turned sharply at right angles and calmly rolled down the lengths of barbed wire.

According to the prearranged plan, the tanks crushed

the mess hall, the recreation hall, the commissary, the supply station, all of which had been evacuated by the Germans. Converging on the guard barracks, the behemoths rolled them under, crunching bones, flesh, skulls, and brains along with wood, asphalt, shingles, and linoleum. The tanks spared only the ammunition shed, which was quickly surrounded by a waiting squad of prisoners and emptied.

Most of the Americans were asleep and, like the radar station inhabitants, never even awakened for their execution. Those who were aroused by the commotion, or who had not yet gone to bed, raced outside to see what the Heinies were up to. They were shot down. Several fled into the dark woods around the camp, still unsure what had happened. To Oberst Otto Werner, these escapees were of no consequence. They could do nothing to mitigate the success of the breakout. Only the Gouldsboro Prisoner-of-War Camp contained the motorized legs to make an army out of willing soldiers, that critical mobility to neutralize a geographic area wide enough to guarantee Rohmer his one perilous day.

Werner reviewed the series of coded instructions smuggled into the camp over the months through Trondheim's plant, who also reversed the process to allow communication from Werner to his unseen correspondent. The last message had arrived that afternoon with the new time of the landing.

Werner knew that there were no plans to evacuate them. They were expendable pawns. After the attack, those not killed would inevitably be recaptured. But for a brief moment, they would be alive again, fighting, far from home, in some unexplained bizarre way, for the Fatherland. That was all they were told. No escape. No deliverance. Only a brief interlude of war with probable death in an alien country. To Werner, these were the sweetest options of all.

The hatch cover flung back, he stood, defiant, in the lead Patton tank. Over the months, he and his men had learned to handle the controls of the American products, and even of a few British Centurions which, like unwanted orphans, must have stowed away in the hold of a Liberty ship bringing damaged equipment back to the United States for cannibalization or repair. The names Chrysler, Allison, and Packard were unfamiliar to him. Although the machines could never be the equivalent of his own Tigers, they were more than adequate weapons. If not, he reflected with bitterness, he would not be standing in Gouldsboro, but would still be in Libya routing the tattered remnants of Alexander's Africa Army.

From his elevated stance over the flat assembly field, Werner could see the vehicles sort themselves into four identical columns with the jeeps attached to the head of each: the tanks still covered with undulating strips of desert camouflage, manned by their complement of four men plus a captain who stood upright in the hatch; the armored personnel carriers, their motors racing as soldiers piled into the back, twenty to each carrier; the half-tracks waiting with empty swivel plates on the rear platforms. Werner's men had spent much effort on these metal blocks, secretly machining and redrilling holes and cams to accommodate the German 10.5-cm L/45, the 3.7-cm. AA c/30, and the 2-cm. AA twin-barrel guns which even now were being detached from the surface decks of the submarines in the bay. Between these deadly weapons and the accessory 3.7-cm. AA M/42s and M/43s carried in the holds of the wolf pack, Werner would have an incredibly vicious spectrum of firepower to protect each of the mobile Panzer units he was constructing on American soil.

Off to one side were the gasoline tank trucks for mobile refueling and dozens of large tractor cabs, each pulling an empty thirty-two-foot flatbed trailer. Next to them, looking like a collection of lurching praying mantises, were the self-propelled derricks used to lift disabled vehicles off the road onto the trailers for transport back to the repair depot.

Werner gave a condescending smile at this accumulation of civilian equipment. What in the world did Rohmer want them for? Considering the short time during which Werner expected his forces to be operational, it seemed silly to haul damaged items back to Gouldsboro for immediate repair. His orders were specific, though. He was to bring these derricks and trailers to the terminal at Adams Point. Werner could not help reflecting that those prisoners who survived the next twenty-four hours would probably spend the rest of the war repatching the equipment stretched before him.

Werner nodded with satisfaction as the military vehicles moved to their preassigned positions, sending up clouds of dust in the process. Within forty-five minutes, the camp's vast storage depot was emptied of all strategic items that Werner had selected in advance. The four columns waited in place, impatient, motors idling in neutral, as the drivers anticipated the order to move off.

From the head of each column, a jeep detached itself and rode to Werner's tank. These would be Hessler, Braunscher, Raasch, and Schnee, the Panzer colonel's prize tank commanders who had fought with him in the sands of North Africa. Like Werner, they knew that their mission was only for a brief moment, perhaps futile, and still a mystery. They did not care. The anger and frustration of years of captivity, living as prisoners of the hated Americans, submitting to the orders of inferiors, forced to be servile to Ukranians, Poles, and even Jews, abraded their sensibilities. Subjected to the ridicule of the stupid peasants who came to stare at them, having to beg and barter for trinkets—these and other indignities too numerous to mention had worn down their humanity. In twenty-four hours, they might be back behind barbed wire, but for now, for the present, they were once again the Masters. Werner recognized the determined look in their faces as a reflection of his own. That is good, he said to himself. The Americans have primed these butchers well.

But men and machines and guns, he worried, are no good without bullets and cannon shells. It was 200 hours, two o'clock in the morning. The radar station should have been taken by now. The freighter and the submarines would be arriving at the unloading jetty at Adams Point, only eighteen minutes away. There, his

Panzers would find the vital munitions, the 90-mm shells for the tanks, the cannons and machine guns for the vacant mounting plates on the half-tracks, the machine guns, hand grenades, mortars, and mortar shells—the fangs for his toothless columns. Enough destructive firepower to allow him to seize and hold the strategic terrain until Rohmer had completed his mission.

They would also acquire the wireless sets, the portable field phones with connecting spools of ground cable, the walkie-talkie sets, the mobile phone exchanges, all as essential as manpower, firepower, and transportation. Within hours, the four columns would separate and spread like waves of killer ants over an ever-expanding perimeter. The copper wires and high-frequency radio waves would follow them, and bind every man and machine to a central command post where Rohmer and Werner would control the operation.

Looking down again at the eager faces of the four tank commanders, Werner could not help thinking how much all of them were like an organism with its vital parts dissevered and strewn all over the landscape. We have the motors, others have the guns. We have the bodies, others have the plan. Now is the time for the enemy to pounce upon us and destroy us. Now is our moment of vulnerability.

Had Werner but known von Eyssen, he would have instinctively recognized the intuitive wisdom of the Grossadmiral's injunction to Rohmer, "Keep the protective cloak of surprise ... and you cannot fail." Like a shielding hand stretched out from three thousand miles away, von Eyssen's words were even now protecting this fragile, shimmering beachhead, so pitifully weak, its jugular bared to any alert foe. With each passing moment, as the parts moved and meshed together, its strength was increasing, until, within hours, the metamorphosis completed, it would itself be transformed into a creature of prey. Then and only then would it herald its presence to the still-unsuspecting Americans.

To his men who had waited silently watching their leader, Werner said, "We should be at the wharf in less than thirty minutes. It will take less than three hours to unload the equipment and ammunition and distribute it to the four columns. By 500 hours, we will be invincible, mechanized, armed, and led. For however long God grants us our tactical superiority, we can do our duty."

Werner watched the columns move out. The men were clean-shaven and wore proudly the patched battle dress that had once earned them the taunts of the guards. Each arm boldly displayed a black armband, with a white circle containing a tilted red swastika—the products of weeks of midnight sewing. As they passed before Werner in review, the dust swirled about him and made him cough. He held his right hand out in a stiff salute, a permanent "Sieg Heil" on his lips. Their arms, too, shot out in unison, creating an endless sea of waving symbols.

As the columns left the compound, each vehicle paused for a moment between pairs of soldiers who were standing in the road. The men quickly pressed to the sides the cardboard templates from which earlier they had removed the centers. With a paintbrush, they stenciled a bright red swastika over the faded white five-cornered star of the United States Army, shaming it by contrast. The teams worked fast and the stencils grew wet and sticky. When the teams were not fast enough to change to a fresh stencil, a rivulet of red paint would drip and run down from the garish emblem. To Werner, it looked as if the Nazi insignia had already achieved its bloody baptism. The symbolism made him shiver with excitement and anticipation. It sent a thrill through his body and his arm stood out rigid for all the world to see.

→ **NINETEEN**

The radar station was now in German hands. There was no longer any need for the U-boats to run silent and scared. Rohmer, back on his boat with full crew manning the upper and lower deck cannons, was slicing through the outer reaches of Frenchman Bay. He had left two sailors at the blockhouse with a wireless transmitter to warn him of any enemy approach. Should the radio fail, they were given flare pistols to use in case of emergency.

The young Germans guarding Stephen Shoemaker were unaware that nothing in von Eyssen's plan allowed for their eventual return to the wolf pack. When the mission was over, they were to be abandoned. Rohmer was distressed at this callousness, but two added to the five thousand already destined to be recaptured did not make a great deal of difference. He smiled against that eventual moment when the poor quaking radar operator would finally realize that he, and not his captors, was the actual master in that room.

Retracing his way around the eastern end of Turtle Island, Rohmer set course three hundred ten degrees north by northwest, to skirt the forbidding silhouette of Ironbound Island. He could see, to port, the red light flashing in periods of five seconds from the unmanned lighthouse on Egg Rock, and he could hear the sonorous, low-pitched horn warning sailors away from this treacherous ledge south of Ironbound. Rohmer sighted the lights of Bar Harbor to portside as he glided between Sheep Porcupine and Burnt Porcupine islands. Straight over his bow, facing his ship across the remaining five miles of open water, he could see the blunt nose of Adams Point.

The bow wave broke evenly as the U-boat sped forward, as impatient as its crew. Rohmer looked behind him. He saw the rest of the pack in line. They had waited until he emerged from the cover of Turtle Island and were now following him through the cold waters, decks prepared. Towering crates of supplies and munitions were stacked near the cannons, searchlights ready to be activated, klaxons and loudspeakers affixed to the bridge.

The clouds parted for just an instant. The third-quarter moon hovered in the north sky, etching a silver-white path to the vessels, lighting their gentle swirling wake like ethereal foam. The land stood out in dark contrast as the surface of the water brightened for a brief moment in the soft moonglow. More than one sailor, viewing the quiet protected body of water surrounded by the crisp indentations of land and sprinkling of islands, could not help, even at night, but be thrilled by the natural beauty of the bay. It seemed almost tragic, Rohmer thought, to bring war to this pacific setting— but then he remembered that the Americans were bombing his homeland. They had no qualms; why should he? At that moment his peripheral vision picked up a glint of light against the horizon. Within minutes, the brightly lit hull of the *Astra* became visible. Like moths drawn to a flame, the U-boats turned in unison, fifteen degrees to starboard, and headed for the pier on the east side of the point.

The U-boats were not the only ones attracted to the illuminated ship this evening. It seemed that all of Adams Point, with a few late-night curiosity seekers from North Sullivan, were down at the old ferry pier, staring up at the silent white freighter. Despite the waiting ambulance at dockside and the restless crowd eager to help the wounded man, the ship appeared deserted. It had moored over an hour before, but had neither lowered a gangplank nor exposed its crew to the expectant onlookers. Right now it was a ghost ship, rising and falling with the waves, bruising the dock and rubbing off barnacles which had multiplied there undisturbed since the last ferry to Bar Harbor in 1940. Not a sound, not a face. The white ship waited.

Barnard Hodgdon looked at the milling crowd, recognizing almost everybody present. Those that he did not, he reckoned must be guests renting the cottages of the summer folk who could not come this season because of the war. He made out his daughter with her white nurse's cap leaning against the side door of the Ellsworth ambulance. She looked happier than she had ever looked before. Hodgdon hoped that her new radiance did not mean what he feared it might. He knew the signs well from Edith's mother in whom they had occurred six times. He had been watching his daughter's figure over the past weeks for the slightest evidence of convexity. Well, there could be worse than a marriage. Some actually turned out pretty good. But by gosh, he'd wish those fellows would learn to keep their peckers inside their pants, or at least save them for the girls down to Bunker's near the North Sullivan train depot.

Edith caught her father's eye and waved to him. She knew what he was suspecting. So far, her resolve had held off Stephen's increasing impatience. How much longer, she did not know.

"This is the biggest excitement we've had here," Hodgdon caught himself saying at least a dozen times, "since the *Corsair* pulled in in 1927." Barnard remembered well that Sunday morning at the wharf when Junius Pierpont Morgan's newest lady friend alit for the drive into Ellsworth to mass. "Oh, how I'd love to hear her confession . . ." he remembered himself saying before his wife angrily hushed him up, pointing to his children who could not understand what all the fuss was about.

The level of excitement increased when the seven submarines were spotted offshore. The moon had backlit their black shadows on the water. The crowd grew quiet, but not apprehensive. With the powerful radar station operating at Schoodic Peninsula, and given the fact that the ships were cruising on the surface, the vessels could not be anything but American, perhaps seeking to aid the stricken freighter.

The townspeople now crowded onto the long pier, eagerly awaiting the berthing. Suddenly, powerful searchlights from all seven U-boats pierced the semidarkness and held the wharf, the people, and the ambulance in their harsh white rings. The hot lights blinded them to the swastikas on the bows and fluttering on the pennants over each bridge. Not daring to move, blinking over and over, shielding their eyes with their hands, the gathered onlookers strained to identify the hulking shapes.

As the submarines docked, armed sailors jumped onto the shore and spread out, forming a tight protective ring around the wharf. One searchlight turned up and lit the deck of the U-201. There, fluttering brazenly for all to see, was the blood-red flag of Nazi Germany with its black emblem. It shocked stillness into the scene. In the quiet, the crowd heard, for the first time, the muffled mechanical clanking of dozens of tanks, the grinding wheels of jeeps, trucks, and cranes, which had turned down the narrow road toward the point and were racing two abreast to the jetty at the end. Rohmer addressed the crowd with a megaphone.

"This is Kapitän Wilhelm Rohmer of the German Reich U-201. You will consider yourselves in occupied territory. You are our prisoners. Do as you are told and you will not be harmed. Disobey and you will be killed."

He paused. As the sailors moved in to cordon off the crowd and make room for the unloading, he could hear angry, incredulous shouts of the people milling about, agitated, yelling and pushing, growing more belligerent by the second. Rohmer signaled his bow gunner. Staccato shots of tracer shells suddenly tore into the aging fleet of lobster boats, trawlers, and sloops moored in the harbor. It was almost like a Fourth of July spectacle with graceful trajectories of fluorescent bullets rising and falling as they set boat after boat on fire. The brilliant flames cast fiery reflections on the water and on the frightening hulls of the U-boats.

The cries of the crowd grew louder as they tensed, weighing the decision to challenge the cordon and save their boats. Hodgdon did not wait. In an impetuous gesture, he grabbed up the man on each side of him and broke through the ring of guards. He shook his fist furiously at the sailors. "You've set our boats on fire," he cried out. "We must save them."

He got no further. Kern waited until the three men were clear of the crowd. He lowered his submachine gun. Three short bursts of bullets tore into their chests, knocking them down as they ran forward. Their bodies slumped onto the dock and were kicked into the water by the nearest sailor.

Rohmer looked on the scene with approval. It was necessary that something like this should happen. He recalled von Blumberg's lecture at Flensburg: "The first thing one must do is provoke an incident and then squash it with blood. The more terror, the better. Remember, gentlemen, we are only a small country. Yet we are holding under subjugation an unwilling population many times the size of Germany. How can we do it? By only one way ... fear! Make them afraid of you. Make them fear you so much that they will not think of questioning your commands." And then the directive that puzzled Rohmer for some time after the lecture, "Be *arbitrary*. Be *capricious*.... *Kill for no obvious reason!* That is what will best control the mob. Believe me, gentlemen, I know."

Von Blumberg had continued, certain of his audience's attention: "Let me give you an example. Suppose you are guarding a concentration camp where touching the barbed wire fence is punishable by death, as is refusing a command of the guard. A new shipment of inmates arrives. What do you do? Take a hat off of one of the new arrivals and throw it on the fence. Order the victim to retrieve it. If he disobeys, shoot him. If he obeys, shoot him. The example of his death will quickly convert the belligerency of the new prisoners to fearful docility."

Edith Hodgdon had never heard such a lecture. All she saw was her father rush forward and die. Without thinking, she jumped out of the ambulance and flung herself at the guard who had pushed her father's body into the water. The corpse still lay there, floating face down, bobbing near the piling in a spreading film of greasy blood. She screamed hysterically as she pummeled the sailor with her fists. Tears coursed down her cheeks. Her head jerked back and forth with unbridled, hysterical hate.

"That woman!" Rohmer barked over the megaphone.

The guard swung the butt of his rifle and smashed her across the face, cracking her lower jaw. She staggered back, with a gasp of pain. Blood spilled from her mouth. The pain lasted only a second before Kern lowered his gun again. A burst of bullets sliced her midriff, lacerating her aorta and puncturing her spine. Her body, too, was kicked into the water to float next to her father's. Her face was turned up, but her open eyes no longer saw the skies she had taught Stephen to love.

Very astute, Rohmer concluded, as a deathly stillness fell over the crowd. They stood there, the women weeping, the men impotent in their fury, paralyzed by fear of what would happen next and who would be the next to die. They all had only one thought—to stand still, be quiet, to obey and live.

Rohmer's admiring reflections on his old War College mentor lasted only a minute. He, too, was listening to the familiar clanking and whining of a Nazi war machine. A moment later, dozens of rings of headlights illuminated the whole terrain as brightly as daylight.

➤ TWENTY

It was unlikely that more than two dozen inhabitants of Hancock County, other than those at the wharf, were aware of the midnight passage of four columns of Panzer troops from the prisoner-of-war camp. Still without shells for his tank cannons nor possessing any heavy armament, Werner was relying on the element of surprise to prevent any unforeseen obstacle to his flight. For protection, he had mounted portable machine guns in the open hatches of the lead tanks. These, along with rifles and handguns, were all that he could supply with ammunition retrieved from the guard supply shed. The remainder of the Korps, while noisy and ominous, was impotent.

Swiftly the columns moved two abreast along the narrow, unlit fifteen-mile road between the prison camp and Adams Point. There were few cars out in the deserted countryside at that time of night. Those who saw the approaching headlights of strange massive hulks crowding both sides of the road turned off the pavement hastily to escape being crushed. As the long, spaced-out columns rolled by, the Germans could see the cars and trucks stranded on the soft shoulder, the angry drivers shaking their fists and hurling obscenities, threatening to report the obviously drunken sailors to the Naval Base in the morning.

Only at the junction of Route 184 did the Panzers encounter what could have been a serious blow to their critical timing. A large gasoline truck was stalled after turning off the side road onto Route 1. Steep embankments on both sides prevented the Germans from bypassing the block. The columns sputtered to a noisy halt.

Accompanied by an escort of soldiers brandishing

machine guns, Werner approached the struggling driver. At first, the driver thought it was a big joke when he saw the men with swastikas ordering him about. Werner cracked the man across the face with the butt of his revolver, tearing open the side of his nose and cheek. The stunned driver touched his face, unable to comprehend the blow and the blood streaming down his lacerated flesh. With a shriek of pain, he lunged for the slight commander, but was stopped with a savage kick to his abdomen and two sharp blows across his head by the two soldiers. The crumpled body rolled into the ditch.

Werner ordered one of his men to start the truck. The motor turned in a coarse rumble, but would not catch. Werner cursed, his pale face twisted with anger and impatience. He waved to the column in back of him. Immediately two tanks rolled forward, kicking up clouds of dust amplified by the solid beams of light slicing the pitch darkness. The tanks strained against the tanker, their metal treads sliding, then gaining, inch by inch, as the motors fought for power. Slowly, the truck moved. Then, faster, faster, until with a loud screech it tipped over the side of the high embankment and toppled head over end, over and over again, to crash on the jagged rocks below.

A thunderous roar split the air as the fuel exploded, sending up fierce currents of heat and fire that seared the Germans standing, hands on their hips, by the side of the road watching the sudden and violent conflagration.

Werner kicked the unconscious American over the crushed metal guard rail. The limp form spun downward until its outstretched silhouette was surrounded by a seething corona of fire. The inferno of flame caught the body and sucked it in. Werner watched the black blot shrink and disappear. Then, with a shrill cry, he climbed back into the tank and ordered his men on to Adams Point.

Rohmer and Werner. Neither man had ever seen the other before. Except for the vagaries of war and the von Eyssen plan, their lives would probably have passed and expired without even a chance meeting. Now, shaking hands, hugging each other, clasping shoulders, they seemed to the sullen crowd like two long lost brothers reunited.

The two men entered a small Cape Cod boathouse. Inside the old building with its dour gray shake sides and roof, they spread out the coastal charts and terrain maps of the area. The cabin was not electrified. A kerosene lamp pitched over their heads. Old paddles, masts, spars, and life jackets hung from the rafters. Anchors, moors, and floats lay strewn about the corners of the room.

So far the plan had gone as directed. Even now, soldiers under Werner's command, stripped to the waist, were unloading the munitions. The U-boat cannons were being bolted onto the mobile carriers. Crate after crate of supplies were being absorbed into the four tank corps. The Germans sweated under their heavy loads as they shuttled back and forth, racing against time.

The townspeople were herded into a large field and compelled to sit on the ground, hands clasped together in back of their necks, bodies bent forward. Only four guards were needed to maintain complete discipline.

Rohmer and Werner pored over the maps—one the plebian, the other a university graduate. The older, coarse sea captain; the younger, almost frail tank colonel. One who, within a short time, would return home, perhaps to glory, certainly to his wife and freedom; the other, if he lived, to face the prison barracks. One who knew what he was going to live for; the other who did not know what he was going to die for. Both German officers, on American soil, carrying out the dictates of a friendless man three thousand miles away who spent his free moments looking into a cameo locket.

The two conversed in hushed tones.

"I see that you have done your homework well," Rohmer said.

"Six months in this hell leaves you lots of time," Werner replied with sarcasm. "Getting the maps was no problem. We were able to study your needs well. Tell me if you agree?"

His tone was deferential, a sign of respect for the older officer, but both men knew that from here on, the success of the von Eyssen plan rested with Werner's ability to deploy his men and limited resources over unfamiliar ground, to secure temporarily a militarily untenable objective.

"This is where we are now." Werner stuck one end of his pencil in Adams Point.

"The railroad depot is here," making a small black ring around a speck on the map only a half-inch away. "For all practical purposes, we shall consider both operations, the preparation of the missiles and the securing of the freight train, as taking place in the same sector." His fingers outlined a pattern. "What we have before us is a triangular salient based for the most part on natural barriers. Look for yourself."

Rohmer stared at the map, but could see only colors representing topographical contour and black lines for rivers and traffic arteries.

"Look here, it is superb," Werner boasted. He placed a pencil on the map at Adams Point and drew a dark line up the coast, paralleling Route 1, for a distance of three-and-a-half inches. It ended at the town of Machias.

"One Korps under Braunscher goes up this way."

He then retraced the line back down to Adams Point and continued it farther down the coast, following Route 1 for another three-and-a-half inches to Rockland.

"The Second Korps, with Hessler, this way." He stepped back for a moment. "There, Rohmer," pointing with pride, "there is one side of your triangle. It faces the sea for one hundred miles. By tonight the entire road will be destroyed. After my sappers have finished, it will take a week to restore it for military traffic."

Rohmer looked at the black pencil line. What Werner had said was true, but what about the land approaches?

Werner anticipated the doubt.

"Look again at Rockland. It sits on the coast at the mouth of the Penobscot River." Werner took his pencil and starting from Rockland, drew a dark line following the river as it penetrated deep into the state. He stopped at each of the major cities which straddled the river and circled them in black...Bucksport, Bangor, Milford, Howland, and Lincoln.

"This is your second side. The river. Schnee, with the Third Korps, will travel up the east bank to Lincoln and blow up the bridges at these main points," indicating the encircled cities.

"There are bridges at other points, but these five are the only ones capable of supporting heavy equipment. I will make for you a moat, one hundred twenty miles long, to secure your southern flank. We will occupy the high banks on the east side of the Penobscot, and with carefully placed field pieces, can thwart any attempt to ford the river or to rebuild the bridges for at least twenty-four hours."

Rohmer's excitement grew as he saw the lines demarcated on the map. In his mind, he closed the last side of the triangle, from Lincoln to Machias. Werner did just that for him with his pencil.

"And, for this last side, there is nothing for fifty thousand square miles but lakes, mountains, and forests. Nothing. They planned this prison camp well. *We* cannot get out, but *they* have no way of getting in. In fact, if you search carefully, there is only one road through the whole triangular salient and it terminates in Aurora. That is where Raasch will be waiting with the Fourth Korps, just in case. No, mein Kapitän, with your radar watching the south and my men destroying the river crossings, we can leave the third side to the black flies for which this state is famous. It would take two weeks for a force to move in this direction down from Canada."

Rohmer looked at the map with astonishment. It was so simple. The seacoast had been secured with eight dead American sailors. The northern flank posed no problem. Werner should be able to seize and contain the river boundary in ten to twelve hours.

"It is good. Very good!" Rohmer looked up at Werner with a pleased expression on his face. He was about to say something more when Werner spoke again, voicing both their sentiments.

"Von Eyssen is to be congratulated. From a strategic standpoint, the ground is ideal. I see no trouble. No trouble at all."

"Remember," Rohmer warned, "I may have the radar scan, but I do not have the firepower to prevent a sea task force from overpowering me. If they should come before we are ready, I cannot stop them."

"Any more than I can repulse a strong force which should cross the river before we have arrived to blow the bridges," Werner agreed. "There too I would be annihilated. No, Herr Kommandant, for the next sixteen hours, we will be vulnerable. But ... but ... after that!"

"After that, the missiles will be in place. Our fangs will be bared."

They laughed together, a nervous relief from the tension, then resumed their discussion, voices relaxed and easy. Rohmer was assured by Werner that the heavy equipment was waiting at the loading dock. The U-boat commander emphasized the critical importance that Berlin placed in the train shipment.

"I do not know why it is so vital, but von Eyssen must have it. Incur any losses you have to, but bring that freight car here from North Sullivan. Everything else is secondary."

The look on Werner's face worried Rohmer, who pictured the tank commander disobeying his instructions and, in the heat of revenge, heading out into the countryside to grind his Panzer columns through flesh and mortar until he ran out of fuel and ammunition or was killed. Men like this one are dangerous, Rohmer thought.

A knock on the partly closed door, and Kern entered, followed by Hessler, Braunscher, Raasch, and Schnee. The men were tired, disheveled, and covered with a mixture of sweat and grime.

"The unloading is finished," Kern reported, with tired satisfaction.

"Herr Oberst," the four tank commanders announced almost in unison, "we are ready. The columns are equipped. It is incredible! The supplies. The firepower.

Berlin thought of everything. We can stop an army for a week. It is good!"

The men spoke rapidly. They were loud, excited, animated. Rohmer and Werner looked at each other, their emotions more constrained. They might never see each other again. They knew that they were just pawns in a master scheme, created thousands of miles away, but the enthusiasm was catching. Suddenly, against their wishes, the exhilaration in the room spilled over them and caught them, too, in its sharp talons.

"The Cognac, Kern. The Cognac," Rohmer ordered.

Kern opened a canvas bag which he had left resting against two lobster buoys in the corner and extracted a bottle of Cognac and a set of glasses.

"Ah, very kind," Werner said, inspecting the bottle.

Kern filled a small glass for each of the men. They clinked the glasses together, spilling the liquor in their haste.

"To the Führer," shouted Werner.

It was not quite the toast that Rohmer had had in mind. "To the Führer," he assented.

With their arms in salute, the officers threw back their heads and downed the fiery spirits. The vapors rose up through their nostrils and seared the backs of their throats. Their faces were flushed as they crashed the glasses against the cement floor in the corner.

Werner turned to Rohmer and Kern. He clicked his heels in a gesture of respect, bowed slightly from the waist, and shook each of their hands in turn. He left, followed at his heels by his Korps commanders.

"Did you notice?" Rohmer asked Kern, after the five had left. "What happened to those men? Was there an accident on the dock?"

Kern looked puzzled for a minute.

"Oh, you mean the red stains and blotches on their tunics? That is only paint from the sides of the tanks. Werner thought of everything. His men even painted swastikas on the tanks."

Rohmer did not answer. It might be paint, but, in the flickering light of the old lantern, it looked to him as if Hitler's new American Army had already tasted first blood.

Now, it was his turn.

Outside, the scene was quiet. Werner's troops and tanks were gone. The townspeople were missing. The *Astra* still rose and fell with the waves on one side of the long jetty. Along the opposite side lay the U-201 with the entire crew standing on deck, and next to it, touching each other the remaining U-boats waiting their turn.

On command from Kern, the tall construction crane brought by Werner from Gouldsboro approached the wharf. It rode up onto the pier and slowly traversed the length of the jetty, braking at the very end. Almost immediately a tractor with an open-platform trailer was backed onto the jetty, coming to a stop in front of the crane, right under the swaying hook suspended from the top.

Kern signaled to the bridge of the *Astra* where the captain and first mate were now waiting for their instructions. The large crane swung over the deck of the freighter. The hook dropped through the open hatchway and was seized by the crew who fastened it to one of the triangular sections of the prefabricated stadium bleachers.

The heavy rigid truss rose into the air. It swung over the trailer and was gently lowered onto the waiting flatbed. The men bolted the three-cornered structure to matching couplings on the body of the trailer. The bleacher stand was a sloped structure, an elongated triangle with a long base of thirty feet resting on the truck bed. The high back of the bleacher rose up twenty feet into the air. A long, slanted reinforced track connected the two ends. The whole unit was ten feet wide and crowded the sides of the trailer platform.

While the launching pad was being secured in place, the crane was busy lifting out of the forward hatch of the U-boat the first of the deadly warheads. With careful monitoring by one of the Peenemünde scientists, the crane lowered the rocket, head end up, onto the sloped ramp. Sailors standing alongside the trailer bolted the side brackets, bracing and locking the rocket to its final bed. These attachments would never be loosened. The tremendous power of the lift-off would rip the rockets from their wooden moorings and shatter the whole ramp in the process.

Without a break in the rhythm, the Mack truck shifted into low gear, tensing for the weight of the load. A row of sailors with red-tipped flashlights guided the trailer to solid ground. The driver paused for a short salute to Kern and started for the concealment of the nearby woods, where the dense fir and spruce formed an impenetrable umbrella over the hidden logging trails beneath. There, the engineers would carry on the delicate and exasperating task of setting the gyroscopic and magnetic compasses. Once their job was completed, only a light touch on the relay and the electrical contact would catapult these aerial dreadnoughts toward their preset targets.

Rohmer watched the whole operation with growing satisfaction. The launching pads of the *Astra,* the trailers from Gouldsboro, the missiles from Kiel, the scientists from the Baltic, all working together. As each individual component, worthless by itself, joined its mate, before his eyes the power of the Third Reich was asserting itself in this foreign land. As he looked upon the mating of the warheads with the wooden ramps, he could not help thinking of their still-temporary fragility. How much he and all his men were dependent upon their new pack members who, at that very moment, were racing across the map in all directions, to expand the protective curtain of clanking steel.

→TWENTY-ONE

Michael knew that it was trouble even before he picked up the phone. The clock said four o'clock. It was Thursday morning. Since meeting Bainbridge the day before, Michael had kept the Naval Intelligence Office on alert around the clock.

"I'm sorry to call, Michael." Liz's voice softened his resentment at being awakened. He grunted an indecipherable reply.

"It's the radar watch at Schoodic." Michael could detect the tone of concern. "Maybe I'm just reading something into it, but this is the first time they have ever had the same wireless operator on duty for eight hours straight. Shoemaker says that everything is all right, but I don't believe him. He wasn't his usual horny self. He sounded as if something was wrong. I can't be certain, but I thought that I'd better let you know."

For a minute Michael did not answer. Maybe nothing was the matter, but if the information obtained yesterday from Trondheim was accurate, Bainbridge be damned, there could be serious trouble up there. How to find out?

Michael gave Liz a series of rapid instructions and then hung up. He dressed quickly and walked to the office. He knew that if the rocket launch was to coincide with the Reichstag opening on Saturday, he still had almost two days remaining. Rohmer would not land any sooner than he had to and hang around like a sitting duck risking military retaliation.

But what if the date was wrong? What if Hitler planned to announce not an attack in progress but a mission already accomplished? Michael knew to expect the unexpected when dealing with von Eyssen. If Rohmer had already landed, the interval during which he could be stopped was running out. However, if that *was* the case, there should be concrete evidence of German military action aimed at securing protection for the missile launch site. O'Malley hoped that Liz would have that information by the time he arrived at the office.

He quickened his pace, washing his sleepy head with the cool morning air. The streets were almost deserted. In the eastern sky, he could see the first brightening of the horizon as the earth rotated under his feet. It looked like a nice day. He could not help giving a wry laugh as he recalled a bit of esoteric minutia that the first place in the United States to get the morning sun was Frenchman Bay.

Michael could sense the tension in the map room. On his orders, Liz had called in the rest of the staff. Only Berkowitz was missing. O'Malley felt a surge of anger.

An enlarged map of northern New England was tacked up on one wall of his small office. Against the other wall, a PBX console had been hurriedly installed. A dozen long black cables snaked through the partly opened door and hooked into the back of the communication set. Michael had ordered private lines connected to those outposts he knew would play a role in the deadly game that had just started.

He sat down behind the desk, prepared for the worst. "What have you found out?"

He was shocked by what he heard over the next ten minutes. The Maine National Guard headquarters in the state capital at Augusta had been besieged all night with calls from Hancock and Penobscot counties about Germans coming from every direction. The reports were garbled and seemingly exaggerated. They spoke of hundreds of tanks, jeeps, trucks, with thousands of German soldiers speeding up and down the coast and along the Penobscot River. There were wild, improbable tales of rape, murder, bombings, and mass executions, all of which served only to convince Augusta of the absurdity of the sightings.

All during the war there had been reports of spy landings, parachute drops, and even invasions. They had all turned out to be fallacious. The persistency of *these* reports, occurring over a period of eight hours, surprised the Guard, but they had no manpower to investigate. The division had been activated after Pearl Harbor and was now fighting in the Marshall Islands. Augusta tried to make contact with their armories in the areas supposedly affected. They were told that the lines were down. They could get no confirming information. It was late at night. Things would be clearer in the morning. So they did nothing.

The Coast Guard in Eastport was deluged by pleas, some by phone, but mainly by wireless from lobster boats and small pleasure craft, telling pretty much the same things as the National Guard had learned, though not as bloody and violent. They were also told of a slaughter at Adams Point and something about a Swedish freighter. The Coast Guard knew about the freighter, so there was nothing alarming about that. As for the rest, they waited for the confirmation that they knew the Army or Navy would have.

The Army First Command had no knowledge of the Gouldsboro disaster whatsoever. They had never initiated periodic fail-safe checks with the prisoner-of-war camp. Why *should* they? The installation was so isolated that, as far as they were concerned, nothing could happen there. There was a liaison officer between the Army Eastern Command and the Navy ConCinch, and dispatches from the Coast Guard and the Maine National Guard were piling up in his office forging an irrefutable monument of evidence. But he was in Washington for a briefing and nobody was manning his desk. What could happen overnight? An invasion?

The Navy had suspicions about a possible submarine landing at Winter Harbor in the person of Michael Francis O'Malley. But how could he confirm what was going on three hundred miles away? The task force from Portsmouth would not make Frenchman Bay until eight o'clock tonight, in about fourteen hours. Until that time, the Navy could only mark time.

The Air Force had the means of obtaining instant knowledge. It would be light in another hour, and if there was no ground fog planes could be sent aloft. The planes stood ready and waiting at Otis Air Force Base on Cape Cod, south of Boston, the onshore breeze moistening their wings in the dawn. Nobody called them.

The burden of the attack fell upon the local police departments and sheriffs. These positions in the small Maine communities were almost entirely filled by part-time and volunteer personnel. In town after town sleeping police chiefs were being awakened by frantic calls from local telephone exchange operators with incoherent messages about German soldiers. "Tell the Army in Augusta" was the usual reply as the men went back to bed again, only to wake up with alarm when the Nazi juggernaut either crashed through their towns without stopping or paused long enough to demolish some facility which would have aided an advancing American counterattack.

As Werner's men sped along their assigned routes like a plague of locusts, they left in their wake a communication and transportation desert. Telephone poles were blown down by grenades, telegraph wires cut. High-voltage electricity pylons were shelled, power substations systematically destroyed, as they rolled through town after town. Road signs were knocked down, culverts crushed, as were overpasses, underpasses, and route interconnections.

Schnee's column, starting at Rockland, traveled north on Route 116 along the east bank of the Penobscot River. At each specified bridge, the Panzers lobbed shells at the spans, severing only one segment if the bridge was long, or the entire structure if it was old and poorly suspended.

The first sign of organized resistance occurred at Bangor, the largest city astride the Penobscot. A steady avalanche of reports had been pouring into the police headquarters during the early hours of the morning telling of the Nazi drive to destroy the river bridges. John Herrick, the new chief, had no idea how a fully equipped German force had gotten onto American soil, let alone invade deep into Maine, without any American attempt to stop it.

Herrick was young, not yet twenty-eight, with a round, almost childish face topped with curly brown hair. He had no expectation of outside help. He had no heavy equipment or even military expertise to deal with the advancing juggernaut. His men were lightly armed. But, if nothing else, he was no coward, he was angry, and he knew his native city.

To reach the bridge in the middle of the city, the Germans would have to travel through the old mill section down in the Flats along the river's edge. This dense industrial area was crowded with high red-brick buildings dating from the 1800s and penetrated only by narrow, crooked streets.

The perspiring young chief explained his plan to those crowded around the precinct map of the city in his office. Within an hour, streams of Highway Department trucks loaded with sand and gravel had been driven to every intersection in the Flats, the motors made inoperative and tires slashed, until the entire square mile was solidly packed with blocked masses of stalled heavy equipment and thousands of tons of earth.

All game and rifle clubs were alerted. Along with every available member of the Police Department, Herrick stationed his deputized "soldiers" in the windows and on the rooftops of the ancient buildings lining the now-impassable streets which blocked every access route to the bridge. The men waited, smoking, laughing with nervous tension, but unafraid, as they heard in the distance the explosions of Schnee's Korps destroying facilities in the suburbs.

German scouts reported the American preparations to Schnee. Resistance up until then had been virtually nonexistent, and the tall, heavy-set tank commander resented the unexpected delaying maneuver. His instructions to his Oberleutnant were concise.

Schnee halted his column short of the trap along the river. With white streamers tied to the aerials of a motorcycle group, he rode along River Street, twisting around the obstacles, skirting the stalled trucks until he was met by several of Herrick's men. Approaching cautiously, they led the Germans to the bridge where the police chief was waiting.

The encounter between the two men was tense. Schnee demanded that the obstacles be removed and the snipers withdrawn. Herrick refused.

"We can clear the streets with much unnecessary destruction," Schnee threatened, knowing that such an action while ultimately successful would waste valuable time with American marksmen picking off his soldiers.

"Go ahead," Herrick retorted, glancing at his men for support.

Schnee tried once again, "This is not your war. Keep your men back and no one will be hurt."

Herrick's limbs were trembling and he wiped his forehead of sweat, but he would not give in.

"I realize that you are in a position to delay my men," Schnee tried to reason. "On any other occasion I would deal with your threat in a conventional manner. But I have neither the time nor patience now," he warned. "My men have captured one hundred of your citizens, including women and children. If within one hour, your men have not cleared a route to the bridge and allowed us free passage, I will kill ten people for each minute's delay after that time." He glanced at his watch and then waited with an implacable expression on his face for the police chief's answer.

The American looked at the German with loathing. Herrick could not believe that this soldier, a man like himself despite their opposing positions, would actually carry out such an incredible, inhuman threat. Scared, uncertain, Herrick nevertheless stood his ground.

Schnee motioned to one of his men. The soldier went

over to the sidecar of the lead motorcycle and returned carrying a small, limp form. He dumped the dead child onto the pavement between the two antagonists.

Herrick could see the young boy's face, now unrecognizable from clotted blood and flesh, a jagged raw crater in the left temple where the bullet had torn through the skull. The child was no more than eight or nine years old.

Schnee smiled at the obscenities hurled at him. His men moved closer to protect him. Their hands tightened on their holsters as the Americans facing them tensed. Herrick's face whitened and he choked back the waves of nausea. Finally he gave a weak nod of assent, and turned his back, his head lowered in shame.

Schnee smiled at the easy victory. He gave one last look at the crumpled form at his feet and then at the backs of the retreating Americans. He could not help commenting to himself on how accurate the Führer was in demeaning the American enemy as a spineless and unworthy opponent.

But if Schnee's victory over Herrick was easy, the bridge itself posed more of a problem. The steel and stone structure was too solid and withstood twenty minutes of cannon barrage. Schnee had his sappers mine the middle pier. It blew, but when the smoke had cleared, the span was still intact, though weakened. He had no more time to waste.

Transferring the cannon shells and fuel out of five tanks, he had them driven onto the shattered segment of the bridge. One by one, the tanks started in a straight line down the center of the bridge. When almost at the breech, the driver jumped out and returned to the column. One tank. Then two. Three. The fourth tank was just about to plow into the rear of the other tanks when the added weight caused a metallic screech to split the air. With a rumble of crunching concrete, the pier, exhausted, gave way. The tanks fell, one after the other, through the now-broken roadbed into the swirling rapids below.

Schnee watched with satisfaction. It had cost four tanks, but that did not matter. His job was not to hold together an army for weeks or even days, but to sever any links across that now-critical torrent of water. The only commodity he must husband was time. With a look at his wristwatch, he motioned to the column behind him. The four tank drivers quickly hitched a ride on one of the armored personnel carriers bringing up the rear, as the Panzer Korps sped on to Milford.

The pattern was the same for Braunscher, who went east, and for Hessler, who went west on Route 1 along the coast, both starting in the middle at Adams Point. As the troops crested the intermittent rises of land, they could see the blue indentations of water setting off the green forests which crowded down to the water's edge. Offshore, the many small islands appeared as the morning sun burned off their camouflage of fog. Every facility which could serve for transportation or communication was destroyed. When the Germans reached the end of the salient, they would stop, sit down, and wait for eventual recapture. What they had achieved was a trail of debris and desolation that lay behind them and would for a time preclude the possibility of revenge.

The exploding salient was like a giant vacuum cleaner. It sucked up the thousands of telephone calls which poured into it, operators valiantly trying to reestablish contact with exchanges in towns and villages which only a few minutes before had called out telling of horrors which no one really believed. In vain were the attempts to find out what had happened. As Werner's men moved, the triangle expanded, slicing off mile after mile of American countryside and converting it into Nazi-occupied territory as surely as if it had been the plains of Pomerania. As the reluctant voyagers from Bornholm struggled with Rohmer's drivers, making them shift the trucks back and forth to line up the firing tangents, Werner's wolves with claws of steel were insuring them Lebensraum.

➤ TWENTY-TWO

For Agreen Crabtree, this was just another morning. Since his wife had died of a stroke several months before, he had tried to spend as much time as he could with his thirteen-year-old son. They had camped the night at the cabin on Tunk Lake. Agreen was oblivious to the recent Nazi incursion as he drove into the North Sullivan depot over the little-used St. Regis Paper Company logging road.

Crabtree busied himself starting up the fire to make a pot of coffee for the two of them. He had noticed nothing unusual this morning except for the strange silence of the teletype machine from the Ellsworth station. He told his son, "I suppose the pole is down again next to Thorsen's Crossing. I told the super that as soon as you get one good blowdown, the rest of the trees are sure to go."

He knew that a car would soon arrive from Ellsworth to deliver the absent messages that could not come through the downed wires. As he stood waiting for the pot to boil, he could feel a faint vibration under his feet. A loose pane of glass rattled in the warped frame of the back door of the depot. He looked up, trying to gauge the direction of the activity. He could not imagine what it could be. No scheduled trains were due to come by till 4:10 that afternoon.

"I guess that must be the one George is makin' such a fuss over."

The bubbling of the pot distracted his attention for another minute or two. By that time, he became aware that the dull, rumbling noise was approaching from the *south*—and then, not even from the direction of the tracks. The noise changed to a clanking and grinding.

"What the heck," he expostulated, looking down at his son. "Let's go see what's coming."

They both went out into the dusty parking yard in front of the small wooden structure. They were dumbfounded when two tanks ground into view, accompanied by Werner in a jeep. Three armored personnel carriers full of heavily armed Germans took up the rear. Without a word, the soldiers jumped off the carriers. They swiftly surrounded the station, quarantining off the area with machine gun implacements concealed in strategic locations. One tank camouflaged itself well in the edge of the woods. The second remained facing the station door.

"The train. From Canada. The unscheduled one. Has it come through?"

Crabtree did not know whether he was more surprised at the unheralded arrival of a Nazi Panzer force or the fact that the thin scholarly German appearing out of nowhere, and waving a gun at him, obviously knew more about the train and its route and timing than he did.

"No, it has not come by," he replied, his manner calm and unafraid.

"Then we will wait for it together, old man. Do as we tell you and there will be no trouble."

He motioned for two soldiers to separate the father and son. Agreen waved Homer away with a forced gesture of nonchalance as if to deemphasize the bizarreness of the situation.

"Don't be afraid, Homer. Just do as the man says and everything will be all right."

He turned to Werner, "What do you want?"

"Set the semaphore to stop the train at the station!"

"What if I don't?"

"Very simple. First your son will die and then you."

Crabtree said nothing. He looked at his son who was trying to act brave. Then at the ring of soldiers who returned his gaze without a flicker of expression.

"Let me go to the control panel."

Agreen entered the depot followed by Werner and

the soldiers. The long metal lever screeched as the station-master pulled it down to the floor.

"Now," Werner ordered, "switch the track onto the spur to Adams Point."

Crabtree looked up in surprise. Side-railing a mysterious train to Adams Point was as puzzling to him as the presence of Germans with tanks in North Sullivan. He did as he was told, pivoting the rusty "X" junction to bring the southbound ore train onto the abandoned rail tracks which terminated at the ferry pier.

"We cannot risk any tricks on your part." Werner's tone was curt. "I do not know a great deal about this operation," indicating with a sweep of his revolver the complicated panels and rows of stick levers, "but we do not intend to take any chances."

He motioned for the soldiers to bring Agreen outside. Crabtree saw the fright on his son's face and tried to comfort him.

"Do not be impatient," Werner assured the father. "You will soon see what we are going to do."

As they moved into the yard, the second tank was already repositioning itself several hundred feet below the junction where the Adams Point spur took off from the main line. The tank rolled up onto the shiny tracks. It spun on its treads, turning to face north, as if daring the expected train to pass by.

Agreen watched with relief. The Maine Central will knock that tin can right off the tracks. Werner must have read his mind, or seen the transient change of expression.

"Oh, no, old man," the German warned. "I hope you have not thought to double-cross us. The tank is not going to stop the train. Your son is."

At a sign from Werner, the two soldiers seized the young boy and lifted him onto the front of the tank. They tied his ankles to the front treads and secured his arms to the projecting cannon. He was not injured and could move about slightly, but he could not free himself from the front of the tank. Homer looked at the long double row of glistening steel tracks which led to the nose of the tank below his legs.

Crabtree cringed back from the scene with horror.
First his wife, now his son. The boy reflected the terrified
expression. His father forced a wan smile.

"Don't worry, Homer, you'll be all right. Don't move.
Everything will be fine."

Werner searched Agreen's eyes. "Do you wish to
change anything in the station, old man?"

"No," was all that Crabtree said, and for the next
hour and a half he waited alongside the tracks, looking
north and then at his son, but always listening intently
for the faint, familiar sounds of the Maine Central.

⟶ TWENTY-THREE

The open lines to O'Malley's office were now spewing
forth a torrent of information which spoke of only one
thing: the German advance on American soil and the
staggering impotence of the authorities to halt it. Looking at the map on the wall, Michael felt helpless. The red
flags were in place, marking last recorded locations of
contact. Every minute the flags moved out farther and
farther, confirming his worst fears. Rohmer and Werner

were succeeding beyond their most sanguine dream of carving out territory which would later be resold to the Americans for the price of time.

Time! Time! That was the crucial factor. How much time did he have left? When did the twenty-four hours begin? Michael interpolated backward. The movement of the tank columns, the prison camp breakout, the radar station landing. He made a guess of midnight, right after the fail-safe check at Schoodic. If his calculation was accurate, it meant that he had barely fifteen hours left before the missiles would be launched.

It was now nine-thirty Thursday morning. The Portsmouth fleet would reach Frenchman Bay eight o'clock in the evening, just as the late May sun was setting. If they managed to get there before the rockets were armed, perhaps they could abort the deadly attack on the armada in Boston Harbor. It was a hope, a feeble straw, but Michael was clutching at anything.

In response to his plea, Washington had alerted the Fifty-first Armored Division of the impending disaster, but so far Michael had heard nothing of Wentworth's movement north. Where was he? Michael looked at his watch again. And . . . why was Bainbridge so quiet?

The Fifty-first Armored Division was not sitting on its ass. That was the last position which its commander, Major General Malcolm S. Wentworth, would have considered salutary. His recurrent swollen hemorrhoids were only part of the problem.

Wentworth had spent the previous day in the requisitioned CCC camp in Marblehead, where his four infantry battalions were bivouacked, cursing the tedious paperwork to split his force into separate units for transport to England. Right now, he had three medium-tank battalions afloat in Boston Harbor, two on the U.S.S. *Mohegan* and the third on the U.S.S. *Patrick Henry*. His engineering battalion was on the U.S.S. *Louisville,* and God only knew where the reconnaissance and artillery battalions were. He was lucky that Stryker knew. In addition to being a damn good G-2 Intelligence officer for the division, John Stryker had served as Wentworth's aide since 1938.

"A German invasion in Maine?" The look of incredulity on Wentworth's face matched the tone of his voice. The overweight, graying general took the urgent message from his aide's hand and read it himself. "What kind of bullshit is this?"

"That's what I felt about it," Stryker answered, "but it's true. The teletype came from Washington less than five minutes ago. Some German subs—they're not sure how many—landed up the Maine coast, near Bar Harbor and all those fancy summer resorts. They knocked out the radar station. That's how the Navy first knew that something was going on up there. It seems that Naval Intelligence, the Anti-Submarine Division, has its headquarters right here in Boston, over near Harvard. Some mick named O'Malley runs it. He's supposed to be pretty good. Well, they check in with the radar station every four hours and they got suspicious. They have been suspecting a landing or sabotage or something, but they didn't know where it would take place or when."

Wentworth interrupted, "So *what* if some U-boats landed? God knows why they or anybody else would want to land in *Maine*, for Christ's sake. Why the hell are they bothering Washington about this? It's the Navy's fucking business."

"Well, sir, apparently the Army has a large POW camp in a place called Gouldsboro right nearby. Five thousand prisoners. It is a repair and maintenance depot for tanks, trucks, jeeps, and all that stuff, and . . ."

"You are not going to tell me . . ."

"Yes, sir. The prisoners broke out with the vehicles. They must have rendezvoused with the U-boats to obtain ammunition and supplies. Right now, they control over five thousand square miles of territory."

"How? How could they?" Wentworth exclaimed, jowls shaking.

"To protect their southern flank, they are destroying the approaches and bridges over the Penobscot River.

The sea guards their east flank. And the third side is nothing but wild forest without even a decent road. That's why the Army put the prison camp there in the first place. It's incredibly isolated. I don't know how they did it, but the Germans have got themselves a real sweet time up there."

Over the next hour, Wentworth learned the enormity of the tragedy which had taken place down east. Stryker unfolded the map and showed the lines of enemy spread. He told of the rockets and the predicted attack aimed at disrupting the huge concentration of men and munitions in the harbor area. Most important, Wentworth learned that Naval Intelligence was hypothesizing a critical twenty-four-hour period to prepare the missiles for launching.

"When did you say they landed?" Stryker could sense Wentworth's anxiety.

"The best that we can guess is about midnight."

"And now they expect us to go up there and stop them?" Wentworth cursed and slammed his fist into his palm. "Goddam fools!" His round fleshy face was flushed and angry. With deliberate sarcasm, he scorned, "Doesn't Washington realize what is going on here? Do they think that we are just sitting around waiting for marching orders? The Fifty-first is scattered all over this fucking state. We're broken into so goddam many little pieces and filed away on so goddam many ships and warehouses that you'd need a whole quartermaster corps to put us together. Goddam it, John, it's not fair."

Colonel Stryker did not try to answer. Wentworth was too good a soldier to complain for long. If anyone could do what Washington wanted done, he could. There was no doubt that the general could extract from the convoy the supply and support units of his division and put them back together again. The question was, how long would it take?

"John, what have we got?" Wentworth asked, suddenly grim and contemplative. He did not wait for the answer. "Fifty-four 105-mm howitzers, eighteen 155-mm howitzers. That will more than take care of the 90-mms on the Pattons which I assume the Krauts have stolen from the depot. We have three hundred seventy-three tanks, which probably is more than the Germans have. Call Washington anyway. Find out everything that was stored in the depot and what was ready to roll. I want to know exactly what we are up against. Have Intelligence give us an estimate of the maximum firepower a U-boat can carry in munitions—on deck and in storage. That will tell us how long they can hold out."

The General thought for a minute, his brow furrowed. "Get Morin," he ordered. "He heads the bridge company in the 114th's armored engineering battalion. Samuel P. Morin. I'm sure the Krauts have dug in along the banks of whatever the damn river is called. Probably have the high ground to prevent us from repairing the spans. I don't care. We don't have the time to build bridges. We'll ford in between. Morin can throw pontoons across the River Styx. He's the best. Beg, borrow, or steal him, but have him at Marblehead by ..."—he looked at his watch —"... by 1100 hours."

Wentworth talked rapidly but his instructions came out sharp and clear. Stryker mentally filled the conduits to expedite the commands.

"The Air Force," Wentworth continued, "call Reilly over at Otis. Tell him to scramble. Shit! I don't know why the hell nobody contacted him before. Goddam Army! I want full aerial reconnaissance of the whole area. Tell him I want to see every fucking Kraut just as sharp and clear as Betty Grable's tits on those pinups. And I want those surveys made hourly, sunrise to sundown.

"So far as we know, the Germans have no planes. And they don't know which direction we are coming from. They can't move by day or we can bomb them to hell. They can only move by night and they can't do that until they know where to go. So," he added with a growing feeling of confidence, "unless you now are going to come up with a rubber raft that the Germans can change into a flying carpet, I think we've got them.

"Remember—Morin, the bridge; Reilly, the photographs. Get those self-propelled field pieces ready. The depot inventory. The anticipated firepower. I want to move out in two hours with whatever we've got ready. The rest can hustle and catch up with us the best they can. Time! We must move!"

"Yes, sir!" Stryker exclaimed, caught up in his superior's enthusiasm.

"John," Wentworth's tone suddenly became less assertive. "Have you ever used our own medic? The way things are going, I'll not have time to get over to Devens. If Greenberg can treat anything else besides the clap, you'd better tell him to get over here and fix my goddam aching asshole!"

→ TWENTY-FOUR

Hugh O'Connell found it hard to concentrate this hot, muggy Thursday morning with the intermittent drone rumbling the air and shaking the windowpanes. Curious at the disturbance, he got up from his desk and went over to peer at the empty sky outside.

"Jennie," he asked, his head cocked up, still listening

to the crescendo now fading in the distance, "is it my imagination, or are there more planes flying overhead this morning?"

"Yes, Mr. Mayor," she replied. "I noticed it myself on the way in from Malden. They are coming from Otis and seem to be flying north. Every ten minutes or so, another one goes back and forth. I wonder what's up." She gathered from his desk the papers he had just finished signing and quietly closed the door behind her.

O'Connell ran his finger down the list of remaining interviews to wade through before the day was over. He was about to press the buzzer for his next appointment when the door opened and Jennie reentered. The mayor was puzzled by her disturbed manner.

"I didn't want to tell you over the intercom, Mr. Mayor," she hunched her shoulder toward the full antechamber. "Too many ears out there. You have an urgent call, and I thought you'd want to take it first before seeing Judge O'Meara."

"Who is it from?"

"A man called Lawrence Bainbridge. He's here in Boston. He said you would know the name."

O'Connell said nothing for a minute. He knew the name all right. Bainbridge. Damn him! Bainbridge and Conant and Vannevar Bush, all members of Roosevelt's National Defense Council. His expression grew bitter. When Roosevelt wanted votes, he sent Jim Farley sucking up to him in Boston. O'Connell had delivered his state on the line for the Democrats. So did the political bosses of the other large cities throughout the country, delivering the ethnic vote. But when it came time to staff the Cabinet, to choose men for the National Defense Council, where were the Irish, the Catholics?

"Don't tell me," he retorted to Roosevelt after the last election. "Don't tell me that the Catholics don't have any brains. You mean that there are no micks in the country who could be secretary of state or secretary of the interior? You picked a *Jew* for treasurer. What do *we* get? Only the Post Office!"

Roosevelt tried to calm him down. "Hugh, this is a

big country. The rest of the United States isn't like Boston. The party must think of the Midwest, the South, Iowa and Alabama. They still think that the Vatican is ready to land troops in Washington. Be patient, Hugh. It takes time. You will get there in the end."

O'Connell accepted the rebuke with reservation. He was basically an impatient man except in the affairs of politics. Had he been aware of the blood-borne colonies of cancer cells gnawing at the nerves of his back, he might not have been so understanding.

"Put him through, Jennie," the mayor told her, "and ask Judge O'Meara if he would mind waiting a few minutes longer."

The call was not a long one. When O'Connell finally lowered the telephone, it was not to see his patient visitor in the outer office. Instead he drummed his fingers on the desk in a savage tattoo. His face was twisted in anger. He stabbed the intercom button.

"Get me Roosevelt," he ordered.

Turning off the intercom, he spoke to an unseen audience in the room, as if making a solemn oath.

"No goddamn Protestant, I don't care how big a fuck Bainbridge is, is going to tell me that my city is going to be destroyed and that nothing can be done about it. I don't know anything about rockets or whatever that goddamn funny bomb is the Germans have up in Maine, but they are *not* going to kill my people. Not if I can do anything about it."

He winced from a spasm of pain in his back.

"Roosevelt will help," he said more with forlorn hope than certainty. "He's got the whole goddamn Army and Navy just sitting on their ass right outside my window. He's not going to tell me that they can't do anything. Hell! If they don't stop this attack, the party can kiss those fourteen electoral votes good-bye for the next hundred years."

His voice turned mean and bitter. "They may not think we Irish have any brains, but goddamn it, we have long memories. One bomb, or whatever it is, on this city and . . . the English know! It is one of our greatest

strengths. We Irish can *hate* for an awfully long time!"
He heard his father's words again, "If I should forsake
thee, O Jerusalem..." O'Connell paced back and forth
in front of his desk, torn between the lacerating pain
burning through his ribs and his fear of the unknown.

"What if they really can't stop this attack? But...
they must!"

He shook his head, not daring to allow the thought
to run to completion. Roosevelt would help. Yes, he said
to himself, his breathing slower and more even. They all
will help. They must.

He gave a sigh of relief and allowed a weak smile of
confidence. Pressing down the button, he ordered in a
voice too tired for this early in the day, "Jennie, keep
trying Washington. Meanwhile, please ask the judge to
come in."

⟶ **TWENTY-FIVE**

At any other time, the knowledge that from 1742 through
1781 Adams Point was a burgeoning industrial community would have little affected the life of Kapitän Wilhelm
Rohmer. Millions of years in its past, or even billions of

years, through a freak of nature, intermixed with the
cooling volcanic magna which composed the bedrock of
the area was an unusual black mineral. Its existence was
well known to the early settlers who fired the crystalline
ore in crude kilns to make hand-forged nails, pans, and
bullets. To the scientists from Peenemünde, the mag-
netite was the one contingency for which the Reich had
not planned.

Rohmer had watched with impatience as the hours
fled by. It was now noon. The German sailors had been
on American soil twelve hours. Still only half of the missiles were ready. The U-boat captain's body strained one
way and then the other in sympathy with the tractors as
they struggled to line up the huge rockets. The scientists
sweated along with the drivers. First, they corrected for
deviation caused by the annual migration of the magnetic
north pole. Next, they allowed for individual variation
caused by the presence of iron and steel in the tractors
and trailers themselves, as well as in the adjacent rockets. Still the gyroscopic and magnetic compass settings
evaded their control. Each time one rocket was shifted
in position, it threw off the settings of every other rocket
in the forest. Shaking their heads, the engineers went
back and forth with their instruments, from warhead to
warhead, like worker bees tending to the swollen bodies
of the queens. They were puzzled. They could not obtain
the necessary corrections. After six wasted hours and
much nonproductive cursing, they discovered that the soil
under their feet was, as Rohmer had been telling them
all along, a "cursed ground."

This delay threw Rohmer off his tight schedule. The
scientists' explanation did nothing to mitigate his mounting anxiety. He walked through the thick, dark forest,
reflexively reaching out to touch the sides of the camouflaged rockets poised on the pads, tips slanted toward the
sky. He was aware of the swooping flights of the Bell
P-39Q Airacobra reconnaissance planes, crisscrossing
Adams Point, trying to ferret out the dark threats. So
far, no bombs dropped from their bellies. When he was
ready, he would no longer require the protective sylvan

covering. The malignant threat of the rockets would then be their own impregnable shield. "That is why we may win yet," he said to Kern. "If I were the Americans, I would not take pictures. I would bomb the whole peninsula—just in case, like the British do in France." He sighed at the wonderful naïveté of his enemy which stayed their hand, and prayed for this paralysis to continue for another few hours.

For a moment, he thought that he had been too sanguine as he heard a loud rumbling. The noise grew louder. The ground began to vibrate. Apprehensive, he looked up and scanned the sky in all directions. The loud, piercing whistle of the sixteen-wheel locomotive shattered the air, over and over again, as it eased itself close to the water, almost touching the jetty at the end of Adams Point. In a hiss of steam, the huge quaking engine finally stopped, dwarfed by the larger white hull of the Swedish freighter.

Rohmer was at the dock within minutes. He inspected the hundred-twenty-five-ton monster trailing its incongruous tail of one sealed freight car. He could see the engineer and the fireman crowded into the cab with Werner and another German soldier. On the engine roof sat four soldiers, legs crossed for balance, with machine guns drawn and menacing. Another pair rode on the front of the engine. The rest of Werner's force followed behind, the forward jeep containing an old man and a small boy.

"All right, Herr Kapitän, here is your train, safe and sound," Werner boasted with a touch of pride. He motioned for the soldiers to take the Crabtrees away. The old man walked with his head held high, looking straight ahead. His son walked beside him, hands tightly clenched. He seemed afraid to leave his father's side, yet would not take his hand. Each walked close together yet separated by some invisible barrier.

"Those two?" Rohmer indicated the father and son.

"It is interesting about them," Werner replied, with a quizzical expression. "The father is the stationmaster. I told him that his son would die if the train was not stopped. You know what he did? He never stopped the train!"

Rohmer looked at the departing figure of Crabtree with disbelief. Werner continued, apparently amused at the story he was telling. "But this one," pointing to the engineer still sitting in the cab, "this one slowed down the train to wave to the old man. He noticed the tank with the boy on it across the tracks and stopped. After we killed the guards, he was very cooperative and switched the train to the spur himself. You know," waving his hand at the disappearing pair, "the old man never said a single word all the hours we waited for the train. And he never said a word after."

Rohmer thought for a minute. He was a father, too. This man probably knew less about the importance of the cargo on the train than he did. Yet he had been willing to sacrifice his son. In his own way, he must have realized that if obtaining the train was important enough to kill his son for, then it probably was important enough for him to die to save. Rohmer shook his head to clear away the disturbing omen and moved to the job at hand.

Acetylene torches were already melting an opening into the car so that the two Norwegian scientists could inspect the contents. Along one side of the wharf, the rows of bright yellow canisters waited, each four feet high and two feet in diameter, ten for each U-boat. After they were filled, all seventy would be spaced evenly in the bulkheads running the length of the seven vessels to facilitate trim.

When that is done, Rohmer thought with anticipation, we press the contact switches and leave. He checked the time. It was now two in the afternoon. "Another ten hours," he instructed Kern, "and it will be midnight. If those two from Peenemünde have finished with the rockets, we leave then. Be ready!"

Excited, he strode off in the direction of the launching site to see what could be done to expedite the work.

→ TWENTY-SIX

Michael looked at the pile of glossy photographs spread out on his desk. He would pick one up and peer closely, only to discard it a moment later with an expression of disgust. Liz waited for the inspection to be over. Her usual vivacity was dampened by the tragic events which were rushing to a crisis beyond Michael's control.

"Are there any more?"

"No, Michael. This is all the courier brought from Otis. The last plane returned at about noon." She registered the worried expression on his face and elected to leave him alone.

Michael glanced at the large clock on the wall. Two-thirty. The afternoon had barely started and it was already half over. He turned again to the reconnaissance pictures. He did not have to be an expert to see evidence of Teutonic thoroughness. Snaking its way through the pile of photographs was the Penobscot River, torn apart with shattered bridges. He could see craters where railway intersections had once existed, torn-up roadbeds and downed telephone poles at highway intersections, toppled electric pylons with their ceramic transformer caps sticking obscenely into the air.

The U-boats were there, next to the *Astra*. The Swedish freighter was officially off-bounds, neutral territory, until they could establish a hostile act. The U-boats were trapped. Any moment now the task force from Portsmouth should be in sonar and radar contact with the only exit from Frenchman Bay. But no sign of the rockets. Where were they?

Michael wished he could pry back the dense foliage on the pictures. Using the trucks from the Gouldsboro depot, Rohmer could have concealed the warheads over the entire county. If he only knew their locations and how they were to be launched, the Air Force could neutralize the missiles by bombing, even before Wentworth arrived. According to the last communiqué, the Fifty-first Armored was making incredible time. Racing across the eastern tip of New Hampshire into Maine, the division was now knifing towards Werner's Penobscot River moat.

Michael felt helpless as if he had dreamed this whole horrible nightmare before and could do nothing to avoid the inevitable finale. However, he did not fathom the full threat of the unfolding tragedy until his two unexpected visitors had come and gone.

Douglas Gatling, the tanned professor from New Mexico, introduced himself. Taken back by his handsome appearance, Liz lingered a minute more than she usually did after bringing someone into O'Malley's office. The young man was very polite and deferential as he shook Michael's hand. There was an awkward pause during which Michael collected the photographs strewn over the desk and stacked them in a neat pile in the corner.

"I am here at Lawrence Bainbridge's request."

Michael's antennae rose. Beneath this visitor's playboy insouciance was purpose. Michael had a premonition that the visit would not be to his liking.

It was less than an hour since Gatling had received an unexpected call of desperate urgency from New Mexico. Shortly after Michael had phoned Bainbridge to report Rohmer's landing, Bainbridge alerted Los Alamos that its precious cargo was riding right into the hands of the Germans. The telegraph wires were down and there was no way of either stopping the train or warning it of the danger.

Gatling could still hear Leslie Grove's words thundering in his earpiece, "Get to O'Malley! You must impress upon him the absolute necessity for insuring that the ore does not leave these shores ... *under any circumstances!* Do you understand?"

"Remember," General Groves continued, his voice high-pitched and nasal, "no price is too high to pay. It is the most valuable mineral in the world today. Not only the Germans but even the Russians are scavenging the world for a cache. *We must have that uranium!*"

It was a welcome relief when Gatling heard Spencer Kissielowsky take the phone. "Douglas"—his voice was solemn and tense—"I realize that we are placing you in a very difficult position. Frankly, I do not know how to tell you to handle the problem. It *may* be necessary to tell Naval Intelligence in general terms what we are doing here. But the heart of the problem is something more elusive than that."

There was a long pause on the phone as Kissielowsky tried to get his thoughts in order.

"How can you buy back something whose value we do not yet know, but for which we are willing to pay any price? How do you persuade others of your belief—and it still is only that, a belief—of all of us in this desert? A two-year-old faith which we do not even know is valid?" His tone was patient and understanding as he concluded, "Douglas, we will respect whatever you are able to achieve."

Gatling looked at his tall, freckled host, uncertain how to begin. He was aware of O'Malley's official reputation, but it was not a simple question of intelligence. How do you explain to a layman, in an hour, the juxtaposition of atoms, the potentials of nuclear power, the blackboard formulas, the years of work in the desert, the fears if the theories work and the fears if they don't? Bravely he grappled with his mission.

The scientist revealed the Manhattan Project, beginning with elementary principles, building gradually, yet avoiding information which was too highly classified. After forty-five minutes, he stopped. Michael had not said a word. He had heard rumors of the vast secret enterprise. If he had been forced to imagine what it concealed, he would have guessed a "secret weapon." He would have been right, to a degree. What was missing and could not be comprehended was the magnitude of the weapon. It was this shocking dimension which Gatling tried to get across, to convince O'Malley of the primacy of the project over all other considerations.

Michael was puzzled and impatient. He did not understand why Gatling had come to see him. True, the scientist's story was an interesting one, but why bother him with it? He already was struggling with one disaster.

"What does this research in New Mexico have to do with us here? We have our own problems—right now some pretty damn serious ones, Professor Gatling."

Gatling was taken back by the tenor of the question. He searched O'Malley's face for some glimmer of understanding. "The train, Mr. O'Malley, the train."

The introduction of the vital ore into the already complex picture was a staggering blow to Michael. Douglas emphasized the strategic importance of the shipment to the desert project and how, if it fell into enemy hands, it must be recaptured. Under no circumstances could the uranium leave the country.

O'Malley was barely listening. Gatling's mission did not have to be spelled out for him like a schoolboy. Michael was angry. Bainbridge knew all along about the shipment and of the risk of its being captured by Germans landing in the vicinity, yet had not bothered to warn him. Had he expected Michael to ferret out this information on his own? And *why?* He was a bastard! But there would be time for recriminations later. Michael now had two problems, the rocket attack and the possible loss of the uranium.

Did Gatling know about the missiles? He certainly gave no indication that he did. Either the scientist knew about them and didn't care, or else he thought the Germans had landed specifically to secure the ore. If he was indeed unaware of the threat to Boston, that meant Bainbridge had not informed New Mexico of the rockets when he alerted the physicists there to the danger to the train. Michael looked up at the young professor who waited for him to speak. The emissary seemed cognizant only of the uranium. Well, damn him and damn Bainbridge! Michael was not going to say anything. Let Bainbridge tell Gatling himself. O'Malley reassured Gatling only that he would keep him informed of further developments as he escorted him out.

Michael kept staring at the closed door. He had the sensation of something sinister and dangerous which he could not identify. It involved Bainbridge. He shook his head, disgusted at his inability to decipher the signal. He was still shaking his head when Liz announced the arrival of his second visitor.

Mayor O'Connell's demeanor was stern. His back pain was upon him, debilitating and eroding much of his composure. Worry consumed the rest. He acknowledged Michael with a half-nod, and spoke angrily.

"Why didn't you people tell me all along that the attack on my city was going to be by long-range rockets? Has all this nonsense about sabotage just been a smoke-screen to make an ass out of me? To lull the city? I'm nobody's fool, O'Malley"—he pounded the table, his face beet-red and sweating—"and I don't like being played for a sucker. Not by you or any of your goddamn big-shot Washington friends!"

Michael looked up at him with a start. Bainbridge again! O'Malley tried to say something, but O'Connell would not stop and ranted on. "How long have you known about this? What are you going to do about it?"

"Mr. Mayor," Michael tried to interject a note of calm and sympathy, "we learned about the missiles less than twelve hours ago. Believe me, if we had known about them earlier, we wouldn't be in this situation now." His tone reflected a heartfelt candor.

O'Connell looked his host over. What he said rang true. And O'Malley, red-haired and Irish as they come—how could such a man betray Boston? O'Connell realized that his outburst had been unwarranted. He had noticed since the pain in his back had worsened that his reactions were often inappropriate.

"All right, Mr. O'Malley," he apologized. "Perhaps I came off half-cocked, but as mayor I ought to have been notified immediately of this new threat to the city. Can you stop it?"

O'Malley laid all the facts in front of him. He felt sorry for the man, but what he was forced to reveal did not at all allay the mayor's anxiety.

"You mean to be telling me that these rockets will probably fire off by midnight? You are saying that the Army can't get there in time, the Air Force doesn't know where they are hidden, and a half-ass fleet is still piddling up the coast? Is that what you have to report to me? Christ, O'Malley, this is the United States of America, not Poland or France, Goddamn it! What do you want me to tell my people?" He looked up, pleading.

Michael could not answer. What was there to say? He hoped that some miracle would erase their mutual fear but could assure O'Connell only that the Germans from Gouldsboro would eventually be recaptured. Of that he had no more doubt than did von Eyssen, Rohmer, or Werner.

"But that is not the point, O'Malley. When? When? That is what matters!" the mayor begged.

Michael could do no more than echo the mayor's mounting panic. O'Connell realized he could get nothing further and got up to leave. He shook Michael's hand with sad resignation. "I don't think this should go to the press. Not just yet. Let me think about it. How to tell my people." His voice grew softer and his eyes clouded over with pain. He caught his breath. He was forced to bend over for relief. "Thanks ... thank you," he said, without spirit, hardly the same man who had entered. He limped out and closed the door behind him.

Michael watched him leave. He realized at that point how detached he had become from the human race. Here, in his sealed office, he dealt with probabilities, not lives. Facts, not emotions. The rockets would land. People would be killed and maimed. He bore no direct responsibility for any of them. They did not figure in his hermetic world. He was answerable to Bainbridge. O'Connell's burden was heavier. Michael's respect for the stooped man increased. This man who was registering in his own heart the cries and tears of a soon-to-be-wounded city.

O'Malley's eyes went back to the desk. It was empty

except for the stack of photographs on one corner. The map with the advancing Nazi positions faced him across the room. The hands of the clock continued their silent pirouette. He could hear the muffled hum of activity in the plotting room below. Liz did not come in. It was quiet, an oasis.

His mind began to wander without direction. He stood aside and let it drift without constraint. He thought of his last two visitors. One the correct scientist, the other the blatant politician. One cloaked in the mantle of the mystery of the universe, the other sitting on electoral votes for his grandson. One caught up in a dream for the betterment of mankind, the other worried over wakes on the waterfront. Michael wondered whether it was possible to weigh people, their instincts, the rightness or wrongness of their actions? Could human motivation be reduced to a quantified scale? If so, which of his two visitors was more deserving of pity, or more worthy of help?

And Bainbridge? He had notified Gatling about the uranium peril, and O'Connell about the rocket peril, but had told neither man about the reciprocal danger to the other. Instead he had sent them both to see O'Malley. Why? Was he supposed to acquaint one with the corollary threat to the other? If so, each man could be trapped into a dilemma of the other's making, like an errant spider caught in the web of his arachnid neighbor.

Michael's mind froze at the next thought. It would not let go. Gatling and O'Connell . . . and Bainbridge. A bizarre image took shape in his mind. A picture of a Solomon sitting on a throne. A strange, hunched-over Hebraic king crouched in a velvet chair, holding a naked child upside down by its feet. A long sword in the other hand. *What if . . . ?*

→ TWENTY-SEVEN

If John Stryker ever had reason to admire his commanding officer's tenacity, it was during those torture-wracked hours Wentworth rode in his lead jeep, bounced and jostled without mercy as the Fifty-first surged north. Never once did the major general allude to his pain. Wentworth had taken a gamble and was now consumed in making certain that his strategic decision did not result in a disaster, not only for himself and his men, but for the convoy in Boston Harbor whose fate hung so precariously in the balance.

"John," Wentworth said after he had folded and refolded the terrain maps piled on his lap and studied for the dozenth time the statistics on the probable German firepower which Washington had provided, "what do you think? Do you agree with me?"

Stryker turned to listen, attentive but knowing from experience that his opinion was superfluous.

"From what we can see from Reilly's reconnaissance, every decent bridge is blown. Intelligence has analyzed the photos and there are strong concentrations of German troops dug in at Bucksport, Bangor, Milford, Howland, and Lincoln. The main road on the east bank between those key points is in shambles. They've done a superb job, those Kraut bastards." His voice took on a tinge of envy. "I'm looking forward to meeting that fucking bastard, Werner, who planned it all." He shook his head with regret. "I only wish we had more sons-of-bitches like him on *our* side instead of all the assholes sitting in the Pentagon. . . . All right," he continued, talking out his thoughts. "So what do we have?" He paused, not really expecting an answer. "We cannot cross at those key spots," he said with a resigned shrug. "If we did, we would be playing right into their hands. We could cross, break their positions, and rebuild the spans. The Krauts know that, and we know that. But that is not what they are after, to prevent us from crossing."

He glanced at Stryker, who stared back, puzzled.

"No, John, hear me out. As I see it, the only thing Werner is after is *time*. That's the hooker here. If the Germans can delay us until they set off their rockets, then they couldn't give a good goddam in hell how and when we get across. So . . ." he ran his index finger along the Penobscot River on the map, "so, this is what we are going to do." His face lit up in a broad smile as he beamed at his now-bewildered companion. "John," he waved his finger at him, "we are going for broke. Twelve hours . . . no more."

This calculated decision meant the deliberate jettisoning of food, medical supplies, fuel, and munitions. Each man was given only the rations he could carry. Enough gasoline was loaded for a three-hundred-mile excursion. One day's supply of ammunition was loaded. The abandoned extra supplies would follow behind. Wentworth was haunted by the fact that unless he achieved a tactical breakthrough within the next day, the eventual American victory over the Germans would be a pyrrhic one.

The Fifty-first was a lean, hungry animal, stripped for speedy flight and short but lethal fight. The vehicles stretched for miles as the column raced relentlessly north. Except for the unusual precaution of having the highways blocked off from civilian traffic by alerted state troopers, it seemed to the Americans in the farming countryside like any other field maneuver.

Morin's vital bridge company was placed at the head of the column. Wentworth realized from the map that Frenchman Bay lay due east of Bucksport. Fording the Penobscot any further north than there would result in a longer drive to reach Adams Point.

"John," he said, waving the map at his Intelligence officer, "South Orrington or whatever that goddam town is called—that is where Morin will cross. According to the topographical maps, there are no bluffs or high ground on either side of the river. More important, it is equidistant from Bucksport and Bangor." He had a triumphant, almost devilish grin on his face.

"John, I want you to split the column. Half will attack at Bangor and half at Bucksport. The minute Morin touches that damned east bank, the men will retire and shift to South Orrington. While we are attacking both cities, it is doubtful Werner will divert men to cope with Morin. Remember," he cursed happily as he pointed out something which had escaped Stryker's attention and was soon to haunt Werner, "even if the son-of-a-bitch wanted to move, how can he? He's destroyed the road between his cities.

"No, John, Werner should have known better," Wentworth said condescendingly. "As a tank commander, his strength lies in mobility. Goddamn it, his own Guderian should have beaten that into him. The Panzer Korps must be able to move and move fast. Blowing the bridges as he did, that was fine. He could have even concentrated his troops at those points. But never, never destroy the transportation arteries which his tanks need to maneuver. Not in this thick forest terrain. No, John, Werner has holed himself up in a series of isolated fortress positions which went out with the invention of gunpowder in the thirteen hundreds."

Werner realized the logic of Wentworth's position too late. In the early hours of the battle, he waited tensely at Adams Point, pacing nervously in the boathouse, impatient for each message to be decoded by the wireless operators who were receiving a constant barrage of communications from his commanders in the field. At first, the reports from Schnee that the Third Korps had made contact with the vanguard of Wentworth's forces at Bucksport and at Bangor did not alarm him. To the contrary, his thin lips twisted in a pleasant curve, inwardly pleased that his American opponent was stupid enough to try to launch a frontal assault against the main bodies of Nazi troops.

As the messages poured in, telling of larger and larger concentrations of American soldiers facing those two cities, his spirits became elated. He looked up at the clock. Time! Time! Let the stupid American general waste that precious commodity. Let him bridge at either point ... but later, later ... when the rockets were already soaring toward the harbor. Then let him come across on a flying carpet with banners streaming and trumpets blowing. Werner allowed himself a broad smile, in itself a luxury rarely observed in this taciturn young German commander.

By the time the first mention of the small excursion at South Orrington made its feeble and unobtrusive way through the torrent of radio and telephone data, Werner's by-now unbridled optimism smothered its lethal significance. But it did not go away. The Nazi twenty-man roving reconnaissance patrol which had first detected the presence of Americans opposite them on the flat marshes south of the small alluvial farming town could not tell whether the enemy force was merely a mirror image of their own assignment or whether it represented the advance of a larger body.

Neither could Schnee, nor Werner. Not that they could have done anything about it. Not until they knew for certain what Wentworth was up to. Was he going to attack at Bangor? Or at Bucksport? Or even at both places? If, on the other hand, South Orrington was *not* a diversionary ploy, but the prelude to the main thrust, from where should the German troops be withdrawn? Bangor? Or Bucksport? Or both?

Werner should have known that there was trouble even before Morin's pontoons touched the east bank and the sequestered Americans started to pour across the wire grid mesh links like an unleashed avalanche. He should have sensed it by the sinister plateauing of action at the two cities. Instead of Wentworth's increasing the artillery pressure at Bangor and Bucksport, the military action illogically peaked and then, slowly but perceptibly, diminished and almost languished as with clever feints

Wentworth withdrew his firepower and shunted his men in a swift maneuver along the inviolate west bank roads toward Morin's bridgehead.

By the time Schnee reported the breakthrough to Werner, by the time Werner could see vividly on his map in the wooden boathouse the full extent of his florid opponent's outflanking strategy, by the time Wentworth realized with a heart-stopping thump on Stryker's back that nothing ... nothing ... could thwart his now-frantic race for Frenchman Bay, Rohmer, panicked by the imminent confrontation with the American armored column, was suddenly confronted by another threat, this time from the sea.

⟶ TWENTY-EIGHT

It all started with a tiny glow, just the faintest glint in the corner of the grid-engraved tube. Each sweep of the radius reignited the phosphors an instant before the chemical darkness extinguished them again. The glint took on mass, divided in two, then became three. The dots moved from the periphery of the tube, making their way toward the center on a tangent of their own choosing. As they changed position, they became larger, seeming to feed upon the sweeping bank of light.

Rohmer was away from his wireless set, deep in the forest. Shouts from the sweating soldiers, working with the missiles, called his attention to the bright flashes of cascading light which rose into the sky and hovered for a moment before falling back in graceful crescendos of fluorescent particles. Again and again, the flares went off from the tip of Schoodic Peninsula.

It took Rohmer no more than fifteen minutes to make the trip across the bay to the radar station.

"How many are there?" he peered over Shoemaker's shoulder in the darkened room.

"Three."

"Are you sure?"

"I can see only three. They have been on the screen for at least thirty minutes."

Rohmer felt the urge to punish the operator for bringing him the distressful evidence of the American move. He paced back and forth, deep in thought. Finally, he asked,

"On what bearing?"

"Approximately sixty-eight degrees, east by northeast."

"Can you tell the speed?"

Shoemaker looked at the screen again. He plotted the movement of the particles of light which spelt rescue for him and perhaps death for his captors. "It's hard to tell. The screen isn't designed for nautical speed. I'd say, at least twenty to twenty-five knots."

Rohmer calculated quickly. The range of the station was about eighty to one hundred miles. The ships had reached the detection zone less than half an hour ago. This meant that within three to four hours they would be at the Porcupine Islands, blocking his escape route. The real peril was even greater. If *he* could monitor *them* electronically, the reverse was also true. When he was ready to leave with the ore, he and his U-boats would be caught in a web of radar and sonar from which they could never escape. A web which would grow more accurate and binding with every passing second. A web which would follow them no matter where they went, how they twisted and turned, surfaced and dived. Even now the electronic antennae aboard the fleet were probably being supplemented by additional radar-equipped planes to tighten the curtain of surveillance. He was locked in a wizard's box from which there would be no escape.

Rohmer looked up at the clock. It was six-thirty. In the east, the light was already dimming. Although night would fall in less than two hours, the darkness would not shield him from the 9-centimeter microwaves.

The U-boat commander scanned the coastal map mounted on the wall of the blockhouse, trying to pinpoint the American fleet which, from a hundred miles away, had pressed an invisible knife to his jugular. Like Werner, Rohmer could see all too well the short distance between the last reported position of Wentworth's troops and the concealed missiles.

More ominous, before he left for the radar station, Rohmer thought he had detected in the tank commander, for the first time, a note of alarm, or possibly even of fear. Now the U-boat captain himself began to shiver, the hairs on his shoulders and back rising in waves. His pupils dilated. His pulse quickened in terror as he saw the sharp leading edge of the American armored dagger draw closer and closer.

Time . . . time . . . that was still the currency of the game. How much longer before Wentworth forced his hand?

The rockets were almost ready. Only one or two more remained to be set. With the deadly warheads primed for their predestined trajectory, he could hurl the death blow to the American city. Yes, that was the answer. His eyes narrowed to thin slivers. He could almost taste the destruction he would unleash. Push the button now. Before Wentworth arrived. While he still had the chance. Race for the sea. Dive! Dive! Dive! Maybe some of his ships could elude the electronic blockade.

The deed could not be done. The primary purpose of

the mission was not the missile attack, but to secure the ore. Despite Rohmer's threats and cajoling, his entreaties and brutal reminders of their fate if they did not hasten, the Norwegians were still hours away from finishing their work. The canisters had been placed in no more than four out of the seven submarines. If only that train had been several hours earlier!

Von Eyssen's injunction had been specific: his mission was to get all of the uranium to Germany, not part, and certainly not by playing hide-and-seek with killer planes and destroyers. The Grossadmiral's instructions did not brook any equivocation. Rohmer's mind worked rapidly, testing potential courses of action. He kept coming back to one alternative, the *only possible solution*. It was a bitter price. He concluded with bitter resignation, like the gladiators of Imperial Rome, that if that is what the Fatherland wants, that is what we who serve to die shall do.

He walked over to Shoemaker and put his hand on his shoulder. The young boy looked up, frightened, half-expecting to see Rohmer's Luger pressed to his temple. He was dumbfounded to find his captor smiling and relaxed.

Rohmer pointed to the wireless set on the table against the wall. "Tell me," he asked, his manner courteous, "is that still operational?"

Shoemaker was puzzled. What did this man want? He replied that the radio still functioned.

"Then, my good friend, raise your superiors in Boston." Rohmer smiled again, now confident in his course of action. "Connect me with Naval Intelligence. With Michael Francis O'Malley. I think we are going to make a deal."

───→ **TWENTY-NINE**

Michael was weary. His muscles were cramped, his mind and mouth stale. He got up to stretch and take a few deep breaths. It seemed as if nobody had moved in hours. Although Douglas Gatling and Mayor O'Connell had been arguing with each other all evening, they still sat in their respective corners like part of the elegant furnishings.

The New Mexico scientist was carrying out some silent ritual on a wedge of aged Stilton. He held the cheese over the low alcohol flame of a silver chafing dish. He would scrape the melted surface off with a knife and turn it onto a hard soda biscuit. He chewed slowly, washing down the pungent mixture with some musty Madeira which he swirled around in his mouth for a long time. He was so engrossed in this task that for those few moments he seemed to elude the tension which permeated the air.

Intent upon his drinking, O'Connell sank deeper and deeper into his corner of the thin, uncomfortable settee. The silver tray with the large water glass full of Irish whiskey stood next to him. The present bottle, soon to be added to the many accumulating nearby, was clutched by the neck as if it would escape if it had the chance. His face was pasty and his eyes clouded, the change due more to pain than to alcohol. He slouched back, except for an occasional forward motion to swallow another large gulp of the dark amber liquid. He stared at his lap, not saying anything.

Michael went over to the window and spread the slats of the venetian blind. He could see the people in the street below entering and leaving the Ritz-Carlton. From his vantage point twelve stories above, they looked like

mechanical bugs. Life was going on down there, unknow-
ing, uncaring, while up in the opulent setting of Bainbridge's suite, two men were fighting for the right to
determine who should die. Not whether anyone should die.
Death was not the option. Only who and where and when.

It was eleven o'clock. Michael looked anxiously
toward the door. Rohmer's ultimatum would expire at
midnight, and still Bainbridge had not returned from his
emergency meeting with the National Defense Council in
Washington. Rohmer's conditions were simple: let the
Astra clear the three-mile limit into international waters
and the Panzers would lay down their arms; let the
U-boats find sanctuary beyond radar range and there
would be no rocket attack. In a desperate gamble, fearing
that the dramatic success of the Fifty-first would panic
Rohmer into a premature firing of the missiles before the
Americans could decide, O'Malley had forced the armored
column to a precipitous halt. Now, he waited.

Against the far wall on a tortoiseshell table a red
phone rested, mute, a discordant note not only of color
but of urgency in this room where time and man seemed
to move so slowly. Michael had the sensation of circles
within circles—like the phone, connected to his office
phone in Harvard Square where it sat next to the wireless
whose electromagnetic waves touched Shoemaker and
Rohmer ... the three ships from Portsmouth, anchored in
the lee of the Porcupine Islands for protection against
direct attack, while their cannons were zeroed in with
exquisite accuracy on the submarines anchored at Adams
Point ... the rockets, silent, poised—just a fingertip on a
relay switch and they would be hurled two hundred fifty
miles to the Boston waterfront ... passing, as they flew,
over cannon shells released at the U-boats an instant after the noise and flash of the missile launching—perhaps
one of those aerial bombs would even land on the hotel,
right in this room with the red phone. And so it went,
around and around and around, just like a dream with
no ending and no beginning. But it was no dream.

Michael shivered. He felt greasy sweat sliding in his

armpits. A dull ache throbbed at the base of his skull. A wave of nausea brought up a few drops of sour, bitter bile which he hastily swallowed. He had the bizarre intuition that he and everyone else present were actors carrying out the directions of some mysterious playwright, potent and malevolent, yet invisible. It could not just be his imagination. Something was wrong. But what?

O'Connell broke the silence. He raised his hand to point at Gatling, spilling whiskey from the glass onto his lap.

"You are going to risk the lives of thousands of people here in this city for a dream?"

"It is no dream, Mr. Mayor," Gatling replied softly. "The power of the atom is real. It is an incredible force. It will change the entire world as we know it today."

"It may change the world. Granted. But not tonight. Not in this room in the next hour. Let the German commander have the ore and leave."

"You do not understand." Gatling's tone was one of tolerance. "If we let the Nazis have the ore, they may be able to obtain the bomb before we do. They could control the world tomorrow."

"Always 'tomorrow.' Always 'maybe,' Mr. Gatling. What we are talking about here is *today*. Right here. Not tomorrow. Do you want the death of thousands of people on your conscience?"

"But the bomb we are about to test could shorten the war and save the lives of more Americans than are killed by the rockets. You saw what the Germans did last summer when everyone thought they were finished at Stalingrad. They came back and gave Russia another six hundred thousand casualties. Do you know that right now when the Japanese pilots have no more bombs in their planes, they commit suicide by diving straight into the decks of our ships? They call it 'kamikaze.' Can you in good conscience accept the fate of a million Americans who will die when we invade Japan and try to capture the sacred person of their divine emperor? No, I am arguing for a greater humanity. To save *more* lives. Let Roh-

mer set off the rockets. Certainly there will be casualties
here. But before those rockets have landed, the U-boats
will have been blown out of the water."

"Rohmer is no fool," Michael interrupted. "He is
aware that the ore is as valuable to us as it is to his
country. He will not leave it on the beach waiting for the
American troops. If I were Rohmer, I would blow up the
submarines with the ore inside. If he can't take it with
him, then he must deny it to us. Provided that is his only
choice, which in this case it is."

"I agree," O'Connell said. "I suspect that is what our
very bright Kapitän will do."

"In that case, there is really *no* choice," Gatling in-
terjected. "We must destroy him and the ore. If we cannot have it, then neither can they."

"That would mean the destruction of the city,"
O'Connell protested.

"That is a small price to pay to prevent the Nazis
from developing a nuclear weapon."

The mayor rose from his seat, unsteadily at first. He
walked over to Gatling and stood defiantly in front of him.

"You don't even know whether the bomb will work."
He paused between each word to let the full import sink
in. He certainly was not drunk.

"You want me to condone your sacrifice of my city.
Why? To deny the Germans some mysterious ore. Ore
that you claim will kill even more people than will the
rockets. Okay. I might buy that. We all would. If ..."—
he threw the words into the room like daggers, not caring
whom they bloodied—"if you could convince us that your
toy works."

Gatling tried to speak. This drunken Irishman had
divined his Achilles' heel. He cast about frantically for
something to say, to redress the balance in the room
which had unexpectedly tipped against him. He *knew* that
the bomb would work. It had to. All the research at Los
Alamos was sustaining that hope. What was more important, he was a scientist. Like Columbus, he knew the
world was round ... before he sailed. Like Copernicus, he

knew the earth went around the sun ... without traveling to the stars to observe it. O'Connell was a politician; he manipulated votes, not atoms. How could Gatling prove to him what he knew in the recesses of his soul? Faith is not a contagion, like a virus. The scientist could not answer, but sat back, blanched and shaken.

"O'Connell swayed in front of him, his hands on his hips, mocking, taunting him with his exposed impotence.

"No, sonny, you can't prove a thing. Not a damned thing. You can only ask us to trade *my* city for *your* toy."

O'Connell sat down again and poured himself another drink. His hand trembled and the liquid overflowed the rim. He downed the portion in one swallow and sank back into place as if he had never left it.

The room was quiet again. No one moved or said a word. The street noises could be heard ... the muted car horns, the drone of traffic, all the distant echoed sounds of normal human activity. The air grew heavy and scented with the acrid odor of sweat and worry.

The three men jumped when the door suddenly opened and Bainbridge entered. Everyone turned to look at him as he shakily made his way toward a purple velvet wing chair, everyone trying to guess what Washington had decided—although they all knew the final decision would be Bainbridge's. Michael had known this all the time. Gatling must have learned it from General Groves's latest phone call from New Mexico. Certainly O'Connell was told by Roosevelt that Bainbridge represented the National Defense Council and would have the final say. Why, then, was Bainbridge putting everyone through this charade? Michael felt like clawing at the substance occupying the velvet chair, to see if it was made of flesh and blood, whether it could cry and scream and bleed. Why was Bainbridge playing with them all?

It haunted him, along with the other riddles, the unmatched pieces that would not fit together: Berkowitz's death, the change in the timing of the U-boat landing, Bainbridge's inappropriate performance at their earlier meeting, even his failure to inform Gatling and O'Connell about the reciprocal threats. Michael clenched his fists in a futile gesture. What was he looking for? What was staring him in the face that he couldn't see?

Bainbridge leaned back, the sheltering wing chair burying him in shadow. His fingers continually tapped together in front of his face.

"Professor Gatling. Your arguments and those of your superiors have validity. Certainly I, if anybody, can appreciate the chimera of Nazi nuclear power. However" —he dropped his voice to a near-whisper—"there is another urgency which must override the primacy of your claim." He motioned with his hand to the up-till-now invisible aide standing in back of him to bring over the red phone. "The invasion of France is almost upon us. The convoy is critical to its success. Under no circumstance will the Pentagon countenance its jeopardy, especially for a weapon whose validity is yet to be tested."

It did not take long to consummate the negotiations with Rohmer. Only a matter of a minute to dispose of emotions which had stirred them all evening. Michael's agile mind was already weighing the logistics of the exchange of perils even as Bainbridge was speaking to the U-boat captain. The arrangements completed, Michael watched Gatling and O'Connell leave.

It is odd, O'Malley thought, one could not tell which of these two antagonists had triumphed. There was an air of resignation upon both faces as the men crossed the room to shake Bainbridge's hand in parting. It is not really a victory, Michael said to himself. Neither man had wanted to place his foot on the neck of his fallen opponent. The war would continue with bloodshed and death no matter who had been victorious. Each hoped that he would not live to reap the bitter harvest of his conviction. The two men looked at each other almost sadly. They had nothing left to say. In unison, they mumbled, "I wish you luck," and left, one after the other.

Michael also got up to leave. He felt exhausted, his emotions drained. It had been a long, difficult evening. He walked over to Bainbridge's desk and said, "Good night."

The old man did not answer. He scrutinized the standing figure for a long time in a rather uncertain fashion, as if trying to decide something. Michael could not fathom the unexplained silence. He waited, a puzzled half-smile on his lips. Bainbridge slipped open the top center drawer of the bureau plat and withdrew a black leather attaché case. Opening it, he handed Michael a large manila envelope with large letters stamped obliquely across its face: "TOP SECRET—MAYFLOWER." Michael opened the envelope and took out the contents. When he had finished reading, his smile had vanished. There was only fear in his eyes.

→ THIRTY

Friday morning Rohmer left the radar blockhouse and climbed down the rocks to the water's edge. The tide was low. He skirted the green, seaweed-covered rocks and piles of kelp, picking his way with care through the exposed ledges with their freshly watered tidal pools. He could observe the starfish, the crabs, the mollusks, all coexisting in harmony within the small reservoirs—until, he thought, the starfish gets hungry. Then good-bye to the clam. It was like this everywhere. Only the sessile barnacle seemed safe, opening its quaint stone house to wave in nutrient-laden water with its fimbriated hands. It must pay for its security, Rohmer concluded sadly, by living within a prison, which serves, in succession, as its christening fount, home, coffin, and tombstone.

The U-boat captain looked at the time. It was a little after six o'clock. The dawn had come to introduce his last day of freedom. Only one more U-boat to depart. Then he, too, would be incarcerated, just like the little barnacle, only on land and away from the sea he loved. He focused his sight on the Porcupine Islands. He could see behind them the two cruisers and destroyer lying at anchor. They had not deigned to acknowledge the silent passing of the submarines, one after the other, through the small hours of the night. Why should they? This was not a minuet they were playing, but a swapping of the means of mutual annihilation, forced upon them by the exigencies of time and place.

The sun was full in the east, bright and warm. The wind was cool, steady from the southwest. It would probably be a beautiful day . . . for others. With a last reluctant glance, Rohmer turned and made his way back to the radar station.

During the night, Rohmer and O'Malley had negotiated on the wireless, but not as strangers. For almost three-and-a-half years, Michael and the Nazi captain had been playing a continuing and deadly game of cat-and-mouse. Rohmer, almost alone, had survived Michael's search-and-kill techniques. They were worthy opponents, reciprocally tested. There was no bargaining between the two men. There is always an irreducible minimum beyond which an opponent will not compromise. Once that threshold is recognized, terms can easily be reached. Both men cut directly to this core of agreement.

The modus operandi personified the mutual fears and mistrust of the opposing sides. As long as the U-boats could be monitored by radar, surrendering the missiles would be suicidal. The vessels could then be destroyed with impunity. On the other hand, to let the submarines escape with the uranium beyond the pale of electronic detection without first neutralizing the rocket detonators risked a German impulse to fire them, even by remote control, once the ore had vanished into the North Atlantic.

O'Malley contacted Wentworth, who only brief hours before had been forced to abort the brilliant maneuver that had carried him to Ellsworth, only fifteen miles short of his goal. The general could not understand why, with Adams Point within his grasp, Washington had halted his tanks. He fumed and cursed, informing Stryker in no uncertain terms his avowed opinion that the Pentagon was obviously a fucking home for goddam Nazi lovers! This cynical appraisal of his native country's strategy was reinforced when Wentworth received instructions that he and forty picked men were to accompany the German tank commander Colonel Werner to the missile launch site.

The American force was taken to the forest where the overlying cover of branches and saplings was removed from the rockets. Wentworth and Stryker marveled at the simple but ingenious launching ramps. The men stood in awe of the long-tapered warheads, each with a strange swollen bulge at the nose. The missiles pointed at the sky, waiting for the electric impulses which, received and amplified, would start the irrevocable closing of circuits, igniting the powerful propellant to shove them aloft. The skillfully intermeshed mechanism designed for a single flight, then destruction at its destination, like the lucky drone who manages to catch the ever-higher-flying queen only to be eviscerated at the moment of ecstatic impregnation. The silent weapons looked like a row of hooded falcons, impatient for someone to uncover their eyes and throw them into the air for their swoop of death.

The missiles were divided into seven groups of six each. Rohmer stayed at the radar station with Shoemaker, leaving Werner and Kern at the launching site with the Americans. Rohmer watched the first U-boat depart, monitoring it by both radar and radio. When the submarine reached the periphery of Schoodic contact, it switched on its Naxos equipment. The dipoles on the bridge swept the horizon, confirming the absence of any enemy ship or plane within radar range. As the luminous spot disappeared off Rohmer's screen, the first group of missiles was surrendered to the waiting Americans, who immediately deactivated the detonators.

During the long, tense hours, Wentworth and Werner moved through the woods in tandem, like medieval lords with their retinues spaced out behind them. Wentworth could see the hurt in his opponent's eyes as each metallic symbol of Nazi supremacy was neutralized. Werner would reach out like Antaeus and touch the missile, but it was a futile gesture. With sorrow, he watched Wentworth's engineers scrambling over the now-impotent steel hulks. Although Werner said not a word, he clenched and unclenched his fists, nails scarring his palms, choking on the desire for revenge, thwarted once on the burning sands of North Africa, and again in the verdant wilderness of North America.

Ironically, as the malignant tokens of Nazi blackmail were nullified, the tank colonel's hostility ebbed. The trim German would look over at his fat enemy with a slightly condescending gaze that made Wentworth uneasy. The major general would suck in his gut and tuck in his unkempt uniform, embarrassed by his ungainly proportions.

However, it was not body image which was sustaining Werner in his moment of bitterness but the gradual realization that his cornered country, from a distance of three thousand miles, with a handful of submarines, had threatened such a mighty nation. When the Panzer leader's eye would rest upon the warheads themselves, his back would straighten, his eyes flash defiantly, as if to say to his captors, "You may steal from us like a common thief, but only we, the Germans, have the brains to conceive of such a creation." Secure in the knowledge that his Führer was possessed of other, more deadly weapons to exact the *final* revenge which must be his, the twice-defeated Nazi, proud and unflinching, threw back at his conquerors their unconcealed scorn which he had now stolen for his own.

As the routine repeated over and over again, Rohmer repressed the fear that one of his men, from emotion or patriotism, would press the relay in violation of his orders. If that happened, he knew that the remaining U-boats, laden with ore, would be blown out of the bay in retaliation. Then would follow the inevitable release of the remaining rockets in a reflex spasm.

In his staff room, Michael paced back and forth unable to shake a feeling of alarm. His channel of communication with Wentworth gave him an exact duplicate of Rohmer's radar apparatus. O'Malley, too, feared that just before one of the submarines broke through the web of detection and vanished over the rim of the oscilloscope tube, the Germans would see a new flash on the screen—an American plane, or ship, seeking to lock the departing U-boat into a new zone of surveillance beyond Schoodic Peninsula's reach. Then would come the retaliatory scenario of destruction. Only first would come the rockets and second the cannon shells landing on the beaches. The result would be the same.

Both men said nothing to their subordinates. They marked the long minutes in silence. The last exchange would be the most tense. Without fear of major secondary loss, each side could spit in its opponent's face—fire the rockets or sink the ore, or both. Rohmer and O'Malley were gentlemen, and the last exchange went as all the rest.

All through the night, Shoemaker monitored the changing patterns on the oscilloscope. Shortly after midnight, the *Astra* cast off and cleared Frenchman Bay. Then in response to new instructions cabled from Göteborg, the ship turned north to return to Iceland. The *Astra*'s captain was very embarrassed when he showed the orders to the Baltic engineers. He assured them that alternative transportation would be arranged when they docked at Reykjavik. To his surprise, the passengers did not seem as upset as he would have expected. However, if the captain was in a hurry to return to Iceland, his subsequent action did not show it. The Swedish boat sailed northeast to a position one hundred fifty miles off the Maine coast, then without explanation stopped dead in the water.

Rohmer watched for the last flicker of radiant energy on the screen to vanish. At that point, he would take out his Luger and hand it, along with his freedom, to the young radar operator. This American boy was a gentle boy. He reminded the U-boat commander of his own son. Pleasant, not yet vicious or callous, drawn into a war he had neither made nor probably even understood. Doing his job and hoping his limbs and life would survive unscathed until it was over.

Rohmer had engaged him in casual conversation. Everything the boy talked about revolved around his girlfriend whom he was going to marry. The older man half-listened to the tale, nodding absentmindedly. At one point, he stopped. A nurse. A vision of the white-cloaked body of a young girl floating in the water arose before his eyes. He looked at the young boy and shook his head in sorrow, but said nothing.

His son dead; this boy's future wife dead; his own freedom lost. Somehow all of them were braided together like a hangman's heavy noose. He reminded himself that too much thinking of such things is bad, and turned to his own predicament. He knew exactly what would happen next. Interned, he would find Werner and Schnee and those heroes of yesterday who still survived. There would be no excitement at the unhappy reunion. No faces flushed with enthusiasm, no schnapps, no glasses smashed on the floor. He was struck by the irony of spending the remainder of the war scrubbing off the red swastikas they had so diligently stenciled on the vehicles.

Rohmer looked through the window. There was one consolation: he had been reconciled to death at sea. However, was incarceration like a common criminal a better option? He was already feeling the claustrophobia that confinement would produce. He began to sweat and breathe in short, rapid gulps. He went to the door for a drink of air, cool and damp, like his native Kiel on a spring day.

He could see from across the room the white phosphor of the U-201 about to be extinguished. His own ship, the last to depart. At least he had accomplished his mission. His personal life was really of no greater significance to the Reich than any of the other millions of casualties sustained since 1938. What counted was that the Fatherland would now possess the vital ore it needed for survival. He felt content and satisfied.

Rohmer stood in the doorway, searching the open sea, breathing again more easily. Von Eyssen had thought of everything. Far out, safe from detection of any type, each U-boat surfaced as it approached the *Astra*. With a speed inspired by cunning, the yellow canisters were transferred to the waiting neutral freighter. The whole process took only a few minutes, after which the U-boat submerged again and glided off for its long, perilous voyage home.

Von Eyssen was brilliant. He had anticipated the curtain of steel that the British would draw across the submarine lanes and approaches to Kiel and Bremerhaven. Now the Allies could chase the returning craft to their heart's content and expend their bombs on simple decoys. It would even be desirable to have them think that they had sent the drums to the bottom of the sea.

This last transfer was inspired. The ore would reach the Fatherland, sailing audaciously by day and illuminated by night, off bounds to Nazi attack and respected by the Allies. Within two weeks, the ore would land at Böknfjord and begin its long, cold trip to Telemark. Everything had worked out well.

Rohmer turned to reenter the blockhouse. His hand was already unbuckling his holster. Perhaps he had not destroyed the convoy in Boston, but he knew there would be other landings, other harbors. His dramatic feat had demonstrated the vulnerability of the American coastline. As he surrendered his liberty to Stephen Shoemaker, his only thoughts were of the success of his mission.

→ **THIRTY-ONE**

Bainbridge watched the expression of incredulity twist on Michael's face as his subordinate tried to reject the evidence of his eyes. The old man extended his arm. His scrawny wrist protruded from the starched cuff. He wrapped his bony fingers around O'Malley's hand in a reassuring manner.

"I know what you've been thinking, Michael," Bainbridge said, giving a short, wry laugh. "No, I am not a Nazi agent or whatever else you might have suspected."

Bainbridge reached across the desk and retrieved the envelope.

"You played your part so expertly that we think you deserve knowledge of the plan."

Michael's ears picked up the use of the plural pronoun. Bainbridge continued, "I wish that I could say the same for your assistant."

"Moe?"

"Yes, Michael, we already knew everything that the English told him. We intended you to learn all that . . . in time. Berkowitz was not supposed to warn you about the rockets until he returned on Thursday. Somehow he got suspicious. He thought that the men tailing him in London were Nazi agents. They were ours."

"Moe? But . . . but . . . Trondheim killed him," O'Malley protested.

"No, Michael," Bainbridge said with a gesture of regret. "*We* killed him. It was such a waste. If only he had stuck to our timetable." The plural pronoun again.

The words hit Michael hard. He gasped at the vivid image of a body, coughing blood, struggling for breath to live.

"We tried to kill him in London once we found out he was taking an earlier plane, but he got away. We had no opportunity to try again until he returned to Boston. He should have been killed in England. Again, but another five minutes in his apartment, he would have died before warning you prematurely of the rockets."

Bainbridge's voice was as dry as his skin. In some perverse way, he was still insulted at Berkowitz's presumption in having flawed some carefully contrived scheme. Michael felt like reaching out across the desk and hitting the seated figure to inflict some measure of pain as revenge for Moe's death. But the nagging suspicion that he himself might have played some crucial role in this macabre scheme mocked his sense of righteousness. Michael could do nothing at all. He just stood there, impatient for the explanation he knew would be forthcoming.

"Yes, you learned about the rockets, albeit too soon, and made the next correct move to bring Trondheim in for interrogation. That was very good. He told you what you needed to know. His knowledge of Winter Harbor, though, was no accident, but a deliberate plant which we knew you would eventually uncover.

"Unfortunately, thanks to your assistant's unscheduled arrival and his prolonged survival, you went after Trondheim too early. That unanticipated blunder imperiled the intricate timing of the scheduled attack on Saturday. With great hardship and completely unnecessary anxiety, we managed to advance the complicated maneuvers twenty-four hours to insure a successful outcome."

Dozens of questions raced through Michael's mind, all pushing and shoving for their turn to be hurled from his tongue and into the room.

"Too *early?*" he protested. "We were too *late*. If we had sent the fleet up sixteen hours earlier, we would have the ore today, and the landing would never have taken place."

Even as the words were being spoken, Michael had the strange sensation that what he assumed to be atypical behavior was actually calculated, and if he reversed his thinking, would turn out to be part of a well-conceived plan.

"Exactly. Exactly!" Bainbridge cried, elated. "That is why we did what we did." Bainbridge watched Michael struggle with this inverse logic. The frail figure rose up in his chair as if to lend support to the cognition of a mental inferior.

"Let me ask you one question."

Bainbridge sat back, happy. "I knew you would."

"You are pleased with the outcome? The loss of the ore, the escape of the U-boats?"

"Yes."

"Can I know why?"

"Of course, Michael, of course. I wondered when you would get around to asking me. Sit down. I have a story for you." Bainbridge leaned back to savor his triumph.

"We are not the only ones who know the Germans are losing the war. There are many high-ranking Nazis who realize that it will all be over soon. They are scurrying around Europe, making deals, setting plans to escape to Africa, South America, and the Middle East. We have been contacted on many occasions. Unfortunately, short of delivering Hitler's head on a silver platter like John the Baptist, these men are of little value to us.

"Michael," he warned, his expression grave, "do not be fooled by what you think is going on in Europe at this moment. We are fighting *two* wars. One with Russia against Germany. The other against Russia itself. The Third World War is incubating. Our agents tell us that right now the Russians are preparing to seize forever all of occupied Europe that their armies enter. Bogus Communist governments-in-exile are already functioning in Moscow for Poland, Rumania, Bulgaria, Germany, Hungary, Czechoslovakia, Austria.

"In the postwar world to come, Russia will be our competition. England is finished, crippled by two wars in one generation. For years to come, she will be only a shadow. Russia strides the world now like a newly awakened colossus. In the next war, our ally will be Germany.

Not this fascist Germany, but a Fourth Reich, a postwar, capitalistic, Christian, anti-Communist Germany. A Germany whose hatred of the Slavs will drive her into our camp. Michael, men like me are in the vanguard of this new struggle which is starting before the present war has ended."

Michael stirred uneasily in his seat. He could not see the relationship of what Bainbridge was telling him to anything that had occurred. The older man's manner became excited, his face flushed, as he was swept up in the drama of his vision.

"Think, for a minute, Michael, think. Germany may be devastated, but she has one treasure still intact. A prize beyond value. *Brains!* Do you realize what benefits will accrue to the country that seizes her scientists and her inventions? Did you know the Germans can turn coal into aviation fuel? Did you know that at this very moment they have invented a plane that does not even have a propeller, that can fly faster than the speed of sound? You do accept, after tonight, that she possesses the secret of hurling a bomb two, three hundred miles into the ether? Within a few years these missiles will span oceans. Who shall get the rocket first? We . . . or the Russians?

"Can you visualize thousands of these weapons hidden across the steppes, in Siberia, all aimed at the United States? Can you imagine blackmail on a global scale? What has happened today is only a taste of the power such a weapon can endow. Yes, Michael. Brains . . . jets . . . missiles. We know that the Russians are preparing to ransack all Europe for every scientist they can cart back to Moscow alive. Like locusts, Russia will devour the technological skills of the Western world and grow omnipotent on its strength."

He paused to let the words imprint on Michael's consciousness.

"Then von Eyssen came to us with an intriguing proposition."

At the mention of Rohmer's superior, Michael looked up, startled, "Von Eyssen?"

"Ah, von Eyssen." Bainbridge smiled. "Yes, von Eyssen realized these facts of life about the same time that we did. He had need of certain personal compensation which is irrelevant to the purpose of this conversation. We contrived an ingenious charade by which, in the middle of the war, he could deliver to this shore forty-two of their most advanced rockets, the fruit of all their missile research since 1934. Think of Rohmer and his men, traveling three thousand miles to hand over to us the most deadly weapon so far to come out of the Second World War. One which will surely determine the outcome of the Third World War.

"Nikolai Martov, my erstwhile young Russian counterpart, has tried desperately the past two years to contact the German engineers who developed these lethal weapons. He has offered them boundless treasure to defect, to be spirited to Sweden, and thence to the land of the tsars, but we ... I ... have succeeded, where he has reaped only bitter failure.

"The plan had to be foolproof. It had to lure the Nazi High Command so that they would approve the scheme. We stripped the northeast coast of defenses and concentrated them in Boston Harbor where they would be vulnerable to rocket attack. We removed the Italians from the Gouldsboro Camp and brought in a complete Panzer corps. We stocked the depot with all the necessary equipment and vehicles. We arranged for the *Astra* to be diverted at exactly the right time with the launch ramps. We set up the ore shipment and delivered it by the coastal route. Hitler took the bait. How he must have salivated over the unique opportunity both to destroy the convoy and steal our uranium in one blow. The decoys were set. The dupes prepared.

"But it was not sufficient that the German High Command buy the plan. Von Eyssen wished his head to remain on his shoulders, to enjoy the fruits of his labors. The intricate plan had to be patterned so that the inevitable exchange of the ore for the missiles was an unfortunate result of a chance chain of events, beyond anybody's prediction, control, or making. Otherwise, suspicions would have been raised on both sides of the Atlantic with dire consequences for both von Eyssen and myself.

"Timing, Michael. Timing. That was the essence of the plan. Consider, for a minute, the consequences if our forces had arrived too late. Rohmer would have loaded the ore and left with alacrity after firing the rockets. If, on the other hand, we arrived too early and frightened him off, he would not have landed. If he landed and we arrived before he had the ore cached away and the rockets ready for firing, there would have been no basis of a logical swap. No, the timing had to be exquisite, and so it was.

"Your deduction about Winter Harbor was inspired. Rohmer was thwarted at exactly the right time. His instinctive response to trade was sublime. It was unavoidable—the only move he could have made within the confines of von Eyssen's injunction. No robots could have performed any better than you two did.

"There was never any reason not to accept on face value the deception we perpetrated. Neither von Eyssen nor I was suspect, nor ever will be. Both of us merely tried to salvage the unexpected tragedy which you and Rohmer presented to us. Think of us in this room only hours ago torn between our compassion for O'Connell and our fear of Gatling's prediction."

Michael interrupted, "But we gave them the ore. According to Gatling, what is contained within those atoms far exceeds the potential of the rockets. Have you not given away your birthright for a mess of porridge?"

"No, Michael. The invasion of France will start within weeks and the Reich will crumble like a rotten shell. We know the state of the German atomic program. Hitler has deliberately neglected it up until now. He is a Bohemian boor and does not understand science. Roosevelt is not much smarter, but he has better advisers and he listens to them. For Germany, the war will be over before that ore can be processed. If those submarines manage to make it through the British blockade we have arranged to surprise them, I wager we will find the same yellow cans, unopened, waiting for us in Berlin."

Bainbridge's voice became strident, "Do you realize what we have done? We are masters of the power of the atom, the most terrifying force known to man. Tonight, in this room, we have bought the means of delivering that threat anywhere in the world. Consider, Michael. Marry the atomic bomb to a long-range missile and the United States can control the world forever." His words became shrill. "Even more, by being first we can prevent any other country from duplicating our efforts."

"You mean by blackmailing Russia?"

"Yes, although I prefer not to use that unhappy term. The only way the world can ever achieve peace, real peace, is to prevent conflict. With a monopoly on atomic power and the ability to deliver it on command, we can ensure global stability, for the first time in history since Augustus Caesar."

"Lawrence, that is the same dream that Hitler promised, and before him Napoleon and Attila, and many others like them."

Bainbridge looked at O'Malley with an air of regret. "Michael, you may be an intelligent man, but you are a parochial thinker." He touched the attaché case. "I have told you all this because I feel that you deserve an explanation. I do not think that you will betray me."

Bainbridge was right. Michael knew that his gullibility could never excuse his unwitting participation. He felt dirty, somehow soiled, not by his role in the sinister scheme, nor by his unjust revenge on the Swedish spy, but oddly enough by Bainbridge himself. He had been violated and cast aside, just like Rohmer. Both of them were discarded pawns, while the strong pieces changed colors and switched back and forth. No, the shame was not his, not any longer.

Michael started to reach across the table to shake his superior's hand in parting. He thought better of it and dropped his arm sharply to his side. He said not a word. His head held high, he turned on his heel and walked out

of the room, leaving Bainbridge with his cachectic limb
still extended.

→ **T H I R T Y - T W O**

The *Astra* was two hundred miles east of Nova Scotia
when its captain, Kristian Skänsen, first spotted the
strange ships on the horizon. It was almost two days
since the *Astra* had departed from Frenchman Bay. Except for the strange absence of complaints from the
Latvian passengers over their detour back to Iceland,
nothing unusual had occurred. Skänsen was sorry to see
the last of the U-boats vanish under the surface of the
ocean. With the twelve hundred pounds of ore stored deep
in the forward hold, all the excitement had gone out of
the voyage. He did not know what was in the drums, nor
was he interested. All that mattered was that he had
carried out his instructions faithfully. Trondheim would
be pleased when he returned to Göteborg and would write
a favorable report to the party.

In the thirteen years since Skänsen had joined the
National Socialist party, he had carried out his assign-
ments without expectation of immediate reward. He had

risen high in the local Gau and his future was bright.
Right now, he knew Sweden was useful to Hitler as a
neutral country, but someday soon, when Russia and
England had been defeated, it would be Sweden's turn.
When that day came, Kristian Skänsen was confident he
would be part of the conquering Nazi hierarchy.

How different his life would have been except for
that night in Kiel in January 1933, when Adolf Hitler
came to speak in the Hanseatic Sailor's Union. The old
hall, soot-stained and with pockmarked floors and walls,
was packed with sailors and students. Overhanging the
raised dais at the front of the room were red pennants,
each containing a white circle with a tilted geometric
symbol he had never seen before. It was an old runic design, the swastika, which Hitler had selected to identify
the National Socialist party for the voters. Flanking the
aisles were phalanxes of longshoremen, each with a
brown shirt, brown jodhpurs, and a leather cross-chest
strap holding thick wooden truncheons.

The audience was impatient and raucous when the
thin, nondescript man in the double-breasted blue suit
entered. His black hair was shiny from too much pomade.
His short moustache was artless. Not looking to either
side, he walked down the center aisle to the front of the
hall. He did not resemble the demagogue the Communist
newspapers had depicted. His face was calm and thought-
ful. Only a simple man.

A hush swept across the room as Hitler started. His
speech was hesitant, almost apologetic. His soft south
German accent was unexpected and pleasant to hear, be-
guiling. His careful praise of local customs and leaders
was innocent and disarming. Without knowing why,
Skänsen listened more intently, his eyes focused on the
speaker. This man was not saying anything new or revolutionary. His words seemed to flow, not from his own
feelings, but from those of the audience, their shattered
dreams, their hopes, anxieties, ambitions.

No, he told them. They were not to blame that foreign powers led by the international Jewish bankers were
squeezing out in reparations the blood and gold that was

theirs. No! Germany's defeat was not a blot upon the conscience of her loyal "folk," but a stab in the back from those elements within the society that had always plotted her downfall.

His voice became charged with power. He was transformed, animated, vibrant, agitated. He walked back and forth, flinging his arms into the air, punching his fists together. His body, devoid of artifice, punctuated his violent message with instinctive gestures.

Suddenly, he broke contact with the audience and soared above them, pulling, tugging, lifting them up to him with all his strength. He *was* the audience and they were him, if only they could speak with his magic eloquence. One man. One voice. One people. All fused together in that room. No microphone. No loudspeaker. No colored lights or music. By consummate oratory and psychological skill alone, he had seized them by their souls and was stretching their emotions to the breaking point.

He promised. He swore. He screamed. Give him. Give him the power. And *they,* not he, would again rule their country. The perils of Communism would be destroyed. The Bolshevik-Zionist taint expunged. The restrictions of the Treaty of Versailles abrogated. The energies and skills of the people unleashed and the destiny of Europe once more restored to its rightful masters. When Hitler had finished and disappeared through the back exit, the sailors, led by the brown shirts, marched into the street outside to bloody the student rally held there to protest the fascist gathering.

Those days were far away, Kristian reminisced as he and his first mate picked out the distant silhouettes of ships steaming directly toward them. The growing black shapes began to alarm him. He had received no warning of a mystery fleet across his course. Perhaps it was part of a convoy returning from England or empty tankers from Montreal on their way back to Venezuela. As the distance closed, he could see with alarm that this was no merchant fleet. The long, low, sleek lines, the stacked layer-cake bridges, the hurling cascades of bowspray as the ships dove into the restricting sea shattering the swells, the swift pace with precise alignment could mean only one thing—naval vessels. Whose? Skänsen could not make out any pennants or markings.

Suddenly he saw a flash of light on the bridge of the ship nearest him. Then another and another. It was too far away for it to be sunlight reflecting off the metal superstructure. It was too bright for signals. A crashing crack of thunder repeated in his ears, making him cover them for protection. Without warning, huge geysers of water shot up in front of him, spraying showers of chilly saline.

He shouted through the speaking tube to the engine room to stop the engines. The fools were shooting at him. The ship was going to be sunk. He felt a sense of panic overtake him, but only for a moment. This was a Swedish ship. There must be a mistake. The *Astra* was neutral territory as surely as if it had been the Djurgärden in Stockholm. They *must* see that as soon as they came closer. He shouted to the wireless operator to radio Göteborg just as soon as he identified their nationality.

This was not to take long, for the racing ships were bearing down upon the white freighter, like a pack of starving wolves cornering a white doe for the kill.

➔ THIRTY-THREE

"My dear Mr. Bainbridge!" Alexander Nikolaievich Ulyanov lumbered through the door across the slippery parquet, hurling his greeting before him. His scalp was shaved clean, his face a pasty white with sloped forehead and high broad cheekbones setting off flat nostrils. Thick lips, thick eyelids, and a heavy black beard which no amount of shaving could lighten gave the man a reptilian appearance. His barrel chest and muscular thighs strained the ill-fitting dark civilian suit.

"Colonel," Bainbridge nodded graciously at him in return. Indicating Michael seated far back in the corner, he waved the Russian to him.

"Ah, yes." The colonel's face lit up. "Mr. Michael O'Malley. We have heard much about you."

Michael rose to his feet to shake the Russian's hand and then slouched back in his seat as the Slav turned again to face his seated host.

Bainbridge's eyes inventoried his guest. Such a strong ox of a man, sadly comparing his own inadequate body. Not stupid, either. Anyone who said that the peasants of the Ukraine were dullards was in for a big surprise, especially in the years to come when the other great powers of Europe would be exhausted. What were the Russians up to? Almost simultaneously with its illegal interception of the *Astra* shortly after it had left American territorial waters, the Soviet Union had sent a harsh communiqué to the Swedish Crown. The short note bore the signature of Soviet Foreign Minister Molotov, the nihilistic robot who had replaced the suave, urbane Jew Litvinov at Hitler's insistence. The tone of the message was curt and menacing. It accused the Scandinavian nation of violating its neutrality by providing sanctuary to certain Soviet defectors and arranging for their escape to the Western Hemisphere. At Bainbridge's request, the Russian embassy in Washington had sent their naval attaché to Boston to explain his country's action.

Throughout the night and into the early hours of the morning, Bainbridge and O'Malley checked all the facts in the bizarre Soviet accusation. Nothing made any sense. The Americans knew all about the Göteborg Trading Company. Recently, it had been receiving large amounts of gold, crudely cast into rough ingots. Much of it was going into banks in South America and the Middle East. The transactions puzzled the Allies. They knew that there were no gold mines in the vicinity of Buchenwald, Auschwitz, and the other small provincial towns where the precious metal was coming from. Even stranger, the Germans had never supported spy operations in the cities receiving deposits of this vast wealth. It was Bainbridge's guess that these caches were intended to sustain those fortunate Nazis who escaped after the war. Each new shipment to places like Bolivia and Panama served to increase his optimism about the eventual outcome of the war. The Swedish Crown had never taken any official action against the company. The Allies had their own equivalent "commercial" enterprises, financed by the British Secret Service and the American OSS. These competing businesses of deceit, incorporated to buy information and sell lies, paid their taxes to Stockholm and broke no laws ... at least of man, if not of God.

As for the *Astra,* after leaving Frenchman Bay the freighter received new instructions from Göteborg to change course and was on its way back to Iceland when it sent its distress signal. Why was it returning? Bainbridge didn't understand. If he didn't know any better, it appeared as if the *Astra* was deliberately trying to make contact with the Russian fleet. Yet if this was intended, then why the panic call from Skänsen when he saw them? More important, why would the Russians fire upon a neutral freighter loaded with paper and wood?

Bainbridge's mind skipped with an agility denied his

somatic frame. Thank God he could still think and reason, although in this case it did not seem to be very productive. The facts did not make sense. If the Russians wanted the defectors—assuming they were in fact defectors and that this was the thrust of the naval interception—they could have arranged for the so-called engineers' extradition upon the ship's reaching port. Why stop a Swedish ship on the high seas in violation of international law? Why accuse the neutral country with such a blatant fabrication?

He looked up at his visitor, wishing he could voice the questions, but the rules of the game were very specific. It was obvious the situation was contrived with some nefarious purpose in mind. His wits and intuition must decipher the mystery.

The Russian watched his antagonist closely, his impassive face masking the active cognition within. He waited for his host to make the first move.

"Colonel," Bainbridge began the playacting, "we are in possession of your communiqué to the Swedish Crown. The charges are certainly grave ones."

"Yes, Mr. Bainbridge," Ulyanov intoned. "Violation of the basic tenets of neutrality is always a grave course to pursue. Especially when carried out in cooperation with fascist groups seeking the destruction of Sweden's close and faithful neighbor to the east."

"Would you be kind enough to elaborate on the allegations?" Bainbridge knew the senseless sparring would continue for at least another few minutes.

"The Göteborg Trading Company is a front for the German Reich. It is permitted to operate with the official consent of the Swedish government and without any restraints on its illegal and immoral activity."

"Am I to conclude from your statement that you accuse the Swedish Crown of cooperating with this so-called Nazi organization for the sole purpose of ferrying to Chile six Russian sailors who do not accept the ideology of Karl Marx? Is that what you believe?" Bainbridge's voice was rising with incredulity.

It all sounded so patently absurd, so ridiculous, that

Bainbridge could hardly mouth the words. Ulyanov was equal to the occasion. He stared straight at the American without a flicker of emotion. "What I believe is of no concern. Is there any other explanation for the facts as my government sees them? At this sensitive time, the Swedish government is unable to refute the charges."

Ulyanov's request was not supposed to be answered. Indeed, Bainbridge did not have another explanation. There was silence for a moment. By pursuing this clever tack, the Russian had, with incredible agility, placed the Swedish government in a very difficult predicament. Ulyanov's case was a simple one: the *Astra* was owned by a German-controlled firm; the engineers had in fact been Soviet naval officers six months before. If they were not deserters, what other explanation would fit the facts? Bainbridge thought of Hitler's propaganda chief. What was it the repulsive, twisted man was always preaching? People will believe a big lie where they would not a little one. Maybe he was right.

Bainbridge could not help but be impressed by the ingenious ploy which placed the Swedish government in the position of trying to defend something that had never happened. The Russians had achieved a tactical victory, but for what purpose?

"Colonel," he offered in a conciliatory manner, "Stockholm is anxious to do everything within its power to resolve this indelicate situation. At the present time, we have been unable to raise the freighter. As soon as radio contact is reestablished, Captain Skänsen and the ship will be escorted by American naval forces to our eastern seacost. The men in question will be detained and a full investigation carried out. Will that be satisfactory to your government?"

Ulyanov was aware that when Skänsen sent his SOS the Allies learned that a Russian fleet, without provocation, had stopped a neutral ship in direct violation of international law. Any suspicion as to their motive had been effectively neutralized by the physical presence of the Russian "deserters" and the ready fiction of the collaboration between the Crown and the Nazi company. Now the

Russian was ready to make his move and bring down the curtain on the pas de deux, an act which broke the American's famed imperturbability.

"Thank you, Mr. Bainbridge. The Soviet Union is deeply gratified at your government's sincere concern for justice. However, the kind offer will not be necessary. Shortly before arriving here, I was informed by our embassy that the fascist ship in question is no more."

The older man's whole body jerked up. He stammered indistinct phrases of alarm and protest.

"Apparently, in their attempt to flee retribution, an explosion occurred aboard the freighter. The ship now lies on the bottom of the Atlantic."

"Were there any survivors?" the inquiry reflected a sincere concern for human life.

The Russian's voice was soft and full of lingering sadness as he answered. His eyes watered. He leaned forward to touch gently, and for a brief second, the American's tremulous hands.

"Unfortunately, the captain and the entire crew were lost . . ."

"Except?"

"Except for the six Russian defectors who will be taken back to the Soviet Union for trial and execution."

Bainbridge could barely restrain himself from asking how six Russians could be rescued from an exploding ship and not a single member of the Swedish crew. He gave the Russian a quizzical stare. Ulyanov could just as easily have said that nobody survived. It was an obvious signal that it was time to stop this silly game and go home. Bainbridge replied, on cue.

"We do regret the loss of lives. My government is pleased that the Russian lives have been . . . miraculously . . . preserved . . . for their execution." He could not resist the sarcasm. He deserved at least that one small satisfaction. "I can assume, then, that the Soviet Union would join us in agreeing that the entire incident is another of those unfortunate happenings of war?"

Ulyanov stood up. "We do sympathize with the loss of Swedish lives. In respect to their memory, we will withdraw our communiqué of yesterday. We will consider the whole affair terminated."

The old man raised himself several inches. With difficulty, he reached his right arm out to the Russian. "My dear Colonel."

Shaking the trembling hand, the Slav bowed from the waist, "My dear Mr. Lawrence Bainbridge. It has been an enjoyable morning together. My respects."

The Russian bowed again in Michael's direction, almost as if surprised to see him still sitting there, and then strode boldly out of the room.

After he had gone, O'Malley and Bainbridge reviewed the events of the contrived deception involving the *Astra*. Hard as they tried to lock onto some cipher which would break the enigmatic farce, they were unsuccessful. As Michael left the hotel suite to return to his office, he was frustrated and uneasy. He had the disquieting feeling that for the first time since he had known Bainbridge, his superior had finally been out-trumped.

────➤ **THIRTY-FOUR**

The young man looked at his companions again and shivered with uncontrollable muscle spasms precipitated by a leaden chill he could not dislodge. Although the air was

hot, his thin, wasted frame still shook from the bitter
cold of the Russian winter. He huddled inside his shabby
brown suit. He held his arms pressed to his sides, fingers
curled shut and shoulders hunched together for warmth.
He was about twenty-one, medium height, and at one time
must have been a handsome youth. Now, the deep lines in
his forehead, the hollow cheeks, the jagged scar across his
chin, and the scattered gaps of missing teeth made him
look ten years older than his chronological age. He was
thin, too thin, and his eyes stared out from dark, sunken
sockets. He shivered again.

Two Russian soldiers, young and well-nourished, sat
upright in the front seat of the car. Two more flanked
the emaciated boy-man in the back. They wore beige
tunics with brown leather belts pinching in the long over-
blouses. In their arms were cradled the dull metallic mech-
anisms of submachine guns. It was unlikely, however,
that their prisoner would have contemplated escape even
if he had not been so anemic and malnourished as to
preclude the effort.

Night had fallen many hours ago, but still the ground
gave off waves of heat which rose like swollen rivers to
suffocate the passengers in the joustling car. The tem-
perature in the city was 109 degrees even at midnight,
and the warm, fetid odors of rotting garbage and offal
stung their nostrils. The car bumped and swerved as the
headlights picked out the ruts in the narrow city streets.
The few streetlights had gone off at eleven o'clock. All
was dark except for an occasional car making its unop-
posed way along the pockmarked roads.

The young man had suffered almost an entire month
of hard travel, day after day, by ship, train, and automobile after leaving the prison camp at Novosibirsk on
the Ob River in Siberia. He had traveled west for weeks
until the flat, still-frozen steppes gave way to the peaks
of the Urals. When they crossed this natural boundary
between Asia and Europe, he felt a sense of elation, as if
he had left a foreign planet. He could now look down,
stare west, and know that his homeland lay somewhere in
the direction of his gaze.

They crossed the Urals at Sverdlovsk and then descended rapidly into the flat, fertile river valley below. They sailed by steamer down the Kama River to its junction with the Volga at Kuybyshev, and then by larger and faster ship to the Caspian Sea. Here, he saw the terrain grow arid and sterile as they circled the shore to the province of Georgia.

The entire trip had been a complete puzzle to him. Taken from the prison camp without explanation, he had been shunted from place to place, always with relays of sullen guards. They did not speak German, and he spoke only a few words of Russian. He could see the disappointment in their eyes that their one prisoner was weak and harmless, so unlike the Nazis depicted on posters throughout the war. He knew that they hated him with an atavistic passion. He suspected that were it not for some powerful directive governing his transit and the hand of some unseen protector, his life would have been in dire peril. Only when they ascended the Caucasus Mountains did they try to talk to him, to tell him with enthusiastic gestures that they were in the birthplace of Stalin. As they crossed the barren border to leave Russia, they grew silent and belligerent again.

He had watched the road signs connecting the major cities of this ancient land as the old 1936 Buick sped along the poorly maintained single-lane highway, leaving in its trail a wake of dust and flying sand. The cities seemed like names from his past, the rich floral floors he had sprawled upon in the many warm rooms of his childhood ... Tabriz, Kashan, Ardebil. So strange and yet so familiar. This was really not enemy country, hostile like Russia, but some exotic land guarding the way to the Orient. He began to relax. By the time the car entered the western gate of the capital with its lofty archway and turrets, the prisoner's anxiety had lessened, though his body still racked with shivers from the cold of his memory.

Although he had asked many times, he was never told where they were taking him. He felt with a desperate intuition that here, in this mysterious city, he would get the answer. Somehow this was to be the end of his long journey.

The car traveled along the western entrance to the city. There were no other vehicles on the broad boulevard. When the car hit a bump, the headlights would rise and light up the rows of handsome poplars which set off the many foreign residences and embassies. The car entered the Maidan Tupkhaneh and slowly traversed the large empty square. It finally came to a stop outside a low white stone building. The guards in the back seat went out and disappeared inside. The prisoner could see the soldiers standing on each side of the portal, immobile in their ornate white dress uniforms with gold epaulets and ceremonial swords.

The Russian soldiers returned with two civilians dressed in gray business suits. A few words were spoken which the prisoner did not understand, and the two Russians remaining in the front seat left the car. The two civilians took their places in the automobile, one in front to drive and the other in back alongside the German. They introduced themselves in a cordial and welcoming fashion. They smiled at him and shook hands with him. They looked at this emaciated, prematurely aged young man, scared and trembling.

Did he realize how his life had been preserved by a gossamer web of power which emanated from the Kremlin itself? They smiled back at each other, thinking how happy he would be within just a few minutes.

The car started up again, only to stop two blocks further down on the same street. All three men got out. Within five minutes, Albert von Eyssen of Königsberg was a free man, and suddenly very warm, for the first time in two years... within the Spanish embassy in Teheran.

→ **T H I R T Y - F I V E**

"It is done?"

"It is done!"

Ulyanov stood in a windowless room in the central headquarters of the Narodny Komissariat Vnutrennikh Del in the Kremlin, facing the unsmiling man who held his hand in front of his mouth. There was no chair in front of the old wooden desk for the standing guest. No carpet on the floor. Only a stern picture of Lenin hung on the wall in back of the seated figure.

Nikolai Martov stared hard at his assistant. "Was there any trouble?"

"No, none at all, although I think the old man suspected something."

"What did you expect?" There were times when this large oaf exasperated him. "Bainbridge is nobody's fool. Of course he suspects. The only question is: Does he know?"

"No, I don't see how."

"The ship?"

"Sunk."

"Survivors?"

"Some of the crew escaped in lifeboats. They were shot and the lifeboats destroyed."

"Our men?"

"Killed with the rest. There are *no* survivors." He could not repress the hint of pride in his voice.

"I am satisfied. You may go." Martov held out his hand. He did not get up but continued to sit alone in the sterility of the empty room, staring at the door which had just closed behind Ulyanov.

Martov was no more than thirty-four, with a pleas-

ant face whose only distinguishing features were a pair
of iron incisors. This prompted him to adopt the disquieting habit of speaking with his right hand held over his
mouth to hide their presence, a harmless trait which un-
intentionally gave him a furtive appearance.

Martov was one of the new breed of Russians rising
through the petrified Soviet hierarchy. The legendary
figures who had forged the Communist state were old and
dying out. A new class was waiting in the wings to take
their place—men like Martov, who went to technical
schools, dressed well, knew no hunger. Men who could talk
the language of the managers who ran the mines, factories, and power plants of this rich, undeveloped land
spread across one-seventh of the earth's surface.

Martov was a technocrat, a conduit between the new
scientific and technical classes and the parochial Old
Guard who still issued forth from the Kremlin in their
black Zim limousines like hard-shelled crustaceans. Martov saw the future. He understood it. He could speak its
language. Someday soon it would be his.

He had seen the future, or at least one small, mind-
shattering glimpse of it, about one year ago at Novosibirsk in Siberia, where the vast hydroelectric power dam
held back the torrents of the violent Ob River. Mixed into
the concrete were bodies of tsarist convicts, Stalinist
political enemies, and, more recently, German prisoners-
of-war captured during the winter campaigns. A river of
energy poured from the six massive turbines to exploit
this bountiful but frigid land.

But it was not for ploughs and pruning hooks that
Martov had traveled those many miles in the winter of
1943. At the Georgi Plekhanov Institute of Applied
Physics, he learned of Soviet progress in weapons of destruction, the scope of which astounded him.

"It is possible to develop a missile to span an ocean,"
Professor Vladmir Rozanov, director of the laboratory,
told him.

"This one here that we have been testing is just a
toy, a Chinese firecracker. Give us the money and we will
be able to hit North America, China, Japan . . . anywhere.

We know that the Germans and possibly the Americans are also working on such a weapon. It is only a matter of time before all of us have intercontinental rockets."

Rozanov looked at Martov, who sat silently, his expression impassive. Dare he reveal his dream to this calculating accountant who somehow had the ear of the Politburo? The scientist could not hold back. "What I am proposing transcends the present, comrade. Let me illustrate." He took four sharpened pencils and held them together with a rubber band. "Suppose we combine two or three or four of these rockets." He pointed the pencils at Martov. "Then we fire them simultaneously. What do you think will happen?"

Martov did not answer. This owl-faced Jew with the large, shiny, bald head and thick lenses intrigued him. He looked at the pencils and waited.

"This rocket will *not* go to America or to China. By combining the thrust of all four engines, we can generate enough power to break through gravity. To lift a man . . ." —he put a paper clip on the tip of the pencils—". . . and throw him through the atmosphere into space." The clip soared off in a long trajectory across the room. Rozanov's eyes blinked with excitement. "Remember, comrade, space is only sixty miles up, not thousands. Why aim the rocket horizontally? Why not straight up, beyond the atmosphere? There, once free of gravity, we need hardly any power at all to place him in an orbit around the earth and keep him there . . . forever! Just think," he boasted, "a floating laboratory, circling around the earth. A Soviet moon. No, Comrade Martov. Forget about earthbound missiles. Give us the money to work with"—he shook the pencils in his listener's face—"and the Soviets will have the first man in space."

Rozanov looked at Martov with disappointment, interpreting his silence as disbelief or disapproval. But Martov was neither skeptical nor opposed. The day before he had learned from Rozanov of the institute's startling advances in nuclear fission.

"We have the theories, Comrade Martov," Rozanov had expounded. "We have blackboards just like the Germans and the Americans. Ideas do not respect borders. We, too, can set off a chain reaction with uranium. The answer to your question as to whether we can exploit this enormous power in a weapon of practical military value depends upon one thing."

"What is it? You can have all the money you want." Martov's impulsive reaction was a rare gesture for him.

"Money is *not* the problem." Rozanov glanced over the top of his glasses at Martov. He had this child-clerk by the balls. He drew the words out to tantalize his listener.

"I could give you an atomic bomb in a year...," he teased.

"If ... ?" Martov urged him on.

"If ..."

In the next two long hours, Nikolai Martov learned that in the whole one-seventh of the earth's surface, in an oversight unworthy of such a Supreme Being, the God of all the Russias had forgotten to place any fissionable material. The only three sites in the world where uranium existed in quantity, Martov was told, were the Permian Shield of North America, the Upper Katanga mines of the Union-Minière in the Belgian Congo, and the worked-out deposits of the Joachimsthal mines of Czechoslovakia still controlled by the Nazis.

"Comrade Martov, we have enough material left from the thirties for our research experiments. For a bomb, for many bombs, we need much more uranium. Get me that ore, even raw and unrefined, and I will give you a weapon that the world has never seen."

Martov's mind was already racing. A bomb? To drop from a plane? No. To put into a missile to shoot across the Atlantic? That was all child's play. If Rozanov had told the truth, he could put a floating bomb up in the sky, so high that no one could ever see it. It would stay there forever, circling like a red sun above Russia's enemies. Then, if he should wish, this new atom bomb could be hurled at the earth with the speed of light, to threaten and annihilate the West without warning.

He grew excited. He could taste the power. Let the

old farts in the Kremlin glory in the days they chased the kulaks out of the Ukraine and stole their cows. He would give to the Motherland the power to control the world!

Martov thought again of the ore making its silent way through the North Atlantic on its voyage to Murmansk. He was forced to admit, with a pang of envy, that only the Germans could have stolen the ore right from under the noses of the Americans, in their own country. Rozanov would be pleased. All it took was one frozen German prisoner. Von Eyssen, that impotent old fool. To betray your country for your son. Even Abraham held his knife over Isaac's heart for his God. What a price, to arm your country's mortal enemy with the ultimate weapon. Well, that was the German's problem. The boy was released as agreed upon, in Teheran. That was the end of that.

Von Eyssen was right, of course, to insist that the *Astra* be sunk immediately after the transfer. The Nazi High Command would never know that the precious ore had not gone down with the freighter. The Americans? They were still chasing the empty decoy subs all the way to Kiel.

Rozanov could now make all the bombs he wanted. Nikolai Martov was very satisfied with himself. He sat long hours with dazzling images of exploding suns and sparkling Roman candles lighting up the dark, windowless room.

→ **THIRTY-SIX**

Liz watched Michael move around his tiny apartment as if he were imprisoned and looking for some way to escape. Although two weeks had elapsed since that fateful meeting with Bainbridge, the memory still rankled his conscience.

"That bastard!" Michael cried out. "Sitting there playing God. Deciding who shall live and who shall die. You know, Liz, Bainbridge called me a 'parochial thinker.' He may be right. I suppose that's why governments are run by Bainbridges and history is made by men like him. But somehow, I can never condone the taking of innocent lives."

Liz tried without success to find some way to break through his funk. Michael would bend his head down to kiss the top of her head or to stroke her hair. There was no sexual desire in his caresses.

Later that evening, Michael ceased his erratic pacing and settled down in a chair in the corner of the room. He reviewed again with Liz the encounter with Bainbridge when he first learned of his superior's duplicity, and later the strange scene with Ulyanov which still left the Americans puzzled as to the significance of the Soviet ploy against the unarmed Swedish freighter. Liz agreed that the Russian naval attaché's performance was a sham, but she, too, could only shake her head as to its ulterior purpose.

Only when Michael, almost as an afterthought, mentioned the message which had arrived that afternoon from London, did she pick up her head.

"Did DNI say which of Rohmer's submarines were sunk?"

Michael was taken aback by her sudden interest in
the effectiveness of the British blockade. "No, we should
be getting that information within the next day or two.
In the meantime, we can cross three off the wolf pack," he
allowed with a measure of satisfaction.

"But Michael," Liz's words were hesitant as if unsure where they would lead, "that doesn't make sense,
either."

He looked at her with a puzzled expression.

"It's just this, Michael," she posed. "If your fanatic
German admiral is all that clever, why does he lose three
of his U-boats which, right now, are probably the most
valuable submarines in the world?" She registered the
sudden excitement in his manner. "I don't understand."

Michael said nothing but sat staring at her. Then a
flush of excitement crept across his face. "You're right,
Liz! Everything was too pat. That is what had me fooled.
But ... ," he continued as he broke out into a mysterious
smile, "if you look at it carefully, it isn't tidy at all. There
is one hole so goddam large you could drive a Mack truck
through it."

Catching Liz up, he gave her a big hug and swung
her around the room. Her glasses fell off and she was
barely able to retrieve them before they hit the ground.

"Michael!" she exclaimed, "one minute you are mop-
ing and then ... the ... next ..."

It was long afterward, when Liz finally lay back and
contemplated the unpredictable redhead alongside her,
that she tried to fathom his erratic behavior. Nothing he
said made any sense, nothing at all. Especially his last
words to her as he fell asleep. Why in the world would
he be interested in knowing from her when it would be
morning in New Mexico?

Bainbridge did not move. He held his body immobile
to reduce to the barest minimum any unnecessary contact
between himself and the worn upholstery of Berkowitz's
sofa. He did not dare look down at the bloodstained carpet. His eyes picked out Liz standing by the fireplace
and caught, for an instant, her hostile stare.

From his armchair, O'Malley surveyed the scene with an easy air which an outsider would have been hard-pressed to explain from the tense atmosphere in the room. It was obvious that he was savoring this moment, feasting on Bainbridge's ill-concealed discomfiture. When Michael spoke, the words hung heavy in the room.

"I knew that you would accept my invitation once you had read Gatling's report. I felt that it would be only appropriate to hold this meeting here. Don't you agree?"

Bainbridge did not reply.

Michael continued, "Think. Think back to that evening when you dazzled me with your Machiavellian tactics. Everything seemed so perfect. Didn't you feel even a little anxiety when you told me of your charade with von Eyssen? Wasn't it inconsistent for your Grossadmiral to construct an intricate pattern of deceit to obtain the ore, and then risk its delivery on almost certain blockade and destruction at the channel ports? Why would the Germans jeopardize that last crucial link? We've already sunk three of the U-boats.

"There had to be a rational explanation for this behavior. Was it that the Germans did not want the ore all along? We have only *your* hypothesis that von Eyssen and the Reich needed the uranium. Perhaps they realized, like yourself, that it was too late in the war for it to be of value. But then, why barter away that equisite opportunity to destroy the convoy in Boston Harbor in order to escape with the ore, and then, by your own words, lose it in the approaches to the European continent?"

Michael walked over to Bainbridge, pressing the words forward as if slicing the air before him with their sharp edges. "What if the Germans never had any intention of taking the ore back to Germany? Remember the Russian fleet? Do you believe Ulyanov's explanation of that charade? Did Martov send his Navy eight thousand miles around the world just to catch six defectors and sink a neutral ship loaded with newsprint? That's too easy, and you know it. But what if the ore was put on the *Astra?* What if—"

Bainbridge's head snapped up. His eyes, like silent semaphores, darted back and forth with O'Malley's as if carrying on their own coded conversation. A look of alarm crossed his face for the barest moment.

"Lawrence, it is routine for the Navy to comb the sites of U-boat sinkings and retrieve all flotsam from the wrecks. I had Gatling flown here from New Mexico to analyze the salvaged material. You read his report. No radioactivity. The wolf pack carried none of your precious cans of uranium. They were empty . . . decoys! And the real uranium? I suspect that your precious dream of nuclear blackmail is halfway to Murmansk by now. I doubt whether even *you* can sink a military convoy of our wartime ally as blithely as you killed Moe Berkowitz in this room."

Michael rubbed his foot back and forth on the carpet in front of him as if to obliterate the stain on his conscience. He looked down at the hunched figure whose slight mass barely seemed to dent the substance of the sofa. "Instead of your being the great architect of the postwar Pax Americana, you have become an unwitting accomplice in what could be construed by some as treachery."

Bainbridge stood up with difficulty, his hands grasping the cushions to help him rise. He was unable to provoke a gesture of support from those around him. Seeing him prepare to go, Liz moved to Michael's side. He held her close without moving, Bainbridge's presence of no more consequence than that of an inanimate piece of furniture.

But the frail figure remained in the center of the room like an ominous vibrating totem. He stood there, examining O'Malley with a patronizing expression on his face, as if saddened by something a petulant child might have done to a father he loved. He spoke in a weary tone of voice.

"Michael, I will not quarrel with you. You have made your point, and, I must admit in candor, more effectively

than I would have given you credit for. Yes," he sighed
again, "perhaps that flash of insight does redeem you, but
not for the reasons that you postulate."

O'Malley was confused. "I don't understand. What
do you mean?"

"Simply this, my dear Michael," drawing himself up
to his full height, his voice assertive. "If the Germans did
arrange to give the ore to the Russians—and the more I
consider your hypothesis, the more plausible it becomes
—then tell me, for what reasons?"

Michael still did not understand. Bainbridge elabo-
rated, once more the omnipotent schoolmaster confront-
ing the errant student. "I am in possession of the knowledge that Nikolai Martov released Albert von Eyssen to
the Spanish authorities in Teheran. That young man is the
surviving von Eyssen heir. He was captured several years
ago by the Russians at Kharkov. His exchange would be
ample motive for our devious Grossadmiral to deal with
our wily Kremlin Mephistopheles. From the Russians . . .
the son. From us . . . the gold."

The old man paused to give his next words sufficient
emphasis. "That explains what the devoted Prussian
father wanted from the plan. But tell me, my good friend,
what did von Eyssen's Nazi *masters* think they would
get out of the subterfuge?"

Bainbridge cast at Liz a glance of wistful nostalgia
out of keeping with his parched demeanor. For an instant,
he looked as if he was going to reach out and test the
softness of her cheek. "Yes, Michael, think about it. You
are younger than I am. You—you both will have many
more years to contemplate that lethal question than I will.
Tell me, why did Adolf Hitler, the Savior of the German
Fatherland, why did *he* agree to the deception?"

The question lingered long behind in that room,
mocking Michael, taunting him, like an evil shadow
which, at the peril of his life, he would never dare exor-
cise.

→ **THIRTY-SEVEN**

Von Eyssen received word of his son's release within an hour of Albert's arrival at the Spanish Embassy. The Grossadmiral's heart rate accelerated from excitement as the familiar squeezing pain started across the left side of his chest and bored deep through to his back. He could not breathe for an instant. The excruciating cramp traveled down the inside of his left arm to the tips of the fourth and fifth fingers. He knew the symptoms well. He removed from his desk a small metal box and extracted a tablet of one–two-hundredth of a grain of nitroglycerine. It was no bigger than a match tip. He placed it under his tongue and waited for the agony to pass. Within seconds, the chemical allowed a flood of fresh blood to rush to the oxygen-starved heart muscle. He sucked in several deep breaths, grateful for the relief. He knew that he could not survive many more of these anginal attacks.

Von Eyssen had spent anxious hours after the radio base at Lorient picked up Skänsen's panicked message to Göteborg, reporting the unexpected contact with the Russian ships. Then Albert was released. That meant only one thing. Everything had succeeded as planned. The ore was now aboard the Soviet ships, destined for its new home, with all witnesses to the clandestine adoption eliminated.

Von Eyssen sat down and counted the pulsations of the radial artery. They were rapid and irregular. He took another tablet of nitroglycerine and let it dissolve slowly against the lining of his mouth. How could he have prevented that long-awaited but dangerous feeling of exhilaration? It had seemed an eternity since Hitler had given his blessing to the plan. Albert's release was but the final act in a macabre drama which had started months ago.

First Klara had died, the breast cancer diagnosed too late to cure. Then Albert, missing in action on the Russian front in the winter of 1942 during the Battle of Kharkov. Finally, the somber realization, in the fifth year of the war, that it was irrevocably lost for the Germans, and with Allied victory Russia would possess the lands in Prussia which she had coveted for five hundred years.

Last June, he had heard that Albert was alive and *for sale*. The price the shifty Russian wanted could have been the moon itself. Von Eyssen was not the first Nazi to have been contacted through Soviet agents in Sweden. Martov was desperate for uranium ore. Many deals were conceived, but never consummated, as the Russian-who-hid-his-words offered money, sanctuary, anything any defecting official wished if only he could deliver the precious mineral. Von Eyssen cast about for some way to satisfy Martov's demands. At first, he had no more success than anyone else. The Gestapo controlled the mines in Czechoslovakia. No one could break their lock on the limited supply. It seemed hopeless.

Then . . . then . . . Bainbridge with his American dollars, trying to buy up German brains like blood sausages. Bainbridge, whose greed and ambition supplied the missing link. One million pounds British sterling to be deposited to his numbered account in the Crédit-Suisse Banque in Zurich. One million pounds for a weapon which could drop from the sky on your enemy. How the American must have gloated that for this paltry sum and some unrefined ore he had purchased mastery of the postwar world for his effete country.

Von Eyssen looked through the window, across the Atlantic, to the room of his distant partner. He could imagine the unknown figure trembling with eagerness while waiting to learn whether the Nazi High Command would accept the plan. The sigh of relief he must have uttered when von Eyssen informed him that Kriegsmarine had bought the charade. How pleased Bainbridge must be with himself at this very minute, blissfully ignorant of Martov's prize.

And the Russian? The German admiral could picture him somewhere on the vast expanse of the Slavic steppes convulsed with joy, still unaware of the American coup.

And the Führer? Deluded by his own mad ambition, Hitler, too, thought he had come out best.

The three who made the plan possible. *All fools!* How naïve. How stupid. But now the Prussian Grossadmiral had his son and his gold and his future, and he would live long to laugh at all of them.

Von Eyssen could still remember those impatient days after submitting his memorandum to the Kriegsmarine. What had happened to it? Was it dismissed as the fantasy of a crank, or filed away by the SS as evidence of treachery, to be used against him? That eventuality did not frighten him. Unless he could insure the future, the present was of no value.

He leaned across the desk to press the speaker button. His secretary answered immediately.

"Yes, Herr Grossadmiral?"

"Tell Hans that I will be ready to go to Obersalzberg within the hour. He will be driving all night. I must be there by morning."

Von Eyssen leaned back in the chair and tried to relax. Another few minutes to calm his skipping heart. He thought of the long, treacherous drive. Tonight, however, it would be different. This time he would be going by invitation from the Führer himself, not by a curt summons from Martin Bormann.

He would never forget his first trip there six months before. So much had depended upon what those overlords high on their mountaintop would say. Could he trap them in his web? His life, his son, his posterity hung in the balance.

He still felt fatigued and tremulous. There was

time.... He leaned back... and closed his eyes... and remembered...

...By the end of 1943 the Autobahn was no longer the great symbol of the National Socialist regime. RAF "carpet bombing" had mutilated vast sections with bomb craters. Streams of people seeking refuge walked along the sides of the road, their heads down, household possessions on their backs or pulled by animals. Observing the tragic scene on his way to meet with Hitler, von Eyssen mused that it must have been like this over and over in history. The generals being driven while the peasants they had betrayed with dreams of conquest trudged to wherever they could find shelter. What disturbed him most was the sad realization that the refugees were going in *both* directions. He crouched back into the seat to close out the distressing field of vision.

At Lamback am Chiemsee, the car stopped at an old inn. The Grossadmiral took a coffee and a pastry and walked around outside to stretch his legs. It was a lovely old wooden building with rustic, weather-beaten tables and chairs spread on a well-groomed lawn that overlooked a crystalline glacier lake. The smell of balsam streamed in from the decaying floor of the surrounding evergreen forest. He drew in deep lungfuls. The air was pure and fresh and his heart pulsed with strength.

The proprietor took pride in von Eyssen's arrival. Not many of the Nazi hierarchy stopped there any more, he confided to his guest. These days, they are in too much of a hurry to get to Obersalzberg, or to leave. Back when, he confided with pride and in a loud voice... you know when... it was different. The Führer himself would stop with the ladies, to enjoy his parties and a glass of tea. The proprietor showed von Eyssen a well-fingered photograph taken in the autumn of 1938, of Adolf Hitler dressed in a Bavarian sports coat, Alpine knickers, and a Tyrolean hat. Von Eyssen nodded graciously. He doubted whether the man would ever again see his leader cavorting in such a grotesque costume.

The car began to climb upward in low gear as it left the valley. Von Eyssen was forced to swallow several times to equalize the air pressure. He leaned out of the window trying to identify the three mountain peaks which towered a full mile higher into the sky. This day the Untersberg, the Berchtesgaden, and the Salzburg were hidden by dense caps of gray clouds.

The Grossadmiral grew uneasy. He felt at home in the flat, boggy wetlands along the Baltic. Heights frightened him. He pulled the shade across the window to avoid monitoring the patient ascent of the car which continued to grind upward to reach its destination at Obersalzberg.

Had he looked, he would have witnessed the final scarification of a primeval wilderness by Martin Bormann. Thinking that his master would approve, he had bought up the entire mountain, confiscated the contiguous State Forest, torn down buildings centuries old, until he achieved a sterile stockade. He then surrounded this mutilated preserve with two high barbed-wire fences, the inner fence two miles long, the outer fence nine, each manned with watchtowers, police dogs, and SS troops. High in the clouds was the private retreat of a master of destruction on a much wider scale, Adolf Hitler.

The road terminated at a wall of solid granite where a private tramway station had been carved out of the rock of the mountain. A cable car ran the last thousand feet to the eyrie perched on the very summit. Von Eyssen shuddered at the thought of this lurching cradle suspended against gravity and a seven-thousand-foot drop to the valley below by only a spidery web of invisible steel.

He left the automobile with hesitant movements, welcoming the engineer's help in boarding the metal cage. He sat down in the corner of the cabin and lowered his head between his legs. He tried to fight the waves of nausea and syncope which flooded over him, drenching his skin with sweat. Not until the car had started and he realized that he was safe did he raise his head and cautiously venture a view of the breathtaking panorama spread out beneath him.

At the top, the car stopped and von Eyssen was assisted out onto the firm ground. Ahead of him, looming like a feudal castle, was the Berghof. Designed by Hitler himself, its clumsy layout and pedestrian lines gave it the grace and comfort of a shingled railroad depot. Even the main dining room, planned around a spectacular window facing the three mountain peaks, was constantly infiltrated by gasoline fumes from the generators situated below. Despite its shortcomings, Hitler was proud of this aerial prison which isolated him both physically and spiritually from the vicissitudes of the worsening war.

Von Eyssen looked around the salon. The cheap oil paintings with bosomy Germanic maidens. The dark carved baroque paneling. The bulky overstuffed furniture which Goering used to claim resembled that of a Jewish feather merchant. Only the massive stone fireplace maintained the majesty of the magnificent mountain site.

This was the Grossadmiral's first visit to the pinnacle of the Nazi hierarchy. He was the only stranger, there by command. The others were constant guests and moved about with ease. Many maintained similar homes nearby, also built and protected by Martin Bormann. Von Eyssen looked about him trying to see how many he could recognize. No one paid any attention to him.

He identified Goering, his once-lean body porcine and corseted, his intelligent mind and courageous instincts dulled and rusted by drug addiction and sloth, his face now rouged and powdered.

Jodl, the correct German officer, tightly groomed, obsequious, whose chief attribute was a slavish devotion to Hitler first, and second to the Army he commanded. It was a standing joke in the Kriegsmarine that Jodl was such an ass that when the day came that the Allies landed in France, he would not even awaken the Führer to tell him.

Ribbentrop and Goebbels, sparring in the corner. Lean, hungry, vicious men, snapping at each other's heels for ascendancy in the pecking order.

Himmler, the ex-chicken farmer, bald, round-faced, with tiny metal-rimmed glasses making him look more like a scalped owl than the chief of the Gestapo.

Bormann, the quiet, busy secretary who spoke to no one and had chits on everyone. Yes, decided von Eyssen, the key to power in this chaotic cult of mediocrity was to file everything away and then be the only person to hold the index. Bormann alone could remember for Hitler the overlapping internecine feuds which the Führer designed to keep his coterie always off-guard and at bay. Only Bormann controlled the unions from which billions of marks could be pilfered and given to the henchmen around Hitler. He had the key to the strongbox and they repaid his largess with their tacit support.

Speer, the urbane, aristocratic architect, who in some unexplained way was ensnared by Hitler at the age of twenty-one to be the First Architect in the New Order. But for his brilliant economic mobilization, the Reich would have run out of munitions and food a year before. Von Eyssen knew that it was Speer's unexpected skill in plundering the material of war from the occupied countries that kept these parasites sitting there enjoying the view for as long as they did.

Von Eyssen was shocked when Hitler finally appeared accompanied by his vacuous blonde mistress. Up close, he could see how severely the war had aged the Führer. There were deep lines etched in his face. Gray tinged the sides of his hair. His right arm hung limp and his right leg dragged as he walked, the result of the abortive assassination attempt by von Stauffenberg in the bunker at Rastenburg.

The deterioration went deeper than mere physical infirmities. Gone was that vital spark, his personal magnetism which had once seduced the most literate and sophisticated nation in Europe. His lower lip trembled. His eyes watered, and he kept dabbing them with a soiled handkerchief clutched in his left hand. His complexion was pallid and unhealthy, the result of life underground and daily injections of stimulants.

Hitler had always dressed simply, but with taste. Now his appearance was disheveled. His dirty jacket hung askew. Food stains soiled the front of his tie. His shirt was dingy and the collar wrinkled.

Even more striking was the callous attitude of the people in the room. They were no longer deferential or even respectful. They barely acknowledged Hitler's presence. They did not rise when he entered the room. They sat down wherever they wanted and ignored him in their conversations. Yet, von Eyssen knew, they all needed him. Without Hitler, there would be anarchy. Everyone in that room had tried at one time or another to deal with the Allies in order to save their own skins, but the rigid preamble of "unconditional surrender" always blocked their frantic efforts. The Allies would not negotiate, and so all of them were trapped with him. They knew that the war was lost. Yet they sat immobile in the darkening gloom of the evening, watching the sun set below the mountains like a curtain falling across a blackened stage.

Hitler was speaking. He was repeating the same speech he had delivered the previous month before the Gauleiters in Posen. It was a speech which von Eyssen alone of those in the room had heard and whose words had fertilized the seed of his plan.

"If the German nation is now defeated in this struggle, it has been too weak. That will mean it has not withstood the test of history and is destined for nothing but doom."

The room quieted with a shock. Hitler sat motionless, deep in his favorite armchair, staring into the roaring flames of the fireplace. He continued, almost in a dream trance.

"Look out that window," he told his audience. "Look at the Untersberg. Who is there? Charlemagne, the Emperor, waiting to be awakened to restore Germany to its deserved glory. Barbarossa, still in his cave, waiting to hear the trumpet to rout our enemies and conquer.... Why? Why do you think the German people have such legends which we teach our schoolchildren?"

No one spoke.

"Because they know, as I now know, that the German people are not ready to be led to greatness. Yes. They ... and I ... have been called before our destined time. We will die, perish. In the future, another leader will arise to claim the success that I have failed to bring to this tainted people. No. The German people have been weighed and found wanting."

Von Eyssen was torn between the drama of the words and the irony of this illusion to Hebraic lore.

"Is there no hope?" The question, like a plea, came from the back of the room.

"There is hope, but not for the Third Reich," he answered with a sigh. "For the Fourth Reich, or Fifth, for them, perhaps. But not for us."

Hitler rose from his chair and walked over to the fireplace. He turned to face them. His voice was soft. This was not a diatribe, but a eulogy. He was not dictating, but pleading for understanding.

"The war is over. What will happen now? England is through forever. The future world will see the final conflict between the Communist rulers of the Slavs in the East and the last flowering of Western civilization, the United States. These two will coexist, but only for a brief moment in history. It cannot last longer than that. It is inconceivable that these two powers, embracing totally different ideological systems, will remain at peace forever."

He grew agitated. He paced back and forth, his body animated once again, suffused with a restored vigor. "They must fight, until one or both are dead. They must!" He paused for a moment. "In that simple law of survival, lies the future salvation of the German Reich. That is our task."

His audience could not follow him. They tried to unlock the puzzle that this enigmatic man had placed before them. Only von Eyssen was at one with the speaker. At Posen, the Grossadmiral had divined the macabre logic of this maniacal genius's thinking. Now in the entire room, only this old man with the bad heart was mouthing the words even before they were spoken.

"What would be most detrimental to our cause? Think. I will tell you. Peace! *The hegemony of one of the combatants!* Let Russia or the United States gain military ascendancy over the other and they will freeze the world into a *pax* like the Romans did for a thousand years. NO!"

His voice tore at the walls.

"These two countries *must* be kept at each other's throats. We must not permit either of them to impose a peace on the world. Each must think it has total military superiority over the other, so it will dare to attack. Only when you believe in final victory, do you encourage mortal combat. In the years to come, we must encourage this competition. Until that inevitable day when the holocaust engulfs both countries. Then ... then ... we shall rise once more and emerge from our lair to reclaim our destiny."

The words rang out.

"Who can tell me how to destroy the world? For in that simple act lies the future greatness of the Fatherland!"

Hitler sank back into the chair once again and was lost in dreams of the future. The fire cast bright, changing lights on the wall and sparkled on the broad expanse of window glass opposite. The rapid reflections consumed the whole room with dancing yellow flames.

The guests drifted off by ones and twos, without even a backward glance in the direction of the brooding man in the chair. It was all right for this decrepit old man to acknowledge defeat, to accept his own suicide, but what of themselves, who had risked *their* all with *his* throw of the dice? They were not prepared to trade their own mortality so blithely in return for immortality in a storybook legend.

Only von Eyssen stayed behind, silent, in his corner of the room. He waited long, wondering whether he dared voice the thoughts which crowded into his mind. He was not thinking of the salvation of the Third Reich, but of the salvation of his family. He reviewed the details, but still hesitated to speak. Then he thought of Albert, dying in a frozen Russian prison camp. The von Eyssen lands gone forever. He accepted the risk. He rose to stand in front of Hitler. The seated figure was lost in contemplation and at first did not notice him. When Hitler lifted his head, there was a sad, compelling look on his face.

"Ah, Grossadmiral von Eyssen. I see that you do not leave like the other rats. Why have you stayed? To read the flames with me? They do not tell of happy times for our country."

The man before him said nothing. For a minute, Hitler wondered what it was that kept his visitor waiting so patiently.

"Ah, yes. The memorandum."

He rose and moved with von Eyssen to a corner of the room and sat next to him. There were very few times in Hitler's life when he felt the need for human companionship. This was one of those times.

"I have read your proposal. There were those who laughed. Most wished to have you hung with piano wire from a meat hook like von Stauffenberg. Tonight I will listen."

Hesitatingly, with fear and uncertainty, von Eyssen began to speak, to choreograph his dance of deceit. Attendants passed through the room to see if either of them wished anything, but were waved away. All the two men sought was privacy and heavy logs to fire the flames high and strong.

The two men conferred far into the small hours of the night. Von Eyssen talked and Hitler listened. By the time the first rays of daylight pierced the cleavage between the mountain peaks, the two men had finished. Hitler got up first, stretched, and smiled. He held out his hand to the still-seated guest. He shook it with warmth and left the room. The Führer had agreed. Operation Mayflower was approved.

Von Eyssen stirred and opened his eyes. The portentous meeting with the Führer seemed like only yesterday. Yet now, six months later, he was returning to Obersalzberg in triumph. All had gone well. The Americans and the Russians had each purchased the necessary ingredients for weapons of mutual destruction. Each believed in both its own invincibility and the total vulnerability of its mortal opponent. The Führer was satisfied that World War III was now certain, and in the wake of the Apocalypse would come the turn of the Reich.

If he left now, he should arrive at Obersalzberg by morning. He could be in France by the following day. The battle there must soon be joined. Every day that America and England waited, another several thousand square miles of Europe passed into Russian hands forever. Churchill was not stupid, even if Roosevelt was. The Allies must make their move now to stake out their claim to postwar Europe. If they delayed much longer, there would be nothing left to invade but Soviet satellites. Bainbridge would help his old friend von Eyssen obtain sanctuary. Otherwise, it would be most embarrassing to the Americans to have their wartime dealings with the Nazis revealed.

Hitler! Bainbridge! Martov! Hate, greed, revenge had made it so easy to dupe them all. Within months, the war would be over, and he would join Albert in Switzerland with the gold. The von Eyssens would rise like a phoenix from the ashes of Europe.

The Grossadmiral rose from his desk and took a last look around the room. The large sedan was waiting below. The driver opened the door for von Eyssen and helped him into the car.

"It will be a nice day, Herr Grossadmiral," Hans volunteered.

"Ach, but the wind has shifted." Von Eyssen shook his head. "The way it is coming now, we can expect a week of bad weather and fog."

He thought of what that might do to the plans for the invasion. The Americans always struck during good weather. Eisenhower was not a gambler like Rommel to risk inclement conditions. It was too late to worry about such things now. With a gesture of resignation for what might come, he settled back for the long, wretched drive to the Alps.

By the time he reached the Berghof, the Grossadmiral was fatigued. Whether it was the exhausting drive or the thin air, he had almost incessant recourse to his pillbox. As he waited in the living room, he wondered how many of the guests knew what had transpired since his meeting with Hitler six months before. The conversation paused and grew quiet. He could hear the muted voices of Hitler and Eva Braun coming downstairs for afternoon tea from the bedrooms on the second floor.

As von Eyssen stood up, eager and expectant, a disquieting chain of thoughts floated through his mind. It was not concern that his deception would be discovered but something more fundamental. Everything had seemed so perfect and yet, what if things did not work out as he had planned? Such an eventuality *was* possible, he decided, though not very probable. Perhaps the atom bomb would not work. Maybe the rockets would never get off the ground. Maybe the Russians and the Americans would get along and not blow each other off the face of the earth.

He gave a silent shrug. The von Eyssens would survive. That was all that mattered. The rest . . . the rest was just the means to that end.

The door opened, and he could see Hitler enter. The Grossadmiral's pupils contracted. His face flushed. His heart raced with anticipation, as with a smile of confidence and a jaunt to his step, he moved forward to receive from the Führer congratulations on a job well done.